Latte Legacies

Sarah's Secrets Mystery – Book 2

by Sarah Macey

Published by Brew & Clue Publishing Ltd in 2025

Copyright © Brew & Clue Publishing Ltd
All rights reserved.

This book is a work of fiction. Names, characters, businesses, organisations, places, and events are either the product of the author's imagination or are used fictitiously. Any resemblance to actual persons, living or dead, events or locales is entirely coincidental.

No part of this publication may be reproduced, stored in a retrieval system, or transmitted in any form or by any means electronic, mechanical, or photocopying, recording or otherwise, without the prior permission of the publisher and author.

By Sarah Macey

Sarah's Secrets Mysteries
Brewing & Betrayal
Latte Legacies

To Tom

My real life Charlie inspiration – barista, dreamer and coffee aficionado extraordinaire. This book will have to do until I can build us our very own Sarah's Secrets.

And thank you, sincerely, for not yet resorting to murder to win a barista contest!

Chapter 1

"Ergh, disgusting!" Sarah Meadows said to herself as a cold, wet tennis ball landed unceremoniously at her feet. She looked down to see Missy, her chocolate lab, gazing up at her with an expectant, soppy grin, her tail wagging wildly. With a sigh, she bent down, gingerly picking up the slobbery ball and giving it another throw across Southsea Common. Missy tore after it with boundless enthusiasm, her ears flapping as she ran.

Since trading her old job for the seaside coffee shop, *Sarah's Secrets*, her mornings had settled into a routine that she loved: beach walks, a shortcut through the Common, and the anticipation of another day at her dream shop. The autumn air was crisp and fresh, the breeze tugging at her hair, but the sun was out, casting a golden glow over the landscape. Though the season was shifting, and the temperature was dropping, nothing could dampen her spirits. Life was good.

As Sarah stomped across the common, the imposing Queen's Hotel came into view, its grand Edwardian Baroque architecture standing proudly against the morning sky. She had seen it countless times before, usually just part of the scenery as she made her way through Southsea. But today, it felt different, more important. In just a matter of days, she would be stepping through its elegant doors, not just as a passerby, but as an attendee of the upcoming latte art competition, one of the most exciting events in the local coffee scene.

Sarah felt a flicker of nerves on behalf of Charlie, her son, who was set to compete. He had poured his heart and soul into perfecting his latte art, spending countless hours at *Sarah's Secrets* honing his craft. His dedication was evident in every silky swirl and intricate design he created, transforming each cup into a masterpiece. She knew how much this competition meant to him, it wasn't just about winning but proving to himself how far he had come.

She could already picture the elegant setting inside the Queen's Hotel, its ornate chandeliers casting a warm glow over the competitors as they showcased their skills. Coffee enthusiasts and industry professionals would be gathered, judging each pour with expert eyes. The thought of it filled her with pride and a twinge of worry. While she admitted that she might be slightly biased, Charlie clearly had talent, but competitions tested more than skill. Could he stay steady under the judges' watchful eyes?

Regardless of the outcome, Sarah knew she would be there, cheering him on and supporting him every step of the way. If he won, they would celebrate. If he didn't, she would remind him that talent and passion mattered more than any title. And perhaps, she thought, they could mark the occasion with one of the hotel's indulgent Afternoon

Teas - scones, clotted cream, and all the trimmings. A small reward for their journey so far.

Missy bounded back once more, dropping the ball at Sarah's feet with an eager bounce. With a smile, Sarah scooped it up and sent it flying again. As the dog tore off after it, Sarah took a deep breath, letting the salt-tinged air fill her lungs. The day ahead was waiting, full of comforting routines and the bubbling anticipation of the competition. Whatever happened, she knew one thing for sure, this new life, this new rhythm, suited her perfectly.

Inside the grand event room of the Queen's Hotel, the air buzzed with energy as staff hurried to prepare for the upcoming Latte Art Competition. Among them were Teddy and Gemma, two of the younger staff, weaving their way through the bustle with trays of pristine white cups.

Gemma, new to both the hotel and the whirlwind of event prep, balanced her tray carefully as she followed Teddy toward the coffee bar stage. "So, what's this competition actually like?" she asked, glancing around at the controlled chaos unfolding around them. "I mean, what are we letting ourselves in for?"

Teddy, who had been working at the hotel just long enough to feel like a veteran in front of a newcomer, gave a knowing nod. "Oh, it's a big deal," he said, setting his tray down with practiced ease. "Second year running that the regional heats have been held at the hotel, and last time the turnout was wild. You wouldn't think people would get so hyped about latte art but trust me, this is serious business."

Gemma's eyebrows lifted. "Really? That many people?"

"Absolutely," Teddy continued, slipping into full tour-guide mode as they turned back toward the kitchen. "You'd be surprised. Portsmouth's coffee scene is no joke. People here don't just drink coffee, they study it. The way they talk about pour-overs and microfoam, you'd think they were discussing fine art."

Gemma bit back a grin as she followed him through the swinging doors into the kitchen. He spoke with such authority that she almost forgot he wasn't much more experienced than she was. Almost.

As they gathered more equipment, Teddy kept going. "See, it's not just about who can make the prettiest pattern in the milk. It's about control, consistency, symmetry. You've got to have a steady hand, perfect microfoam, and…"

Behind him, the head chef, who had been busy at the prep station, glanced up and rolled his eyes. Gemma caught the moment and let out a quiet giggle.

Teddy, oblivious, turned sharply to her. "What?"

"Nothing," she said, stifling another laugh as she lifted her tray.

Teddy narrowed his eyes, clearly unconvinced, but after a brief pause, he straightened up, adjusting his posture like a man with important knowledge to impart. "Anyway," he continued, undeterred, "the real magic happens when the competitors get going. You'll see. The tension in the room, it's something else."

Gemma smirked, but as Teddy kept talking, a small spark of curiosity crept in. Maybe he did know what he was talking about. Or maybe he just talked a good game. Either way, it looked like this weekend was going to be a lot more entertaining than she'd bargained for.

She shifted a cup on her tray and glanced toward the stage. "So, who won last year?"

Teddy scoffed. "Oh, that's the thing. It doesn't always matter who's *best*."

Gemma raised an eyebrow. "Meaning…?"

Teddy lowered his voice slightly, his tone shifting from confident banter to something more conspiratorial. "Last year, he…" he tipped his head toward the banner with Roger Alton's name printed on it "kicked someone out just because they got on his nerves. Said their technique was 'insulting to the craft' or something, but everyone knew it was personal."

Gemma frowned. "He can just… do that?"

Teddy shrugged. "When you're Roger Alton, you can do whatever you want." He set a stack of cups down with a little too much force. "There was this guy, Theo something, he wasn't just good, he was *great*. Came up from nothing, working in some hole-in-the-wall café, but his pours were insane. People were saying he was a real contender for the finals."

"What happened?"

Teddy exhaled sharply. "Roger happened. First round, he gave Theo some scathing critique about 'lack of soul' in his work. By the second round, Theo had to redo his pour three times because the judges kept 'mishearing' his call on the pattern." Teddy made exaggerated air quotes. "By the third round? Disqualified for 'unacceptable technique'."

Gemma blinked. "But if he was so good..."

"That's the thing," Teddy said, shaking his head. "It had nothing to do with skill. Apparently, if Roger doesn't like you, you're done. Doesn't matter if you're the next big thing in coffee or just some nobody trying to prove yourself. He picks favourites, and the rest?" He gestured vaguely. "They get crushed."

Gemma studied the competition floor, where the stage was still being prepped. It suddenly looked less like an arena for artistic mastery and more like a battlefield where only the chosen survived.

"So, the winner…" she began.

Teddy sighed. "Sometimes they deserve it. Sometimes… they just have the right connections."

Something about the way he said it made Gemma glance back at the banner where Roger's name was printed in bold letters. "That's messed up."

Teddy smirked, balancing his tray on one hand. "Welcome to the coffee industry."

The cool morning air of Southsea was fresh with the tang of sea salt as Sarah made her way down Castle Road, Missy trotting contentedly at her side. The familiar turn into the street where *Sarah's Secrets* nestled brought a flutter of excitement in Sarah's heart each time she approached. It was here, in this quaint part of town, that her dream had taken root and blossomed.

Reaching the coffee shop, Sarah bent down to unclip Missy's lead, watching with a smile as her faithful chocolate lab made a beeline for the front door. Missy sat, her tail thumping happily against the pavement, clearing away any stray leaves in eager anticipation. "Good girl, Missy," Sarah chuckled, stepping up to the cheerful blue door that marked the entrance to her new world. "Thanks for the tidy doorstep!"

Unlocking the door, Sarah pushed it open, allowing Missy to bound inside ahead of her. The shop was still shadowed and quiet, untouched by the day's bustle. Sarah flicked on the lights, the warm glow chasing away the night's last shadows. Missy made herself comfortable in the snug, a cosy nook Mike had built specifically for her, tucked between the bustling shop space and the small office where Sarah managed her business.

For a moment she stood at the threshold of the main café area, her eyes sweeping over the carefully chosen decor, the neatly arranged tables, and the polished counter where soon the espresso machine would hum to life. But before she set about her morning routine, she turned her attention to the small stack of leather-bound books scattered across the tables. Inside each cover bore the same inscription: **Tell me your secrets.**

Gathering them up, Sarah allowed herself a small thrill of anticipation. Every night, she placed these books on the tables, inviting customers to jot down their secrets - small, big, funny, scandalous. Some days, she imagined finding something truly juicy, a mystery unravelling right in the pages of her café. But as she flipped through them on her way to the counter, she sighed, her fingers tracing the familiar handwriting of a regular who had, for the third time this week, confessed an undying love for someone named "J."

"Another round of secret loves and hidden crushes," Sarah murmured with amusement, turning another page. One entry simply read: *I stole my sister's jumper and told her the washing machine ate it.* Another, in particularly neat handwriting: *I'm afraid to tell my best friend I love him.*

"No murders, no shocking scandals, just romance," she mused, tucking the books under the counter. Perhaps today would be different. Perhaps someone would finally spill a truly thrilling secret. With that thought lingering, she moved behind the counter to begin her morning ritual.

As she prepared the espresso machine, setting it up just as her son Charlie had taught her, her thoughts drifted to the upcoming latte art competition. It was not just a competition; it was a celebration of the craft she loved, a craft that Charlie had embraced with equal passion. The prospect of watching her son compete, to see him stand proud among his peers, was thrilling.

The quiet of the shop during these early hours was sacred to Sarah. It was a time when she could connect deeply with her venture, reflecting on the journey that had brought her here. From the spark of an idea to the reality of

Sarah's Secrets, every step had been a labour of love, supported by her family and fuelled by her community.

As she finished setting up, Sarah's gaze fell on a framed photo by the cash register, a snapshot of her, Charlie and her niece Robyn at the coffee shop's opening. It was a reminder of why she had embarked on this adventure: not just to fulfil her dream, but to build something that her family could be proud of.

As Sarah adjusted a display of freshly baked muffins, she looked up just in time to see Charlie breezing into the shop. A playful smile spread across her face as she caught his eye.

"Well, well, if it isn't my favourite troublemaker," she teased, brushing her hands off on her apron. "I was just thinking about you."

Charlie grinned, raising an eyebrow. "Oh yeah? What were you thinking?"

Sarah leaned against the counter, giving him a mock-serious look. "I was staring at your photo, trying to manifest you into the shop. Looks like it worked."

He chuckled, running a hand through his tousled hair. "Could be, Mum, or maybe it's because I know it's nearly time to open, and you need all hands on deck!" His eyes twinkled with good-natured humour, softening the edges of his morning grogginess.

Leaning against the counter, he watched as Sarah finished her preparations. In just a matter of months, the coffee shop had become a second home, a place that not only reflected his mother's dreams but had begun to weave itself into the fabric of his own aspirations.

"So, how are you feeling about the competition?" Sarah asked, her tone mixing motherly concern with genuine curiosity as she wiped her hands on her apron and turned round to face him.

Charlie exhaled slowly, rolling his shoulders as if shaking off the weight of the competition. He rubbed his palms together, a nervous habit he hadn't quite shaken. "Honestly, Mum, it's a mix of excitement and nerves. More nerves at the moment, I suppose," he confessed, scratching the back of his neck. "I've studied the rules, watched countless videos, and practiced my pours a thousand times, but watching something on YouTube and doing it in front of an audience are two very different things."

Sarah nodded, her expression understanding. "It's perfectly normal to feel nervous, especially before your first big event. But you've prepared as much as you can, and remember, it's not just about winning. It's about learning, participating, and enjoying the experience."

She glanced at the clock, noting the time. "We've got a few more minutes before the morning rush. Why don't you head into the kitchen and do some last-minute practice? It might help settle your nerves."

Grateful for his mother's encouragement, Charlie agreed. "Yeah, that sounds like a good idea. Thanks, Mum."

He made his way to the kitchen, pulling out his tools and a fresh jug of milk. Setting up his station just as he would for the competition, Charlie began to steam the milk, focusing on the soothing sound of the frother and the familiar feel of the pitcher in his hands. Each pour was an opportunity to improve, to turn his anxiety into artwork.

As he practiced, Sarah watched from the doorway, her heart full of love and admiration for her son's dedication. She knew that whatever the outcome of the competition, Charlie was gaining invaluable experience. More importantly, he was following his passion, something she had always hoped for him. Watching her son pour his heart into each swirl and design, she felt a surge of joy for his burgeoning talent.

The coffee shop soon began to buzz with the early birds seeking their first cup of the day. Sarah returned to her post behind the counter, ready to greet each customer with a smile. As she reached for one of the journals, a folded note slipped free from between the pages, fluttering to the ground. Heart pounding with sudden curiosity, Sarah retrieved it and unfolded the page. One sentence stared back at her, written in hurried, almost frantic script:

I know what you did

Chapter 2

As the morning progressed, *Sarah's Secrets* began to stir with life, the quiet serenity of dawn giving way to the vibrant hustle of a new day. The cool breeze that drifted through the open windows carried with it the crisp scent of autumn, a gentle reminder that the seasons were turning. The golden hues of the falling leaves outside painted the streets of Southsea in warm, inviting colours, creating a picturesque backdrop for the cosy coffee shop.

Inside, the atmosphere mirrored the changes unfolding outdoors. The menu board, once dominated by refreshing iced lattes and citrusy cold brews meant to soothe the heat of summer days, now boasted a new array of comforting autumnal delights. Sarah had spent the past week perfecting her own blend of pumpkin spice syrup, infusing it with real pumpkin puree and a harmonious mix of cinnamon, nutmeg, and cloves. The result was a rich, aromatic concoction that added a delightful warmth to their lattes, quickly becoming a favourite among their regulars.

The shift in seasons also brought a change in clientele. The summer months had seen a steady stream of tourists and beachgoers, their sun-kissed faces and sandy flip-flops adding a laid-back charm to the shop's ambiance. Now, with autumn settling in, a fresh wave of energy flowed through the doors as students from the local university returned to Southsea for a new academic year.

The young patrons brought with them an infectious excitement, their lively conversations and animated debates filling the cafe with a vibrant buzz. They huddled around the rustic wooden tables, laptops and textbooks sprawled alongside steaming mugs of spiced lattes and indulgent hot chocolates topped with whipped cream and a sprinkle of cinnamon. The air was thick with the mingled scents of fresh coffee, warm pastries, and the distinctive aroma of Sarah's signature pumpkin spice blend.

Charlie emerged from the kitchen, a satisfied grin on his face as he carried a tray laden with freshly crafted drinks. He weaved through the bustling cafe, delivering orders with effortless charm, engaging in light-hearted banter with the customers. The students, in particular, seemed to gravitate towards him, their faces lighting up as he recommended new flavours or shared stories about the origins of different coffee beans.

"Here you go, two pumpkin spice lattes with oat milk," Charlie announced cheerfully as he placed the steaming mugs in front of a pair of students engrossed in a spirited discussion about their upcoming philosophy lecture. "Let me know what you think; it's a new blend we're trying out."

One of the students, a girl with bright purple hair and a nose ring, took an eager sip and closed her eyes in delight. "Oh wow, this is amazing! It tastes like autumn in a cup," she exclaimed, her friend nodding enthusiastically in agreement.

Charlie's grin widened. "Glad you like it! It's our secret recipe," he replied, nodding towards Sarah, who was busy ringing up orders at the counter.

Sarah caught the exchange and felt a swell of pride. She loved seeing the joy their creations brought to people, and the lively atmosphere that the students fostered filled her with renewed energy. The influx of young, enthusiastic customers also presented new opportunities for the shop to evolve and adapt.

Later that afternoon, during a brief lull between the morning rush and the after-class crowd, Sarah and Charlie found a moment to catch their breath. They sat together at a corner table, steaming mugs of coffee warming their hands as they surveyed the cozy interior of their shop.

"It's been a busy morning," Sarah remarked, a satisfied smile playing on her lips. "I think the new pumpkin spice latte is a hit."

Charlie nodded, taking a thoughtful sip of his drink. "Definitely. The students love it. And did you notice how many of them were asking about vegan and gluten-free options? Maybe we should consider expanding our menu to include more of those."

Sarah's eyes sparkled with interest. "That's a great idea. We could collaborate with some local bakers or even try our hand at creating our own recipes. What do you think about a vegan pumpkin muffin or a gluten-free spiced apple cake?"

Charlie's face lit up with enthusiasm. "I love it. And speaking of new ideas, I've been thinking more about those espresso martinis we talked about. With the evenings getting cooler, it might be the perfect time to introduce a little something extra to our menu. Maybe even host a special autumn-themed evening event to launch it."

Sarah considered the suggestion, picturing the cozy evening ambiance with soft lighting, mellow jazz music, and patrons sipping on elegant espresso cocktails. She leaned back in her chair, staring thoughtfully at the wall as she let the idea simmer in her mind. Opening up *Sarah's Secrets* in the evenings… It was a big step, something that would require more planning and investment than she had originally intended, but she couldn't deny that the thought of it thrilled her.

There was a certain magic that coffee shops had in the daytime. The hustle and bustle of caffeine-fuelled mornings, the relaxed comfort of afternoon chats, but the idea of transforming her shop into a nighttime haven had an undeniable appeal. It could work. It could be something really special - a niche that would set her café apart from all the others in the area.

But then reality came crashing back. This wasn't just about a new menu or some fresh décor. She'd have to apply for a liquor license, for one. And more staff would be needed. They'd only been open for a few months, and while things were going smoothly, taking on more hours would be a gamble. Still, a big part of her felt like this was the right move.

Sarah sighed, tapping her fingers on the counter. "It could be wonderful," she murmured to herself. "We could decorate the place, create a special menu for the night... espresso martinis, coffee cocktails, maybe even some non-alcoholic versions for those who just want the vibe. It would draw in a whole new crowd."

Her thoughts turned to Robyn, whose knack for mixology that had already proven popular among friends and family. Robyn had a natural flair behind the bar and loved experimenting with flavours, coming up with cocktails that balanced the rich bitterness of coffee with sweeter, unexpected notes. If anyone could help bring this vision to life, it would be her.

As if on cue. Robyn strode in, a colourful scarf wrapped around her neck and her cheeks flushed from the crisp outdoor air. She carried a basket brimming with fresh produce, the vibrant colours of pumpkins, apples, and cranberries peeking out from beneath a chequered cloth.

"Look what I found at the farmer's market!" Robyn announced gleefully, setting the basket down on the table. "I thought these could inspire some new recipes. Maybe a spiced mulled apple juice or a cranberry-infused cake?"

Sarah's face broke into a delighted smile. "Perfect timing, Robyn. We were just discussing expanding our autumn menu, and these look absolutely gorgeous."

Charlie leaned forward, inspecting the produce with interest. "And we were also talking about launching those espresso martinis we've been brainstorming. Think you're up for crafting some magic?"

Robyn's eyes sparkled mischievously. "Are you kidding? I've been waiting for the chance! Imagine this: a pumpkin spice espresso martini, rimmed with cinnamon sugar and garnished with a twist of orange peel. It would be like a cozy sweater in a glass."

Sarah laughed, the sound warm and full of joy. "That sounds divine. I think our customers would love it."

Outside, the late afternoon sun cast long shadows across Castle Road, the golden light accentuating the rich colours of autumn that adorned the street. The scent of woodsmoke began to mingle with the salty sea air as locals lit their fireplaces against the evening chill.

Inside *Sarah's Secrets*, the last of the afternoon customers lingered over their drinks, savouring the comforting warmth of the café. Charlie moved between tables, clearing empty cups while exchanging easy conversation with the regulars. At the counter, Sarah handed over a takeaway order with a friendly smile, while Robyn wrapped up a sale with a couple debating the merits of a cinnamon-infused espresso.

As the final customer stepped out, Charlie flipped the sign on the door to Closed, and Robyn pulled the latch, shutting out the growing evening chill. With the world outside sealed away, the cozy hum of the shop softened into something more intimate, just them, a quiet space, and the promise of creative experimentation.

Sarah wiped her hands on a tea towel, glancing around the warmly lit café. "Right," she said, a spark of excitement in her voice. "Now that we've survived the afternoon rush, let's see what we can come up with for the seasonal menu."

Charlie moved back behind the counter, setting out fresh milk and espresso beans, ready to refine his latte art. He adjusted the steam wand, already picturing autumn leaves swirling across the surface of a latte. "I've been playing around with foam texture," he said, rolling his shoulders before reaching for a pitcher. "If I can get this right, we could have signature designs that people actually ask for by name."

Robyn, grinning, spread an array of syrups, spices, and liqueurs across the counter. "And I've been working on a few... let's call them *bold* variations of espresso martinis." She picked up a small bottle, drizzling a few drops into a glass before passing it to Sarah. "Try this, black walnut bitters. I think it adds just the right depth."

Sarah took a sip, her brows lifting in appreciation. "That's... unexpected," she said, licking her lips. "Not bad, but maybe a little too smoky?"

Robyn grinned and reached for another bottle. "Right, let's try again. Maybe a maple-infused espresso with just a touch of cardamom?"

Charlie glanced up from his steaming pitcher, watching the two with amusement. "At this rate, we'll need to introduce an entire tasting menu for espresso martinis."

Sarah chuckled, settling onto a stool and watching as Robyn adjusted her ingredients with a flourish. "I don't hate that idea," she admitted. "Imagine this place in the evenings. Dim lighting, soft music, a little cocktail menu to go with our coffee selection."

Robyn's eyes lit up. "Exactly! We could do themed nights. Espresso martinis with seasonal twists, maybe paired with little dessert bites."

Charlie nodded, returning to his milk frothing. "And I could still do my thing with the coffee side - signature lattes that feel just as special as the cocktails."

The three fell into a comfortable rhythm, lost in the excitement of their ideas. Glasses clinked as they tasted each new concoction, some greeted with nods of approval, others with laughter and exaggerated grimaces.

As the evening stretched on, the shop remained quiet but alive with creativity. The rich aroma of coffee and warm spices lingered in the air, and for a moment, the trio could see it, the future of *Sarah's Secrets*, transforming from a cozy daytime haven into an intimate evening retreat.

When the final test batch was poured, Sarah lifted her glass with a grin. "Here's to possibilities."

"To a little chaos," Robyn added with a mischievous twinkle in her eye.

Charlie smirked, raising his cup. "And to making it all work somehow."

They clinked their glasses together, the clatter a quiet promise of what was to come.

Sarah stood behind the counter of *Sarah's Secrets*, stifling a yawn as she wiped down the espresso machine for what felt like the tenth time. The comforting hum of the shop surrounded her: the soft chatter of customers, the rhythmic hiss of steamed milk, the faint clatter of cups, but this morning, even her beloved coffee sanctuary couldn't chase away the sluggish fog in her brain.

She'd had two drinks the night before. Two. And yet, here she was, moving like she'd run a marathon in quicksand. *How had it come to this?*

Once upon a time, being a lightweight had been economical. A glass of wine, and she'd been happily tipsy for the entire evening. But now? Now it was downright laughable. Two glasses, and she felt like she'd been hit by a slow-moving train the next morning. *Age was a cruel, cruel thing.*

The door opened, and Sarah glanced up, mid-sip of her much-needed coffee. Two customers stepped inside, their presence subtly shifting the café's energy. The first, a petite woman dressed in sleek black, carried herself with sharp confidence. Her piercing grey eyes flicked across the room, assessing. Beside her, a lanky man towered in contrast, his easy-going stance softening the stark intensity of his companion.

Still feeling half-human at best, Sarah took a deep breath. If she couldn't banish the fog in her head, she could at least fake alertness until the caffeine kicked in.

"Good morning," she greeted them, silently praying that her voice sounded more *perky barista* and less *exhausted woman questioning her life choices.*

As they approached the counter, the dynamic between the two became more apparent. The young woman took charge, her voice clear and assertive as she spoke, while the man seemed content to follow her lead, his body language supportive but decidedly more reserved.

The young woman, with a critical eye and a clear vision of what she wanted, detailed her coffee preferences meticulously. Sarah listened intently, repeating the order back to make sure that she had got it right. Having placed their orders, they found their seats by the window, providing them with a picturesque view of the passersby in Castle Road.

Overhearing the conversation, Charlie glanced over from where he was practising his latte art.

"It's all right, Mum, I've got this one," Charlie called out, wiping his hands on a cloth as he moved towards the espresso machine with a confident stride.

Carefully, Charlie crafted the coffee according to the woman's specifications. The precision in his movements, the careful calibration of the machine, and his focused expression all spoke of his passion and skill. With a final flourish, he completed the drink and carried it over to their table.

"Here you go," Charlie said, setting the cup before her with a polite smile. "Just as you ordered."

The woman took a tentative sip, her eyes assessing over the rim of the cup. After a moment, she set it down and nodded, her approval not effusive but evident. "It's good," she admitted reluctantly, her tone suggesting she had hoped to find fault.

As Charlie turned to leave, he caught a snippet of their conversation. "It's decent, but it's still not as good as when I do it myself," the woman remarked to her companion, a hint of smugness in her voice.

Her companion, a man with an easy-going manner, gave a half-smile that bordered on apologetic. "Maybe not, but it's a nice place, isn't it? Besides, not everyone can meet your exacting standards, but this is really good coffee."

Charlie adjusted the steam wand, half-listening as the woman critiqued her coffee. The words barely registered until:

"It's all fair in the coffee wars."

His grip on the milk pitcher tightened slightly. So, she was competing too. And she wasn't just confident, she was ruthless. Charlie glanced at her from the corner of his eye, sizing her up. The competition just got a lot more interesting.

Her companion laughed, a sound mixed with both admiration and challenge. "Clearly, we're both in it to win it," he said, raising his coffee cup in a half-toast. "But let's remember, it's supposed to be fun too."

She responded with a smirk, her eyes sparkling with competitive fire. "Oh, it will be fun. Winning always is."

But then, almost as an afterthought, her companion tilted his head and asked, "Is your family coming to watch you compete tomorrow?"

For the first time in their conversation, her bravado seemed to falter. She hesitated, her confident expression slipping just slightly. "I'm not sure," she said, her voice softening, a hint of uncertainty creeping in. "They've… never been too interested in what I do."

Her companion frowned sympathetically. "That's tough. You'd think they'd want to be there to support you."

She shrugged, the sharpness of her earlier tone dulling as she glanced down at her cup. "Yeah, well, some things you've just got to do on your own."

Charlie noted the shift in her, realising that behind the confidence and bravado, there was a vulnerability that she clearly wasn't eager to show. Returning to his preparations, the woman's words echoing in his mind. The competition tomorrow had just become more interesting. Charlie knew tomorrow wasn't just another day; it was a battleground, and he was more ready than ever to show what he could do.

Sarah brushed past Charlie, noticing his focused gaze on the customers. "Who are those two?" she asked quietly, nodding towards the window where the young woman and her companion were seated.

Charlie wiped his hands on a cloth, glancing briefly at his mother. "Competitors for tomorrow's Latte Art competition," he explained, his voice low.

Sarah nudged Charlie playfully. "Should I have 'accidentally' spilled coffee on them? Take out the competition early?"

Charlie snorted. "Appreciate the gangster moves, Mum, but I think I'll take my chances the old-fashioned way."

Sarah grinned, adjusting the espresso machine. "Just making sure you've got all your options covered."

Chapter 3

Charlie adjusted his apron for the third time, staring at his reflection in the coffee shop's window. His stomach was a knotted mess of nerves, but at least his hands – thankfully - were steady. The glass reflected the tense set of his jaw, the slightly too-wide eyes of a man on the edge of overthinking himself into a spiral.

He hadn't slept well. Every time he'd closed his eyes, his mind had replayed the same restless loop, steaming milk, pouring patterns, judges scribbling on scorecards, the sharp clang of a cup hitting the saucer too hard. At some point, he must have drifted off, but the sleep had been shallow, broken by flashes of competition nerves and the vague, nagging feeling that he was about to walk into something much bigger than a latte art contest.

Now, standing in the cool morning light, the weight of the day pressed heavy against his chest. It was too quiet in here. The usual comforting hum of the espresso machines, the chatter of regulars, the rich scent of ground coffee, none of it settled him the way it usually did. His reflection blurred slightly as Sarah approached behind him, her voice soft but firm. "Charlie, you're going to wear a hole in that thing if you keep fidgeting."

He exhaled slowly, forcing his fingers to unclench from the fabric. "I barely slept."

"I know," she said, tucking her phone into her bag. "I heard you pacing at 2 a.m."

Charlie let out a weak laugh. "Was it that obvious?"

"You sounded like a ghost haunting the kitchen." She nudged his arm playfully, but her gaze was searching. "You, ok?"

Charlie huffed out a breath, forcing his hands to still. "I just…this is the first big competition I've ever done. And I've seen the lineup. These guys aren't just baristas. They're professionals."

Sarah gave his arm a reassuring squeeze. "And so are you. Just because your name isn't on some coffee blog's Top Ten Baristas to Watch list doesn't mean you don't belong there."

Charlie exhaled, forcing a nod. "Right."

Still, his nerves gnawed at him. It wasn't just about competing, it was about who was judging. Roger Alton had been a fixture at these events for years, and his decisions were anything but fair. Charlie had been watching videos of past competitions, studying the winners, analysing their performances, and learning from their mistakes. And more than once, he had seen truly talented baristas snubbed simply because Roger didn't like them.

"Remember Javier Vasquez?" Charlie muttered, glancing at Sarah.

She frowned. "The guy who did that insane tulip and swan combo at the finals two years ago?", she asked, secretly impressed that she'd managed to remember.

Charlie nodded, his expression darkening. "Should've won. Hands down. But Roger hated him. Said his 'attitude' wasn't right for the industry. Gave the title to some guy whose pours were sloppy but who happened to be his mate's protégé."

Sarah sighed. "That's frustrating."

"It's worse than frustrating," Charlie muttered. "It's unfair. Everyone knew Javier was the best, but Roger made sure he lost. And now, Javier's working some hotel chain's breakfast shift instead of running his own café."

"Roger's still judging today?"

Charlie nodded. "Yeah. And that's what's messing with my head. He's unpredictable. One year he favours the classic, traditional styles, the next he acts like he's all about innovation. There's no way to know what he'll go for today."

Sarah studied him, then said quietly, "Win or lose, we know the truth. And that's what matters."

Charlie let her words settle over him, but the knot in his stomach didn't loosen. He wished it were that simple. He wished skill alone determined the outcome, not the whims of one man's personal preferences. But wishing wouldn't change anything, and all he could do now was step up and hope for the best.

Just as they turned toward the door, Robyn emerged from the kitchen, wiping her hands on a tea towel. The mid-morning crowd had settled into a steady rhythm, customers lost in quiet conversation or hunched over laptops with their drinks. She gave Charlie a once-over, her sharp gaze catching the way he was holding himself too stiffly.

"You'll be fine, you know," she said, crossing her arms. "Nerves are good. Means you care."

Charlie sighed. "Right now, I'd rather care a little less."

Robyn smirked. "That's not how it works, cuz." She reached over and gave his shoulder a firm squeeze. "Good luck today. You're gonna smash it."

"Thanks, Robyn." Charlie mustered a small smile.

"I'm going to try and pop over later," she added. "Amy's covering the ceramics shop this morning, but she said as soon as she gets a break, she'll swing by here so I can escape for a bit and catch the rest of the competition."

Charlie's brow lifted. "You sure you want to do that? Sounds like a solid excuse to get out of watching me flail around in front of a crowd."

Robyn snorted. "Flail? Hardly. You've been practicing for this for weeks. You've got the skills, Charlie. It's just about keeping your head in the game."

"Easier said than done," Charlie muttered.

Robyn pointed a stern finger at him. "Just breathe. Get in the zone. You know how to do this."

Charlie nodded, absorbing her words even as his stomach twisted with nerves.

"Besides," she added, smirking, "if you do mess up, at least I'll be there to laugh at you in person."

Charlie groaned, rolling his eyes. "Appreciate that, Robyn."

Sarah chuckled and nudged Charlie toward the door. "Come on, let's go before your support system starts making bets on how fast you spill milk on yourself."

Robyn called after him, her voice warm. "You've got this, Charlie! And don't forget, when I get there, I expect to see you in the final round."

Charlie threw a hand up in acknowledgment as he and Sarah stepped out of Sarah's Secrets and into the crisp morning air.

They climbed the canopied steps and passed through the grand entrance of The Queen's Hotel, where the hum of voices and the faint hiss of steam wands carried through the air. The rich aroma of freshly brewed coffee wrapped around them, a warm contrast to the crisp morning outside.

Inside, the Elizabeth Rooms had been utterly transformed. A long U-shaped arrangement of espresso stations gleamed beneath the glow of intricate chandeliers. Each setup was immaculate. Polished tampers and gleaming milk pitchers lined up in perfect symmetry, ready for the competition ahead.

At the far end of the room, the judges' table sat elevated slightly, like a panel of gods surveying their domain. The sight sent a cold ripple of anxiety down Charlie's spine.

"This is very real now," he muttered to Sarah as they wove through the crowd.

Sarah didn't slow. "You'd never forgive yourself if you left."

"Yeah, yeah." He squared his shoulders, inhaling deeply. He could do this.

Around them, competitors were already staking their claim at their designated stations. A few glanced his way, some sizing him up, others indifferent. And then there was Eleanor Wren, who Charlie recognised as the girl he has seen in the shop only a matter of hours ago.

Eleanor's eyes flickered to a nearby competitor whose family stood just beyond the barricades, waving excitedly. A mother, a father, a younger sibling bouncing on their heels with enthusiasm. A tightness clenched at her chest. She'd never had that kind of support. Her family had dismissed her passion as a frivolous waste of time, something she'd never fully admitted aloud. She pushed the thought aside, masking it with a sharp focus as she adjusted her milk jug.

"Roger," Eleanor called out, her voice steady, but her pulse hammering against her ribs.

Roger turned, raising an eyebrow at her. "Ah, Miss Wren," he said smoothly, the hint of condescension in his tone as he folded his arms. "What can I do for you?"

Eleanor's fingers tightened around the milk jug she was holding. "I wanted to ask you something. Why is it that no matter how well I do, I never seem to be in your favour?"

Roger gave her a knowing smile, the kind that made her skin crawl. "Favour? I don't deal in favouritism, my dear."

A sharp laugh escaped Eleanor's lips. "Really? Tell that to Victor. Or to Olivia, who you adored five years ago.

Or Martin." Her voice sharpened as she gestured across the room. "Every year, you pick a favourite. And the rest of us? We're just here to make the competition look legitimate."

Roger sighed, adjusting his jacket. "That's quite the accusation, Miss Wren." He took a step closer, lowering his voice. "Maybe you should spend less time blaming me and more time improving your work. I saw your pour last year. It lacked elegance. A little stiff, like you were trying too hard."

Eleanor's breath caught slightly. It was a slap in the face, because she had been trying. Harder than anyone else in the room.

Roger smirked, as if satisfied by her silence. He turned on his heel and took a step away.

"I should disqualify you for such an accusation," he mused over his shoulder. "But that would be a waste, wouldn't it? Some people can redeem themselves. Others…" He glanced back at her. "Well, let's see if you fall into the former category."

Eleanor stood frozen, her heart pounding with fury and humiliation. Her gaze flicked to Charlie. Not friendly. Predatory.

Charlie forced himself to look away, but the message was clear: You're not a threat.

Sarah leaned in, voice low. "I don't like her."

Charlie let out a quiet chuckle. "You don't even know her."

"I know that look." Sarah sniffed. "She's already decided she's better than you."

Across the room, Martin Acton stood near his station, laughing a little too loudly at something one of the event coordinators said. His stance was easy, relaxed, exuding the confidence of someone who had already decided he'd won.

Charlie felt frustration coil inside him like a tightening spring.

"Looks like he enjoys the spotlight," Sarah noted.

"Yeah. And it looks like Roger is happy to give it to him."

Charlie's attention landed on the head judge, Roger Alton, who was deep in conversation with Martin. The older man's expression was indulgent, his hand resting on Martin's shoulder, his nods carrying an air of approval, the kind of silent endorsement that was impossible to miss.

But then, something flickered in Martin's expression. As Roger turned slightly to speak to a fellow judge, Martin's smile dropped for the briefest moment. His jaw tensed, and his body shifted just enough to drop Roger's hand from his shoulder, as if the weight of it had become unwelcome. The movement was quick, practiced. Barely noticeable. And then, just like that, the smile was back, bright and effortless.

The exchange was subtle. Calculated. A keen observer might have seen it for what it was, something just beneath the surface of Martin's polished exterior. Charlie, however, wasn't watching him closely enough to catch it.

"Hey, it's Charlie, isn't it?!"

He turned at the familiar voice, spotting Victor Chan making his way over. Unlike Martin and Eleanor, Victor's excitement was genuine, not calculated.

"You ready?" Victor asked, adjusting his apron.

"As I'll ever be," Charlie replied.

Victor grinned. "Good. I'd rather lose to someone cool than one of those" he jerked his chin toward Martin and Eleanor, lowering his voice, "coffee snobs."

Charlie couldn't help but laugh. "Thanks for the vote of confidence."

Victor wiped his hands on his apron. "You know, my grandma always said coffee and tea are just two sides of the same coin. I started mixing them to honour her. Kind of my way of keeping her traditions alive."

Charlie nodded, appreciating the sentiment. "That's a pretty great reason to be here."

Victor shrugged, smiling. "Gotta do something to make a name for myself, right?"

The buzz of conversation dipped as Roger Alton stepped forward, microphone in hand.

"Welcome, competitors," he announced, his voice rich and commanding. "You are the best and brightest of the South heat, and today, you will prove your worth. This is not just about skill, it's about artistry, passion, and mastery of craft."

Sarah muttered, "He clearly loves the sound of his own voice."

Charlie bit back a smile.

Roger's gaze swept the room, lingering just a second longer on Martin. "Remember, every pour, every swirl of milk, every microfoam texture will be scrutinized. The smallest detail separates excellence from mediocrity."

Charlie exhaled, the tension thick in the air.

Sarah nudged him. "Ready?"

He inhaled deeply. "Yeah. Let's do this."

The announcer stepped up to the microphone.

"Competitors, take your positions. The South heat of the Latte Art championship is officially underway."

And just like that, the competition had begun.

Charlie stood at his station, carefully aligning his milk pitchers and adjusting the grind on his espresso machine, forcing his hands to remain steady. The hum of conversation filled the Elizabeth Rooms, an undercurrent of anticipation as competitors fine-tuned their setups and spectators settled into their seats.

Sarah had found her place in the audience, strategically positioned where she had a clear view of her son. She crossed her legs and leaned forward slightly, her keen gaze scanning the room. Though she wasn't competing, she felt a tight coil of tension in her stomach, as if she were the one about to step into the spotlight.

From her seat, just a few rows from the judges' table, the low murmur of their conversation drifted toward her. She wasn't deliberately eavesdropping, but the occasional sharp whisper caught her attention.

"Alton's being obvious about it again," Judge Evelyn muttered, barely lowering her voice as she shuffled through the scorecards.

Sarah glanced over. Evelyn looked to be in her late thirties, younger than Sarah but with an air of quiet authority. Her neatly braided dark hair and crisp blazer gave her a polished, no-nonsense look, though the tight press of her lips suggested she was holding back irritation.

Judge Paul, seated beside her, cast a quick glance toward the head of the panel, where Roger Alton stood, already basking in the authority of his position. Paul leaned back slightly, adjusting the rolled-up sleeves of his linen shirt, a touch of amusement flickering behind his glasses. He had the unmistakable air of a hipster, salt-and-pepper beard, leather watch strap, and a casual-but-calculated style that suggested he probably knew the best single-origin espresso within a ten-mile radius.

"I noticed," Paul murmured. "He's barely looked at half the competitors, yet I bet he already has Martin Acton in the semi-finals."

Evelyn exhaled through her nose, frustration evident. "He's not even trying to be subtle. And if I hear him talk about 'balance and texture' one more time..."

Paul smirked, shaking his head. "It's always balance and texture when it's someone he likes."

Sarah hid a small smile, shifting slightly in her chair. If nothing else, it seemed she wasn't the only one keeping a close watch on how things unfolded today.

Roger's voice rang out over the general hum of the room. "Ah, Martin! I see you've brought that exceptional blend from your shop. You're not just here to compete, you're here to educate, I imagine?"

Martin smirked as he adjusted his apron. "Well, someone has to set the standard."

Charlie, finishing the final tweaks to his setup, exchanged a glance with Sarah. "Is it just me, or does Roger already have a winner picked out?"

Sarah kept her voice low, her eyes still on the judges' table. "It's not just you. But don't let it throw you. Stay focused."

Across the room, Eleanor Wren straightened a row of cups at her station, her expression cool and unreadable. But her fingers pressed a little too hard against the ceramic, a flicker of irritation betraying her thoughts.

"Every year," she muttered to Olivia Green, who stood at the next station. "Every year, he does this."

Olivia, with the ease of a past champion, merely raised an eyebrow. "If you're good enough, even Roger Alton can't ignore you."

Eleanor's jaw tensed. "We'll see about that."

Olivia adjusted the steam wand on her machine, her movements measured. "It should be enough just to be good enough," she said lightly, but there was an edge beneath the words. "But some of us know that's not always how it works."

Eleanor shot her a glance, catching the flicker of something unsaid in Olivia's expression. She knew Olivia had butted heads with Roger before, he didn't like how she pushed boundaries, how she insisted on bringing new products into the competition space when he preferred tradition. It was a quiet battle, but an ongoing one.

"He hates change," Eleanor said.

Olivia let out a short, dry laugh. "He hates anything he doesn't control."

For a moment, their eyes met in silent understanding. Then, with a small shake of her head, Eleanor exhaled and picked up her tamper. "Well, he's going to have to deal with it."

Olivia smirked. "That's the spirit."

A hush fell as Roger Alton took the microphone. He adjusted his tie, savouring the moment before he spoke.

"Welcome, competitors, to the South heat of the Latte Art championship," he announced, his voice practiced and theatrical. "Today, we are not just judging technique, we are celebrating artistry. True talent will shine through."

Sarah caught Judge Evelyn rolling her eyes.

"We have a spectacular lineup this year," Roger continued. "Some familiar faces, some bold newcomers. And as always, we expect excellence." His gaze flicked briefly to Eleanor, then away, as if she weren't worth more than a passing mention.

Eleanor's fingers tightened around her milk pitcher.

Roger's voice turned warm as he continued, "Now, Martin Acton, your shop has been making waves lately. We're all eager to see what you bring to the table."

Sarah didn't miss the slight shift in the crowd's energy, a few exchanged glances, a murmur here and there. It wasn't just her noticing Roger's bias.

Evelyn's fingers drummed against the clipboard now, her frustration barely concealed. "For God's sake," she muttered under her breath. Paul smirked, but there was no humour in it. He flicked his gaze toward Roger, who stood at the front of the room, basking in the attention as if he were the main event.

Further down the table, one of the newer judges shifted uncomfortably, eyes darting between Roger and the competitors. They were catching on.

Roger, either oblivious or simply enjoying himself, smiled. "Now, let's begin."

The atmosphere in the room crackled with nervous energy. Competitors poured, etched, and swirled, their creations coming to life beneath the intense scrutiny of the judging panel. The audience leaned in with quiet murmurs of admiration and critique, while the espresso machines hummed their rhythmic tune.

Martin Acton stepped forward first, gliding to the judges' table with the confidence of a man who already knew he had won. His latte art, a stunning swan, was technically perfect, and even before Roger tasted it, his approval was obvious.

"Superb. Absolutely superb," Roger declared after a single sip. "Balance. Texture. Depth. This is craftsmanship."

The murmurs from the crowd weren't just whispers now, they were open, simmering discontent.

"He's not even hiding it," someone hissed behind Sarah. Sarah crossed her arms, uneasy.

Eleanor Wren stepped up next, her design immaculate, her pour flawless. The audience tensed, watching as she slid the cup towards Roger. Roger lifted the latte to his lips, took a sip, then immediately set it down with a sharp clink. His expression twisted, just slightly, but enough.

"The temperature is off," he said, voice clipped. A ripple of disbelief coursed through the room. Even Judge Evelyn stiffened in her seat.

Eleanor inhaled sharply. "Excuse me?"

"The temperature," Roger repeated, adjusting his glasses. "It's half a degree too cool. It dulls the overall effect."

The competitors stilled. Everyone knew Eleanor's precision was near unmatched.

Evelyn, not bothering to hide her exasperation, leaned forward. "Roger, come on…"

"I trust you'll respect the panel's expertise, Evelyn," Roger interrupted smoothly, his smile thin. He picked up his glass of water and took a long sip, then turned back to the competitors, completely unfazed.

Eleanor clenched her jaw. "Right."

Charlie could feel the tension radiating from her as she turned away. He swallowed hard - that could be me in a moment.

Judge Paul scribbled something onto his scorecard with more force than necessary, shaking his head.

Charlie stepped forward next, steadying his breath as he worked quickly. His signature piece was coming together, an intricate phoenix rising from flames, the delicate contrast of espresso and microfoam forming sharp, elegant wings. The moment he placed his cup on the judges' table, Roger Alton reached for it first.

"Ah, intriguing," Roger murmured, swirling the cup gently. "A phoenix. Ambitious."

Charlie held his breath as Roger took a slow sip. His expression remained unreadable for a beat too long.

"Quite bold on the vanilla," Roger finally remarked, tapping a finger against the ceramic. "But confident. Intentional."

Charlie exhaled slightly, but then something changed. Roger's expression shifted.

The change was so small at first that no one noticed. Roger's fingers twitched, the cup slipping slightly in his grasp. His throat bobbed as if he were trying to swallow something thick and impossible. His breathing became laboured.

For the first time that evening, Roger Alton's mask of control faltered. He gripped the edge of the table, blinking rapidly. His chest rose sharply, as if trying to expand against an invisible weight.

Judge Paul noticed first. "Roger?"

Roger exhaled through his nose, a short, sharp sound, but then his knees buckled. The room gasped as he stumbled backward, knocking over a chair. His hand clutched at his throat, then his chest.

Then, he collapsed.

Silence fell over the ballroom, followed by pandemonium. A woman screamed. Someone dropped a cup. The audience surged forward, stopping just short of where Roger lay sprawled on the floor. His breath came in sharp, ragged gasps. His lips parted, as if he wanted to say something, then his body shuddered violently. Sarah pushed through the crowd, instinctively reaching for Charlie. His face was pale, his eyes locked on Roger's convulsing body.

"He…he just…" Charlie stammered.

"Call an ambulance!" a voice yelled from the judges' table.

A man from the crowd pushed forward. "I know first aid! Let me through."

He dropped to his knees beside Roger, looking alarmed at the severity of what he was seeing. "Does he have an epi pen? This looks like an allergic reaction."

People glanced around frantically.

"Helen!" someone called out. "Helen, his assistant has his epi pen!"

Helen, who had been frozen in shock, snapped out of her stupor and hurried forward, fumbling with her bag. "I…I have it somewhere in here," she said, digging through the contents with trembling hands.

"Why doesn't he carry it himself?" the man asked incredulously, trying to keep Roger's airway open.

Helen's voice turned bitter as she dug through her bag. "He refuses. Says it's not his job, that it's everyone else's responsibility to keep him safe."

Her fingers probed frantically past notebooks, loose receipts, and what felt like a tangle of charging cables. The seconds ticked by as Roger's breathing grew more laboured.

"We need that pen now!" the men urged, his knuckles white as he maintained Roger's position.

Helen cursed under her breath and, with a sudden motion, upended the entire bag onto the nearest table. Items clattered across the surface, keys, a purser, sunglasses, and a dozen other personal effects scattering in all directions. She scrabbled desperately through the pile, shoving things aside with increasing panic until her hand firmly closed around the plastic tube of the epi pen. But as she gripped it, her movements became oddly hesitant, her eyes fixed on Roger's face with an unreadable expression. For a moment, just a moment, she seemed to pause before handing it over.

By the time the man administered the injection, Roger shuddered once more. Then stilled.

The first aider felt for a pulse, his face growing pale. A long, horrible pause. Then, he looked up. "He's gone."

The room stood frozen in collective shock. Roger Alton was dead.

The competition floor, once alive with motion and excitement, had transformed into something cold.

Judge Evelyn pressed a hand to her mouth. Paul turned away, jaw tight. Martin Acton took a full step back, his face unreadable.

And then, the first murmur of suspicion slipped into the silence.

"He had just taken a sip of his drink."

Sarah's stomach dropped. Charlie flinched. Another voice, sharper.

"No, wait, wasn't it one of the competitors' drinks?"

Someone turned to the table. Roger's last cup, the last thing he had tasted, still sat there.

Charlie's cup. Sarah's breath caught.

And then, a single, terrible accusation broke the air.

"Did someone poison him?"

A new kind of tension settled over the room. A different kind of competition had begun.

Chapter 4

In the hour after Roger's death, the air buzzed with hushed speculation and uneasy glances. The shock of his collapse had rippled through the crowd, leaving behind an eerie sense of disbelief. Conversations, once lively and full of competitive camaraderie, had turned into frantic whispers and exchanged looks of concern.

Sarah clutched the edge of her chair, her fingers tightening against the cool wood. Her heartbeat thudded in her ears, an unsettling rhythm that matched the nervous energy filling the ballroom.

She'd come here expecting an afternoon of friendly rivalry, a showcase of skill, precision, and passion for coffee artistry. And now, instead of celebrating Charlie's success, she was watching him wilt under the weight of silent accusations.

Then, the room stilled as Detective Inspector Luke Stanley stepped through the hotel's double doors, his shoes clicking with purposeful determination against the polished floor. Though young for his rank, his presence commanded immediate attention, and the gravity in his sharp gaze silenced the nearest onlookers. Dressed in a crisp suit, he wasted no time establishing control.

Near the stage, Mr. Henderson, the hotel manager, was engaged in a flustered, ineffective attempt to usher people away from the area. His hands fluttered in vague gestures, his voice strained but yielding little success as guests craned their necks for a better look.

"Please, if everyone could just…just move back…this is not…" His words faltered as yet another person ignored him, stepping forward in morbid curiosity.

He turned, exasperated, only to exhale in something like relief as he spotted the police entering. The weight of responsibility slipped from his shoulders the moment he saw Stanley striding in, his assured presence cutting through the uncertainty like a knife.

"No one leaves this room," Stanley instructed the hotel staff, his voice calm but firm. At his signal, officers moved with practiced efficiency, securing the exits and fanning out to begin their meticulous task of gathering evidence. The heavy doors swung shut behind them with an air of finality.

Henderson took a step back, deferring instantly, his hands dropping to his sides. The control he had so desperately tried to assert now shifted seamlessly to Stanley, who took it without hesitation.

Sarah exhaled shakily. She had met Inspector Stanley before, under equally grim circumstances at a local spa, where, by sheer misfortune, she had been present at the scene of a murder. At the time, she had taken one look at his youthful face and doubted whether he had the experience to handle such a case. But he had proved her wrong in the most decisive way, arriving just in time to prevent her from being attacked. His quiet determination and sharp instincts had left a lasting impression, and over time, she had come to respect his no-nonsense approach to policing.

Since then, he had stopped by *Sarah's Secrets* on occasion, not for idle chatter, but for the briefest moments of respite, sipping his coffee while his mind clearly remained preoccupied with work. He was a sincere young man, one utterly wedded to his job.

Even now, as his gaze swept over the ballroom and met hers, he gave only the slightest nod of recognition—no smile, no warmth, just a brief acknowledgment before returning his attention to the investigation. Sarah didn't take offense. This wasn't a social occasion. But she couldn't ignore the nagging thought that he might find her repeated presence at crime scenes suspicious.

She inhaled slowly, willing herself to stay composed. As the murmurs around her grew softer, Stanley stepped forward, his voice cutting through the anxious silence.

"Ladies and gentlemen, I understand this is a distressing time," he said, his steady tone carrying the weight of authority. "However, I must ask for your full cooperation. Given the circumstances of Mr. Alton's death, we will be conducting individual interviews. It is vital that we gather as much information as possible."

A ripple of unease spread through the room, but no one dared argue. Stanley's sharp gaze moved between faces, assessing reactions. Then, he turned to his officers. "Start with those nearest to the victim when he collapsed."

Sarah sat with Charlie, her mind racing through the events of the afternoon. She had seen Roger Alton bustling about earlier, playing the role of esteemed judge with his usual pompous flair. But had there been something in his expression? A flicker of unease? A hesitation? She replayed every detail, worrying she had missed something vital.

Charlie sat beside her, uncharacteristically quiet, tracing idle patterns on his leg. He had been excited for this competition, his passion for coffee artistry on full display. Now, that excitement had been replaced by a nervous energy that he struggled to contain.

Charlie exhaled slowly. "What are you thinking?" he asked, his voice low.

"That I might have seen something important without realizing it," Sarah murmured. She absently turned her coffee cup in her hands, staring at the swirling liquid as if it might hold the answers she sought.

A snippet of hushed conversation caught her attention.

"…they knew about his nut allergy, right? How could someone serve him that drink?" one competitor whispered to another.

"Yeah, but who would've thought he'd actually drink it? I thought he'd just taste and judge… not actually swallow," the other responded, a nervous tremor in his voice.

Sarah's breath caught. If Roger's allergy had been common knowledge, then someone might have deliberately used it against him. A chill ran down her spine as she considered the implications.

Across the room, Stanley continued his systematic inquiries, his sharp gaze sweeping over the gathered competitors and spectators. The assistant overseeing the competition approached him hesitantly, wringing her hands.

"It was Charlie Meadows' coffee that Mr. Alton sampled last," she admitted in a near whisper.

Stanley turned, his expression unreadable as he took in the information. Before he could move, another figure approached, Helen, Roger's long-time assistant.

Helen had regained her composure since the frantic search for the epi pen just a short time earlier. Her trembling hands were now steady, her breathing controlled. She'd quickly tucked her blouse back into place and smoothed her hair, erasing most traces of her earlier panic. Now, she carried a clipboard tucked tightly against her side, her expression a careful balance between concern and weary exasperation. If any remnants of her momentary hesitation with the epi pen remained, they were masked behind the professional veneer she'd clearly perfected over years working for Roger.

"I thought you should have this," she said, offering the clipboard. "I keep a record of Roger's interactions during the competition, who he spoke to, what he tasted. It confirms what she just said. Charlie Meadows was the last person he interacted with before... well." She exhaled, shaking her head. "Before this."

Stanley studied her, assessing. She wasn't flustered like the others, concerned, yes, but not distraught.

"You don't seem surprised," he observed.

Helen gave a small shrug. "Let's just say Roger had a way of making a scene. This one just happened to be his last."

There was no malice in her voice, just the resignation of someone who had spent years managing a man prone to dramatics.

"Beyond Charlie, did Roger mention anything about the coffee? Any complaints?"

Helen pursed her lips, flipping through a few pages on her clipboard. "No, but that doesn't mean much. He was opinionated, but if he wanted to make a point, he'd do it when it suited him." Her gaze flickered toward Roger's motionless form. "And now, I suppose we'll never know."

Stanley held her gaze for a moment before nodding. With a final glance at the clipboard, he handed it off to one of his officers. Then, with deliberate steps, he moved toward Charlie Meadows.

"Mr. Meadows," he said, his voice carefully neutral, "can you walk me through exactly what happened when you prepared Roger Alton's drink?"

Charlie swallowed hard. "I...I followed the same process I always do. I steamed the milk, pulled the espresso shot, poured the latte. I didn't add anything extra." His voice wavered, and he quickly added, "I wouldn't. Why would I?"

Stanley studied him carefully. This didn't sound like the Charlie he had come to know through visiting *Sarah's Secrets*. The young barista was serious about his craft, meticulous and precise. He wasn't reckless. And he wasn't cruel.

But Stanley could not afford to make assumptions. He had learned that lesson early in his career, people were not always what they seemed. No matter how much he wanted to believe Charlie wasn't capable of this, it wasn't his job to believe in people. It was his job to find the truth. His expression remained unreadable as he flipped to a fresh page in his notepad.

Stanley turned to the hotel manager. "Each contestant selected their milk type upon registration?"

The manager, a stout man with a perpetually worried expression, stepped forward hastily. "Inspector, I can assure you, we are not that negligent," he said. "We knew Mr. Alton's allergy was severe. When we arranged for the competition, we specifically removed all nut-based milks from the options. We couldn't take any risks."

Stanley's gaze narrowed. "And how was the milk distributed?"

"We prepared individual trays for each competitor, clearly labelled with their chosen selection. There was no almond, cashew, or hazelnut milk anywhere in this competition," the manager continued. "We made absolutely sure of that."

Stanley was quiet for a moment, tapping his pen against his notepad. "Then we have a bigger problem," he said finally. "If nut milk wasn't an option, then how did it get into his drink?"

Silence gripped the room.

Charlie sat slumped in a quiet corner, his heart pounding as former friends and competitors cast wary glances his way. Sarah sat beside him, her body rigid with barely concealed anxiety.

"Charlie," she said softly, "whatever happens, I'm here for you. We'll get through this."

Charlie forced a weak smile. "Thanks, Mum."

But as they waited for Stanley's inevitable call, Sarah could feel the tide turning. The world outside their little café had never felt so far away, and for the first time, she wondered if they would truly make it out of this unscathed.

A quiet scuff of a shoe on the polished floor made Sarah glance up. Gemma had drifted closer, standing just within earshot. There was something hesitant in her posture, as if she wasn't sure whether to step forward or keep her distance.

"Sorry," Gemma said suddenly, shaking her head. "I didn't mean to eavesdrop, I just can't believe this is happening." Her voice was tight with frustration, her gaze flicking between Charlie and Sarah.

Charlie let out a humourless laugh. "Join the club."

Sarah leaned forward. "Gemma, did you see anything?"

Gemma bit her lip, thinking. "I was running around all morning, same as everyone else, but one thing I *do* know is that no one was guarding the milk in the kitchen. I mean, why would they? You don't go around assuming people are going to swap stuff out. It just, it doesn't make sense."

Sarah's pulse quickened. "So you're saying someone *could* have tampered with it?"

"I'm saying that if someone *wanted* to, they would've had plenty of chances." Gemma's expression darkened. "People were coming and going constantly, competitors, hotel staff, suppliers dropping things off. No one was watching every single movement."

Charlie swallowed. "But why? Why would anyone do that? It's not like I had a chance at winning, not really."

Gemma hesitated, then spoke carefully. "Maybe it wasn't about winning."

A heavy pause hung between them.

Sarah could feel the tension shifting, the pieces of a puzzle shifting into place, though the final picture remained out of reach. But one thing was clear, someone had planned this. And if they had gone to the trouble of swapping out the milk, then they had done it with intention.

This wasn't an accident. This was murder.

Chapter 5

Crime scene tape glittered under the ornate chandeliers, an incongruous reminder of the tragedy that had unfolded in the elegant ballroom. The once lively competition space was now subdued, its attendees huddled in small groups, their whispers heavy with unease.

In the midst of the tension, Gemma and Teddy moved with quiet urgency, tasked with shepherding people away from the crime scene. Under the watchful eyes of the police, they guided competitors, judges, and spectators into designated side rooms, where they would wait to be interviewed. Some followed without question, dazed by the sudden shift in events, while others hesitated, casting nervous glances back toward the ballroom.

"Through here, please," Gemma said firmly, holding a door open as a small group filed past. Teddy hovered nearby, his usual easy-going manner replaced by a rare edge of tension.

"We need to keep this moving," he murmured to her, eyeing the growing number of people still lingering near the ballroom entrance.

Gemma nodded, already scanning the room for the next group to usher away. The faster they got everyone settled, the sooner the police could begin piecing together what had really happened.

Gemma, her brow furrowed, turned to Teddy. "When you said this would be a weekend to remember, this wasn't quite what I had in mind," she murmured, her voice barely audible above the low murmur of the crowd.

Teddy huffed out a breath, dragging a table into place. "Yeah, well, I didn't mean it like this either." His eyes scanned the room, taking in the scattered groups of competitors, judges, and spectators now waiting to be interviewed. "It's just unreal."

They worked quickly, pulling tables into the side rooms to create makeshift interview stations. The tension in the air was palpable, every movement from the lingering attendees edged with unease. As Gemma adjusted a chair, she caught a sharp voice cutting through the hushed atmosphere.

"This was supposed to be my year. What am I supposed to do now if it gets cancelled?"

She glanced toward the doorway, where Eleanor Wren stood, arms folded tightly across her chest, her frustration evident. Across from her, Roger's assistant, Helen Williams, let out a sharp breath, her expression a mix of exhaustion and disbelief.

"If it has escaped your notice, something a little more important than your 'supposed year' has happened here, Eleanor," Helen shot back, her tone laced with sarcasm.

Eleanor recoiled slightly, her face flickering between annoyance and shock. "I know that, but…"

"But nothing," Helen interrupted, her patience wearing thin. "Every competitor thinks this is their year. You're not the only one affected by this tragedy."

Eleanor let out a short snort, unimpressed. "They can think what they want, but I know I'm right."

Gemma exchanged a look with Teddy as they continued setting up, both silently acknowledging the sheer audacity of Eleanor's words. Even in the wake of a man's death, ambition, it seemed, was not so easily shaken.

Charlie paced backwards and forwards in a secluded corner of the hotel's conference room, transformed temporarily into a holding area for competitors. The sounds of hushed conversations and the intermittent clicking of camera shutters from the crime scene investigation team filled the space, each click amplifying his growing anxiety.

'It was just supposed to be about the art, the flavour... How could this have gone so wrong?' Charlie replayed the moment he handed his crafted latte to Roger. He had chosen the ingredients meticulously, aiming to impress with a harmonious blend of espresso and a touch of vanilla. *'I didn't know... I just didn't know about his allergies.'*

His hands shook slightly as he thought about the consequences. The competition had been his chance to shine, to bring something positive to *Sarah's Secrets*, not a disaster that could overshadow their hard work. *'What if they think I did something on purpose? It was just a normal latte, nothing that could...'*

'No, stop,' he chastised himself. *'You didn't do anything wrong. It's a horrible accident, that's all. But why did it have to happen with my coffee?'*

Charlie felt a heavy sense of isolation as eyes occasionally flicked to him, whispers barely masked behind cupped hands. The room felt colder, the air thicker as the weight of unwarranted suspicion settled on his shoulders. He knew he was innocent, but the reality of the situation was daunting. The idea that he could be implicated in a tragedy over a simple cup of coffee he had made was overwhelming and surreal.

'Just hold on,' he told himself, trying to muster a semblance of calm. *'The truth will come out. It has to.'*

Robyn stormed into the hotel lobby like a whirlwind, her breath coming fast from the sprint across town. The moment she'd heard what was happening, she'd practically thrown off her apron and bolted from the coffee shop, barely pausing to lock up behind her. The news had sent her heart into overdrive, Charlie, in trouble? Accused of something criminal? It was absurd. And she wasn't about to stand by and let him face it alone.

She shoved her way past a cluster of onlookers, her voice ringing out over the low hum of speculation. "I need to see my cousin and Aunt Sarah, now!"

Hotel Manager, Mr Henderson, a wiry man with a permanently harried expression, stepped in front of her, holding up a hand. "Miss, you can't just barge in here."

"I can, and I will!" Robyn shot back, her frustration mounting. "This is ridiculous. My cousin is in there being accused of God knows what, and you expect me to stand here and wait for scraps of information like some nosy bystander?"

"Miss, please, this is a police investigation," the manager started again, but before he could finish, a voice cut through the tension.

"Let her through."

Inspector Stanley stood a few feet away, arms crossed, his gaze fixed on Robyn with a mixture of resignation and something else, something softer, though he'd never admit it. He knew her well enough by now to realise that if he didn't let her in, she'd probably find another way through. And, though he wouldn't say it aloud, he also didn't quite like the idea of her looking at him with the same kind of fury she was currently directing at the hotel manager.

The manager hesitated, looking between them, then finally stepped aside with a sigh. Robyn didn't waste a second. She brushed past him, muttering something under her breath, and made a beeline for Sarah and Charlie.

She barely stopped before throwing her arms around them, gripping tight as if to reassure herself that they were really there. "What's all this about?" she demanded, pulling back just enough to scan their faces. "Why is everyone acting like Charlie's done something terrible?"

Sarah exhaled, rubbing her temple. "It's complicated. They think…" She hesitated, eyes darting to Charlie before continuing. "They think something happened with a coffee that Charlie made. And until they figure out what it is, it's… well, it's not looking good."

Robyn's expression darkened, her hands balling into fists. "That's ridiculous. Charlie wouldn't hurt a fly, let alone sabotage a competition. And why would he want to do a thing like that?"

Before either of them could stop her, she whirled around and marched straight towards Stanley, who had returned to overseeing the evidence collection.

"Inspector," she called, her voice carrying a sharp edge.

Stanley turned, and the moment he saw the storm brewing in her expression, he sighed internally. He had known, even as he let her in, that he'd regret it.

Robyn came to a halt in front of him, folding her arms. "You know Charlie. You've been to the coffee shop. You know what kind of person he is."

Stanley met her glare with an unreadable expression. "Robyn, this is a serious investigation. While I understand your concerns, we have to follow where the evidence leads us."

"But there is no evidence against him!" she shot back, her voice rising. "Just because it was his coffee doesn't mean he had anything to do with this. Someone could have tampered with it after he made it, have you even thought of that?"

"Every angle will be investigated," Stanley said, his tone firm but calm.

"Then why does it feel like you've already made up your mind?" Robyn challenged, stepping closer. "Charlie has worked his arse off for this competition. And now, because someone decided to mess with his coffee, you're treating him like a suspect? How is that fair?"

Stanley held up a hand, trying to keep his own patience intact. "I haven't accused him of anything. But I need to look at this objectively."

"Objectively?" Robyn's voice pitched higher. "So you're saying you're just going to ignore what you know about him? About us?"

Sarah, sensing the shift in tone, quickly stepped in, placing a hand on Robyn's arm. "Robyn, enough."

"No, it's not enough," Robyn snapped, her frustration boiling over. "Charlie is being treated like a criminal, and I'm supposed to just stand here and let it happen?"

Stanley's jaw tightened. "No one is treating him like a criminal."

"Oh really? Then why does he have people watching his every move like he's about to make a run for it?" She gestured sharply toward the officers near the evidence table.

Stanley exhaled, running a hand through his hair. He had let her in because he cared, because some part of him didn't like seeing her upset. And now she was standing in front of him, fire blazing in her eyes, making him regret his moment of weakness. He had seen her fierce before, but not like this. Not with her fury turned on him.

Sarah tightened her grip on Robyn's arm. "Robyn, please. This isn't helping."

Robyn turned back, her chest rising and falling in quick, uneven breaths. For a second, she looked like she wanted to keep arguing, to keep pressing Stanley until he admitted she was right. But then she looked at Charlie, his face drawn, his hands gripping the edge of a nearby chair like he was holding himself together by sheer force of will.

She exhaled, some of the fight bleeding out of her. "Fine," she muttered. "Fine."

Sarah softened. "Listen, Robyn… I think it's best if you go back to the shop."

Robyn's head snapped up. "What? No. I'm staying."

Sarah offered a small, weary smile. "I need someone to keep the coffee shop running."

Robyn's brow furrowed, about to protest, but Sarah pressed on. "And… I think it might be best if you weren't here right now. We need Stanley to be on our side, and, well…" She glanced meaningfully at the inspector, whose expression remained carefully blank.

Robyn scowled. "Oh, so now it's my fault?"

"Of course not," Sarah said gently. "But you know what you're like when you get wound up."

Robyn exhaled through her nose, looking between them all. Then, reluctantly, she nodded. "Fine. But this isn't over."

Sarah squeezed her hand. "I know."

Robyn cast one last glare in Stanley's direction before turning on her heel and striding toward the exit. Stanley watched her go, resisting the urge to pinch the bridge of his nose. He had a feeling that letting her in had been a mistake, but at the same time, watching her storm out, he couldn't quite bring himself to regret it.

Sarah had been loitering near the competition area long enough to overhear most of the contestants being questioned. She knew she should probably be sitting down somewhere, acting inconspicuous, but she couldn't help herself. Every answer, every hesitant pause, every flicker of emotion on the competitors' faces could be important.

Her mind buzzed, unable to settle. Even as she focused on the police's movements, part of her kept circling back to Charlie. He had been visibly shaken when the chaos first erupted, his normally steady hands trembling as he was pulled aside for questioning. She had caught glimpses of him speaking with one of the officers, his responses quiet, almost mechanical. He was rattled. But was it just the shock of witnessing a death up close, or something more?

Sarah exhaled slowly, trying to ground herself, but her brain refused to quiet. Every sound, every movement in the grand ballroom fed into her restless energy. The hum of conversation from lingering guests, the scrape of chairs being pushed back, the quiet efficiency of hotel staff clearing away abandoned cups, all of it kept her senses on high alert.

Her gaze kept drifting back to Inspector Stanley. He moved with an assured purpose, weaving through the room, methodically gathering pieces of the puzzle. Sarah watched as he finished up with one of the junior baristas, his notepad flipping closed with a decisive motion before his sharp eyes lifted toward Gemma.

Sarah's pulse quickened. She took a slow sip of her now-lukewarm coffee, using the movement as an excuse to reposition herself near the seating area. If she was too obvious, Stanley might notice her watching, and the last thing she wanted was to draw unnecessary attention to herself.

The room was still full of movement, competitors reluctantly packing up their tools, guests murmuring in hushed voices, police officers stationed near the exits. It wasn't difficult to blend in. As she casually adjusted the sugar packets on the refreshment table, her focus remained locked on Stanley.

He took a step toward Gemma, and Sarah braced herself, her fingers tightening slightly around the coffee cup.

Gemma looked flustered as Inspector Stanley approached. Her dark eyes glittered, not quite clear whether from excitement or stress, as she straightened instinctively, brushing a stray curl away from her face. Her makeup, once carefully applied, now bore smudges where she had absentmindedly rubbed at her skin throughout the day, likely while moving furniture and managing guests. Despite the exhaustion that clung to her posture, there was a steadiness in her gaze, a clarity in the way she squared her shoulders and faced the inspector.

Stanley stopped in front of her, his notebook in hand. "Miss Smith, I'd like to ask you a few questions about the moments leading up to the incident," he said, his voice steady but not unkind.

Gemma nodded quickly, though her eyes flicked away for a brief second, as if mentally sorting through the jumble of the past hour. "Of course, Inspector."

Sarah moved slightly, keeping to the edges of the conversation but careful not to be seen hovering too obviously.

Stanley flipped through his notes. "You were standing near the competitors' stations just before the incident occurred?"

"Yes," Gemma replied. "I was watching the final pours, trying to see what everyone else was doing."

Stanley nodded. "And did you notice anything unusual?"

Gemma hesitated, wrapping a curl around her finger tightly. "I think I saw something... but I'm not totally sure if it's important."

Stanley's expression didn't change, but Sarah could see the way he leaned in slightly, pressing just enough to make Gemma continue. "Tell me what you saw."

Gemma bit her lip. "Well, I remember seeing Maya near someone's station. She was..." she paused, pressing her lips together. "Fiddling with something."

Sarah stiffened. Maya?

Stanley's eyes sharpened. "Can you be specific?"

Gemma's gaze darted around the room before settling back on the inspector. "I don't know what she was doing exactly. I was walking past, and I saw her sort of... adjusting something? At first, I thought she was just straightening things up, but she was hunched over like she didn't want anyone to see her."

"Whose station was it?" Stanley asked.

Gemma furrowed her brows. "Not Charlie's... No, it was... Eleanor's! Yeah, I'm sure of it."

Sarah's heart pounded. Why would Maya be messing with Eleanor's station?

From across the room, Sarah caught sight of Maya. The young woman was sitting alone, gripping a half-empty bottle of water, her fingers twitching slightly against the plastic. She looked paler than she had earlier, her gaze unfocused.

A prickle of unease ran down Sarah's spine. Had Maya been trying to sabotage Eleanor? Or had she seen something she wasn't supposed to? Either way, she was hiding something.

But before Stanley could move toward Maya, Gemma's gaze shifted, her attention snapping to something just beyond the inspector's shoulder. Sarah followed her line of sight and spotted Teddy.

He had been hovering near the drink station, but now his movements were frantic. His hands twisted together, his foot tapped anxiously against the polished floor, and his face had gone an unhealthy shade of white.

Sarah's stomach tightened. He looked like a man about to break.

Gemma's fingers curled tighter around her apron. "Inspector," she whispered, just as Teddy suddenly took a step forward, his voice cracking.

"I think... I think I did it."

The room seemed to pause. Inspector Stanley turned slowly to face him, arching a brow. "Did what, exactly?"

Teddy swallowed hard. "I...I was supposed to restock the milk," he stammered, his voice barely above a whisper. "But I might've mixed up the bottles. What if I put the wrong one out? What if it was my fault he drank something he was allergic to?"

Sarah's grip tightened around her coffee cup. His fear seemed genuine, but something didn't add up.

"You didn't see anyone else near the milk station?" she asked before she could stop herself.

Teddy hesitated. His breath came in quick, shallow bursts. "I... I thought I saw Olivia nearby, but I don't know... maybe I just assumed."

Stanley's eyes narrowed slightly. "You're saying you didn't see her actually touch anything?"

"I don't know!" Teddy burst out, his voice cracking. "I was moving fast, trying to get everything stocked before the next round. I didn't think...I didn't." He shook his head, pressing the heel of his palm against his forehead. "Maybe I mixed them up. Maybe someone else did. I don't know anymore."

Sarah and Stanley exchanged a glance. Was he panicking because he was guilty, or was he covering for someone?

Stanley regarded Teddy for a long moment before flipping open his notebook. "All right, let's go through everything you remember, step by step."

As he guided Teddy toward a quieter corner, Sarah exhaled slowly, her mind racing. This was something. But whether it was the truth, or just another layer of deception, was still unclear.

Across the room, Maya shifted in her seat, gripping her water bottle even tighter. Sarah's instincts told her that one confession wasn't enough to explain everything.

Someone else in this room was still hiding something.

Chapter 6

The late afternoon light slanted through the large windows of *Sarah's Secrets*, casting long shadows across the café's wooden floor. The usual warmth of the shop, the comforting blend of rich coffee and caramelized sugar, did little to soothe Robyn's unease. The day had been a blur of orders, distracted conversations, and half-hearted smiles, but now, with only a few stragglers left, she found herself lingering near the counter, arms folded, debating whether to close early.

    She hadn't heard from Charlie since midday. She knew Sarah would be doing everything she could to help him, but that didn't stop the worry gnawing at her. The soft crackle of the radio, usually just a mindless hum in the background, suddenly pulled her attention.

    "…and in local news, the recent tragedy at the Queen's Hotel has left the community in shock. As details continue to emerge, questions are being raised about the safety of public events and the potential negligence involved. Speculations abound regarding the involvement of one of the contestants in the mysterious death of Roger

Alton, a prominent judge and well-known figure in the coffee competition circuit…"

Robyn stiffened, her hand tightening around the dish towel she'd been absentmindedly twisting. *Fantastic. Just what Charlie needs, his name dragged through the mud by some amateur journalist who doesn't know a thing about him.*

Scowling, she reached over and turned the volume down with a sharp flick of her wrist. The last thing she needed was customers overhearing and adding fuel to the gossip mill. The bell above the door chimed, and Robyn instinctively straightened, forcing herself to push the tension aside. An elderly man shuffled in, tapping his cane lightly against the floor.

Edward Barnes. Her shoulders relaxed just a fraction. Edward was a regular, one of the good ones, never in a hurry, never anything but kind.

"Evening, Robyn," he greeted, his sharp eyes taking her in. "You're looking like a woman carrying the weight of the world."

She huffed a quiet laugh. "Just a long day, that's all."

Edward gave a knowing nod. "Well then, best end it on a good note. Got my usual?"

"Of course." She moved to the espresso machine, hands finding their rhythm, letting the familiar motions soothe her. "One flat white, extra hot, and a warm cinnamon roll."

He chuckled. "You always remember."

"Barista's intuition."

She worked in silence for a moment, listening to the last murmurs of conversation from a couple lingering at a table by the window. They left a few minutes later, the bell jingling softly as the door swung shut behind them. The shop felt even quieter now, the soft hum of the machines the only sound as she slid Edward's cup and plate across the counter.

He accepted them with careful hands but didn't move away immediately. Instead, he watched her with the kind of patience only age could bring.

"Don't let trouble get in your head too much, young lady. It has a way of twisting things."

Robyn blinked, caught off guard by his words. "What makes you think I'm worried?"

He gave a small chuckle, nodding at the counter. "You're wiping the same spot over and over. Always a dead giveaway."

She glanced down at the cloth in her hand, realizing he was right. Letting out a breath, she set it aside. "It's just been a… complicated day."

Edward tapped the side of his cup. "Complicated days have a way of sorting themselves out. You'll figure it out."

Her throat tightened slightly. "I hope so."

"Hope's a good start," he said simply, before turning and making his way to his favourite seat by the window.

Robyn let out a slow breath and watched as he settled in. He placed his coffee down with careful precision, exhaled, then lifted his gaze, just as he always did. Above the coffee counter, in its simple but elegant frame, hung the picture of Margaret, his late wife.

Sarah had hung it there after hearing Edward's story, a quiet tribute to a woman who had once dreamed of opening a coffee shop of her own. Margaret had never lived to see it happen, but in some way, Robyn liked to think her dream had found a home here, within these walls, within every perfectly poured cup.

Edward traced the rim of his mug with absent fingers, his expression softening. She had seen this moment so many times before, the quiet remembrance, the way he always chose that seat. Not for the view of Castle Road, not for the warm glow of the evening sun, but because from there, every time he looked up, he could see Margaret.

Robyn wiped her hands on a towel and let him have his moment. She glanced at the door, then at the quiet, empty café. The day had been long. The worry still gnawed at her. But as Edward took his first sip, his small smile lingering, she felt something settle in her chest.

Maybe she didn't have all the answers yet. But for now, she could hold onto this, this little corner of peace, this café, this moment. And tomorrow… tomorrow she would face whatever came next.

Later that afternoon, at the Queen's Hotel, the atmosphere was tense. The grand ballroom, which had been filled with excitement and anticipation the previous day, now felt heavy with uncertainty. The hotel manager, Mr. Henderson, paced the lobby, his worry evident in the furrowed lines of his forehead.

The door opened, and Inspector Stanley entered, his expression as serious as ever. Mr. Henderson stopped pacing and looked at him, a mixture of desperation and hope in his eyes.

"Inspector, this is a disaster," Mr. Henderson began, his voice tight with anxiety. "The media is having a field day, and bookings are already dropping. We need this resolved quickly."

Inspector Stanley nodded. "I understand, but we need to conduct a thorough investigation."

"I know," Mr. Henderson said, rubbing his forehead. "But the hotel's reputation is on the line."

Stanley nodded, understanding the pressure. "We're doing everything we can, but these things take time."

As the day turned to evening, contestants began making their way to their rooms, hoping for a bit of rest before the next day's competition rounds. The corridors were filled with hushed voices and nervous laughter, the events of the previous day still fresh in everyone's minds.

Shattered after the panic of the day, Sarah and Charlie made their way up the grand staircase, the plush carpet muffling their weary footsteps. Just yesterday, Sarah had looked forward to a night at the Queen's Hotel, imagining an evening of celebration in its grand halls, surrounded by the buzz of the competition. Now, the same lavish setting felt suffocating, its chandeliers casting a harsh glow on their exhaustion, the plush carpets swallowing their steps like ghosts of their earlier enthusiasm.

Reaching the landing, they paused for a moment, taking in the quiet of the hallway. Sarah turned to Charlie, her eyes filled with concern and love. "It'll be ok, you know," she said, pulling him into a comforting hug.

Charlie, his shoulders sagging under the weight of the day's events, hugged her back. "Inspector Stanley will figure it out," Sarah said, squeezing Charlie's shoulders. "You know the truth, and so will everyone else soon."

Charlie pulled back slightly, looking into his mother's eyes. "I really hope so, Mum," he said, his voice tinged with exhaustion and a hint of fear.

Sarah squeezed his shoulders, trying to infuse him with some of her own strength. "It will, Charlie. Just try to get some rest tonight. We'll face tomorrow together."

Charlie nodded, taking a deep breath. "Thanks, Mum. I'll try."

Sarah pushed open the door to her room, stepping inside as the warm glow of the bedside lamps cast soft pools of light across the space. The room was inviting, plush bedding, thick curtains drawn against the darkening evening, and a small tea tray resting on the desk, but the tension that clung to them dulled any sense of comfort.

She turned back toward Charlie, who hovered uncertainly in the doorway, rubbing a hand over the back of his neck. His shoulders were tight, his posture slumped as if the weight of the day had settled between his shoulder blades.

"Come in," Sarah said, nodding toward the tea tray. "Have a last cuppa before you turn in."

Charlie hesitated, then gave a small nod. "Yeah. Thanks."

She busied herself, flicking the kettle on and opening small packets of instant coffee and tea bags, her movements measured, deliberate. Anything to keep her hands busy. The quiet hum of heating water filled the silence between them as Charlie stepped further inside, glancing around the room as if he wasn't sure where to settle.

Sarah stirred her tea, watching as the steam curled in the dim light. "It's funny," she said after a moment. "This morning, I was looking forward to this part of the day. Coming back here, debriefing, celebrating a little."

Charlie let out a breath that was almost a laugh but not quite. "Bit different now."

"Just a bit," she agreed, passing him his drink. "But at least we're in it together."

Charlie wrapped his fingers around the warm ceramic, staring into his cup as though the swirling liquid might hold the answers he needed. Sarah turned away, giving him a moment, and began pottering around the room. She straightened the edge of the duvet, tucked a stray sock into her bag, then sat on the edge of her bed, flicking absently through the notepad she'd brought with her. She could feel the exhaustion pressing in, but her body remained restless, her mind unwilling to quiet.

Charlie took a slow sip of his tea before exhaling heavily and setting the cup down on the desk. "I should try to get some sleep," he murmured, running a tired hand over his face.

Sarah nodded, not pushing him to stay. "Yeah. Probably for the best."

He hesitated, as if there was something else he wanted to say, but in the end, he just gave her a small nod and headed for the door. "Night, Mum"

"Night, Charlie."

She listened as his footsteps faded down the hall, quickly climbed into her pyjamas and slipped under the covers. Staring up at the ceiling, she tried to will herself into sleep, but her thoughts wouldn't settle. The echoes of the day still lingered, the whispered conversations, the sharp looks, the lingering feeling that something was still just out of reach.

She let out a slow breath, shifting onto her side. The hotel's heating hummed softly in the background, filling the quiet. She closed her eyes, waiting to see if sleep would come.

Sleep eluded Sarah. She lay staring at the ceiling, her mind replaying the day's events in an endless loop. Doubts whispered at the edges of her thoughts, refusing to quieten. Then, just as exhaustion began to take hold, a muffled voice seeped through the thin hotel walls.

Sarah eased out of bed, holding her breath as she tiptoed to the window. Carefully, she pushed the curtain aside, just enough to see. Moonlight bathed the hotel grounds in silver, and there, on the balcony below, two figures stood close, their hushed voices threading through the night air like secrets.

She strained to hear their conversation, pressing her ear against the cold glass.

"Unbelievable," one figure whispered, their voice thick with unease. "You really think he'd do it?"

The second figure let out a slow exhale. "Desperation drives people to madness. And with the stakes this high... I wouldn't rule it out."

A pulse of adrenaline surged through her, quickening her breath. She pressed her palm against the cold glass, straining to catch their words. Below, the two figures moved with restless energy, shifting, gesturing, their conversation punctuated with sharp glances toward the hotel.

"Remember what he said yesterday?" the first figure continued. "Something about how he'd do anything to win?"

The second figure scoffed. "Talk is cheap. But this... this is something else."

Sarah's mind raced. Were they talking about Charlie? She had to find out more. She quickly glanced around the room for something to write on, grabbing a notepad and pen from the desk. She scribbled down what she had heard, her hands shaking slightly with the adrenaline coursing through her veins.

Just then, one of the figures on the balcony turned slightly, and the moonlight caught their profile. Sarah squinted, trying to make out their features. It was hard to tell, but the person seemed vaguely familiar, someone she had seen earlier that day at the competition.

As the conversation below continued, Sarah's thoughts swirled with worry and fear. She knew she needed to get closer, to hear more. She slipped into her robe and quietly opened the door to her room, stepping out into the dimly lit hallway. The soft carpet muffled her footsteps as she made her way towards the balcony, careful to stay hidden in the shadows.

She crept down the corridor, her heart pounding in her chest. The voices grew louder as she neared the balcony, and she pressed herself against the wall, listening intently.

"I'm telling you, if anyone finds out about this, it's game over," the first figure said, their voice tinged with panic.

The second figure nodded. "We need to be careful. No more slip-ups. We can't afford to get caught."

Sarah's breath caught in her throat. What were they planning? She peeked around the corner, trying to get a better look at the two figures. They were still huddled together, their faces obscured by the shadows.

Suddenly, the door to the balcony swung open, and the figures turned towards the noise. Sarah quickly pulled back, pressing herself flat against the wall, her heart hammering in her chest. She held her breath, praying that they hadn't seen her.

"Who's there?" one of the figures called out, their voice sharp with suspicion.

Sarah's mind raced. She needed to get out of there before they discovered her. She slowly inched her way back down the corridor, careful not to make a sound. As she reached the end of the hallway, she glanced back over her shoulder. The figures were still on the balcony, but now they were looking around, clearly on edge.

Sarah slipped back into her room, shutting the door with careful precision before leaning against it, exhaling shakily. Her fingers clenched around the notepad. She needed to tell Charlie and Robyn what she had heard. Sliding back into bed, her mind swirled with questions, her body thrumming with leftover adrenaline. The whispered conversations, the secrets, the suspicion, it was all building toward something. And deep in her gut, Sarah knew this wasn't over. Not by a long shot.

Chapter 7

The early morning light streamed through the window, illuminating the hotel room with a hazy glow. Beyond the glass, the vast stretch of the common led towards the seafront, where the waves shimmered under the soft, golden hues of dawn. Sarah's tired eyes lingered on the view for a moment, but the sight did little to ease the exhaustion weighing her down.

The dining area was half-full, business travellers nursing their first cups of the day, a few lingering guests flicking through newspapers over plates of toast and eggs. She bypassed the food entirely and made a beeline for the coffee urn, pouring herself a dark, unrelentingly strong cup. She needed coffee. Strong coffee. No frothy cappuccino or leisurely latte art this morning, just caffeine in its purest form, something to jolt her mind back into focus.

The night had been a restless blur, shifting between fitful dozing and staring at the ceiling, her mind replaying the events of the competition on an endless loop. Every snippet of overheard conversation, every hesitant glance between competitors, every flicker of unease she had dismissed in the moment now felt like a clue she had failed to grasp. Worse still, she had spent the time lying in the dark, half-convinced she had missed something vital.

Murmuring her thanks to the server, she took her cup and wove her way back through the maze of tables, nodding politely to a few familiar faces. The atmosphere in the hotel had shifted. The buzz of the competition was gone, replaced by an uneasy quiet, the kind that settled in after something had gone horribly wrong.

Back in her room, she set the cup down on the compact kitchen worktop and pulled out her notepad. The pages were a mess, filled with hastily scribbled thoughts from the night before. Disjointed phrases. Underlined names. Doodles where she had let her pen hover, trying to force her tired brain into making connections.

She traced a finger over the words she had scrawled in the early hours, her tired mind attempting to slot them into some kind of order. *What did I see? What did I hear?*

She had written it at the top of the page, underlined twice, as though demanding herself to remember something crucial. But nothing had come to her in the dark. Just fragments of conversation, whispers that had seemed important in the moment but meant nothing without context.

Taking a sip of coffee, she pressed the mug into her palm, letting the warmth seep into her fingers. She needed to focus.

She flipped to a fresh page in her notepad and tapped the pen against the paper, letting her thoughts spill out in a stream of quiet urgency. She realised that she was going to need to do some digging around if she wanted to make any sense of the situation and racked her brain for anyone that she might know who could help her.

She could ask Oliver, one of her local coffee suppliers, he might have heard something, he always knew what the latest gossip was. If there were whispers in the industry, he'd be the one to catch them. Or maybe Mark, the bar manager, who she had chatted to briefly while loitering between rounds. Staff like him saw more than they let on. The guests who came and went, the arguments in corridors, the late-night phone calls. He might have clocked something without even realising it was important.

And Helen… Helen would have the inside track on the competition itself. If there were complaints, if anything had gone missing, if someone had pushed too hard, she'd know. She always knew.

Sarah underlined a phrase she'd scribbled at the top of the page:
What didn't I see?

She stared at the words, then added another beneath it in a firmer hand:
Protect Charlie. Find the truth.

The pen paused for a second longer before she closed the notebook. It was time to start asking the right questions. This wasn't just about understanding what had happened, it was about protecting Charlie's future. The thought of him, sitting upstairs, still reeling from the accusations, sent a fresh wave of determination through her.

She folded the notes and tucked them into her bag. Her half-full coffee was now lukewarm, but she drained the rest of it anyway.

She tucked the notebook under her arm, grabbed her key card, and headed out. The corridors of the Queen's Hotel were unusually quiet, no customers wheeling luggage, no chatter from the conference rooms. Just the thick, muffled silence that follows scandal.

Sarah made her way down the main corridor. She didn't know exactly what she was looking for, only that she couldn't sit idle another minute. She wandered past the competition room, now sealed off with police tape. A member of hotel staff stood nearby, arms folded, guarding the threshold as though Roger Alton might rise from the dead and make a dramatic return.

She kept moving. As she rounded the corridor towards the back offices, she spotted the kitchen swing doors ahead. She slowed her pace. There it was again, that quiet pull of instinct. She needed an excuse to be here. Something that wouldn't set off alarm bells. The universe obliged.

A young porter came out of the kitchen, arms laden with stacked linen napkins. He nearly collided with her.

"Oh! Sorry, Miss," he said, blinking in surprise.

Sarah smiled brightly. "Not your fault. Actually, could you help me? I left my cardigan in the back kitchen during the competition set-up. I think it got swept up with the event laundry."

The young man frowned. "Uh... sure? I guess you can check with the prep station. No one's using it right now."

"Perfect," Sarah said, breezing past him before he could change his mind.

Inside, the hotel kitchen was cooler than she expected. Quiet, but not abandoned, half-set-up, as if the space was recovering from a dinner service that never happened. A few metal prep stations gleamed under the strip lights. The hum of a refrigerator was the only sound.

Sarah made a show of glancing around for her fictional cardigan, then slipped toward the staff cubbies and supply corner. A clipboard hung by a wall-mounted crate near the fridge. She flipped it open.

There. A delivery invoice, speckled with coffee stains, folded slightly out of sight behind a stack of stock receipts. She tugged it free and scanned the print. Her stomach clenched.

ALMOND MILK – BARISTA BLEND – 6L
NOTES: *Substitute with oat milk if unavailable*
Scrawled beneath in heavy pen:
"No substitutions. Req. original."

Her fingers tightened around the paper. Footsteps echoed from deeper in the kitchen. Sarah quickly folded the invoice in half and tucked it inside her bag.

A figure emerged around the corner. Chef Luca. He froze mid-step when he saw her. "Looking for something?"

Sarah straightened. "Yes. My cardigan. I thought it might've been taken back here by accident."

He narrowed his eyes. "Haven't seen it."

Realising that the cardigan ploy wasn't going to get her anywhere, Sarah decided just to ask outright, "Are you the man who signs for deliveries," she questioned, stepping closer. "Like this one, for example."

She pulled the invoice from her bag and placed it carefully on the nearest counter. Luca glanced at it, then back at her.

"So?"

"Almond milk was delivered to your kitchen," Sarah said. "Then someone wrote a note saying to substitute it. And then someone else crossed that out and insisted the original be used."

Luca shrugged, going back to his chopping. "I don't manage the drinks. I manage the kitchen."

"But you do control the deliveries. And this invoice has your signature."

"I sign whatever gets dropped off." He didn't look up. "It's not like the dairy guy and I have deep chats."

Sarah's fingers tapped the counter. "So you didn't notice someone specifically requesting almond milk? Despite the competition rules? Despite the head judge having a nut allergy?"

"I notice a lot of things," he said. "Like how half the competitors walk in here like they own the place. Or how Roger Alton treated staff like we were his personal servants." He leaned on the counter, arms crossed. "You think I wanted him dead?"

"I don't know what I think yet," Sarah replied calmly. "But I know someone went out of their way to make sure almond milk got into this building."

Luca held her gaze for a long moment, then huffed. "I didn't write that note. But if I had, I'd have used better handwriting. Looks like it was written by a caffeinated toddler."

Sarah gave a small, reluctant smile. "Noted."

He leaned in slightly. "You didn't hear this from me…but ask the girl on the events team. The one with the clipboard and the attitude. She's the one who insisted on having it on the list."

Sarah blinked. "You mean… Gemma?"

Luca snorted. "No. Older. Blonder. Wears perfume strong enough to be a fire hazard."

That gave her pause. Helen Williams. Roger's assistant. Always hovering. Always managing. Always watching.

She nodded slowly. "Thanks, Chef."

As she turned to go, he added, "And don't bring this into my kitchen again. I've got enough mess to clean up."

Sarah found Helen sitting alone in the Queen's Hotel staff lounge, a rare moment of stillness in the aftermath of chaos. The polished space smelled faintly of stale croissants and lavender hand cream, and Helen looked like she'd slept every bit as badly as Sarah had.

She was typing something on her phone, one finger jabbing at the screen with tight, controlled movements. Sarah stepped inside and closed the door behind her.

Helen glanced up. Her smile was tight and weary. "Unless you've brought a double espresso and a time machine, I'm not really in the mood."

Sarah raised an eyebrow. "No time travel, I'm afraid. Just a few questions."

Helen sighed. "Of course. Why wouldn't there be more questions?"

Sarah walked over and laid the crumpled invoice on the table between them. "Do you recognise this?"

Helen glanced at it, then froze. Her eyes skimmed the handwriting, then flicked up to Sarah's.

"Where did you get that?" she asked, voice crisp.

"In the hotel kitchen," Sarah replied. "Right after finding out that nut milk wasn't supposed to be anywhere near the competition. And yet... here it is. Specifically requested."

Helen blinked once, slowly. Then she leaned back in her chair, exhaling with more exhaustion than guilt.

"I wrote that note," she said plainly.

Sarah's eyebrows shot up. "So you did bring in the almond milk?"

"Yes. But not for Roger." Her voice softened, and something unexpectedly raw slipped into it. "It was for... someone else."

Sarah folded her arms. "I'm listening."

Helen paused, then reached into her bag and pulled out a crumpled photograph. She hesitated before handing it over. It showed a small girl, maybe seven or eight, beaming at the camera, holding what looked like a homemade birthday cake covered in pastel icing.

"My niece," Helen said. "Milly. She has severe sensory issues. Won't touch cow's milk, oat milk, soy... Only almond."

Sarah blinked. "Wait, what?"

Helen gave a tired laugh. "She and her mum were coming to visit me after the event. I was going to surprise her with her favourite hot chocolate, made just the way she likes it. I had the kitchen keep a small bottle in the fridge under my name. Separate from the competition stock." Her expression hardened. "It wasn't even in the prep area."

Sarah let out a slow breath, the tension in her shoulders loosening. "You're telling me this has nothing to do with the judges? Or the drinks being served?"

"No," Helen said. "Roger didn't even *look* at me unless I was handing him his itinerary or carrying a tray. Believe me, if I wanted to poison him, I'd have done it ten years ago."

Sarah almost smiled at that. Almost.

Helen added, more softly, "I understand why you're asking. And if I were you, I'd be doing the same. But that almond milk… it was personal. Just a small kindness in a day that ended in disaster."

Sarah stared at the invoice, now just a scrap of paper again. No smoking gun. No twist of betrayal. Just… an aunt trying to do something nice.

"I'm sorry," Sarah said. "I was jumping to conclusions."

Helen shrugged. "We all do these days."

Sarah turned to leave but paused at the door. "Just one more thing. Did anyone else know the almond milk was here?"

Helen's pause was telling. "I told the sous-chef when I asked them to keep it separate. And maybe, maybe one of the floor staff. But I never announced it."

Sarah nodded. "Thank you."

As she stepped out into the hallway, her mind raced again. The almond milk wasn't planted for Roger… but someone still got their hands on it.

Which meant the real question wasn't who ordered it, but who used it?

The air was crisp as Sarah stepped out of the hotel, leaving behind the lingering weight of yesterday's chaos. Charlie had chosen to stay behind, lost in his own thoughts, and for the moment, she let him. He needed space, and truthfully, so did she. The short walk to *Sarah's Secrets* was a welcome reprieve, the rhythmic sound of her footsteps grounding her as she moved through the quiet streets of Southsea.

As she unlocked the coffee shop door and stepped inside, the familiar scent of roasted coffee beans and warm pastries wrapped around her like a comforting embrace. This place, her place, was steady and unchanging, even when everything else felt like it was spiralling out of control. Letting muscle memory take over, she moved with purpose, setting up the counter, switching on the espresso machine, and preparing for the first customers of the day. The hum of the coffee grinder and the gentle clink of cups against saucers provided a soothing rhythm, a contrast to the overwhelming thoughts swirling in her mind.

As she worked, she took a moment to set her plan into motion. With the coffee shop's quiet ambience as her backdrop, she pulled out her phone and began drafting messages to her contacts in the coffee industry. Each message was carefully crafted, blending casual conversation with subtle probing questions about the recent competition and any odd occurrences or overheard whispers.

Just as Sarah was about to send her last message, the coffee shop door flew open with a clatter that made her jump. Robyn stormed in like a gust of wind, cheeks flushed, eyes blazing.

She marched straight to the counter, dumped her bag down with a thud loud enough to rattle the sugar jar, and exhaled sharply through her nose. Her hair, normally pulled back for a day in the shop, was half-unravelled, and her coat swung open like she hadn't bothered with the buttons.

Sarah raised an eyebrow. "Morning, Robyn. You all right?"

Robyn didn't answer straight away. She yanked off her coat, tossed it over the back of a chair, and paced a tight circle in front of the counter. When she finally looked up, her face carried a look of barely restrained fury.

"I'm fine," she snapped, then immediately winced. "Sorry. I'm just…ugh, I can't believe this."

She planted both hands on the counter, leaning forward as if bracing herself. "I cannot believe they're still trying to pin this on Charlie. And Stanley? He's not investigating, he's already made up his mind. It's like talking to a bloody brick wall."

Sarah reached for the kettle, already anticipating the need for a calming brew. "So… same as yesterday, then?"

Robyn let out a dry laugh and slumped into the nearest chair. "Worse."

Sarah nodded sympathetically, her heart aching for her niece. She could see the frustration and hurt in Robyn's eyes, especially with the additional sting of feeling let down by someone she'd started to care about. "I know, I feel it too. It's a tough situation, and it's easy to feel overwhelmed. But if you want, you could channel some of that energy into helping me with this."

Robyn raised an eyebrow, curiosity piqued despite her frustration. "Helping you with what?"

Sarah gestured to the counter, where her notebook and phone were surrounded by a flurry of scribbled notes and half-drunk coffee cups. "I couldn't just sit around doing nothing," she said. "So I've been reaching out to local coffee shop owners and baristas, trying to see if anyone saw or heard anything that could help."

Robyn raised an eyebrow, her interest piqued.

Sarah glanced at her. "Do you want to help? I could keep going with contacting people, and maybe you could… make a few calls?"

Robyn recoiled like Sarah had suggested she juggle flaming espresso cups. "Phone people? Me? You have to be kidding."

Sarah gave her a look of exaggerated pleading. "Not even for Charlie?"

Robyn groaned, dramatically collapsing into a chair like she'd been mortally wounded. "Ugh, you fight dirty."

Sarah handed her the list, a small smile tugging at the corner of her mouth. "That's the job description. I make coffee and guilt people into doing the right thing."

Robyn took the list with a theatrical sigh. "Fine. But if anyone cries on the phone, I'm hanging up."

As they took to their respective tasks, Sarah dialled the first number on her list, pressing the phone to her ear as she scanned her notes.

"Hi, it's Sarah. Sarah Meadows? From *Sarah's Secrets*. I know things were hectic yesterday, I was just checking in with some of the folks who were at the competition. Wondered if you noticed anything... unusual?"

There was a pause, then a cheerful voice replied, "Oh, hi, Sarah. No, I mean, just the usual nerves and people stressing about tamp pressure. Poor Roger, though, what a shocker. Such a shame."

Sarah offered a soft "Mmm," jotting down nothing.

The next few calls followed the same pattern, expressions of sympathy, a few vague observations, nothing concrete.

One barista said, "Honestly, I thought Roger looked a bit off before the event even started. Like he was already having a bad day."

Another chuckled lightly. "I kept my distance, judges always make me nervous. He was on the warpath with those scoring sheets, though."

Still, no one had anything useful. Just feelings. Just vibes. Sarah's next call connected after only two rings.

"Hi, it's Sarah from..." she began, but the voice on the other end cut in sharply.

"Oh. You."

Sarah blinked. "Yes, I…sorry…?"

"I just think it's a bit rich," the caller said, tone cold. "You calling around like you're some kind of detective. Isn't your son the prime suspect?"

Sarah's jaw tightened. "I'm just trying to get a sense of what people saw. If there's anything that might help clarify…"

"Help clarify?" The laugh was bitter. "Maybe you should be looking a bit closer to home."

There was a long pause. Sarah's fingers gripped the edge of the counter.

"I see," she said flatly. "Thanks for your time."

"No problem," the caller snapped. "Good luck clearing *his* name."

Sarah hung up with a sharp jab of her thumb and let out a low, frustrated sound that was halfway between a growl and a sigh.

Across the room, Robyn looked up mid-call, eyebrows raised. She caught the storm brewing in her aunt's expression and quickly turned away from the window, rushing to finish the conversation she was on.

"Uh-huh, yep. Totally understand. Ok, thanks so much, I'll let Sarah know. Bye now."

She hung up and crossed the café just as Sarah dropped her phone onto the counter with an exasperated groan.

Robyn didn't say anything at first. She just opened her arms and pulled Sarah into a firm, wordless hug.

Sarah let herself lean in, just for a moment, before pulling away with a wry smile. "Well. That was productive."

Robyn snorted. "We've got about three pages of people saying it was 'sad' and 'such a shame.' You?"

"A handful of sympathy and one personal attack," Sarah muttered. "I'm counting it as a draw."

As the morning gave way to the afternoon, Sarah, still restless and unsatisfied with leaving things entirely to the police, checked her phone. A message from Charlie flashed on the screen:

Police are still here. Slowly working through questions. Nothing new yet.

Sarah exhaled sharply, her frustration mounting. At this pace, they could be waiting forever for answers. Rationally, she knew that twenty-four hours wasn't a long time in an investigation like this. The police needed time to work through evidence, to ask the right questions. But this wasn't just any case, this was her son. And rationality had no place where he was concerned. Calling around that morning had helped scratch the itch slightly, but it wasn't enough. She needed to go faster than the police, to start pressing people herself.

A momentary lull in the coffee shop gave Sarah the chance to pause. The morning rush had passed, and the quiet hum of customers enjoying their drinks filled the space. She exhaled, rubbing the back of her neck, before grabbing herself a coffee and sliding into the seat opposite

Robyn. For the first time that day, she allowed herself to slow down, if only for a moment.

Robyn, sitting across from her, seemed to sense the shift in Sarah's mood. "We can't just wait for them to figure this out," she said, her voice full of conviction. "We need to keep digging."

Sarah nodded, wrapping her hands around the warmth of her cup. "I was thinking of heading back to the hotel under the pretence of retrieving a bag I left behind."

Robyn smirked. "Very subtle, Aunt Sarah. What if they get suspicious?"

"They won't," Sarah said confidently. "I'll just be a concerned mother who happens to ask a few questions. Besides, I've got the charm of a coffee shop owner on my side."

She glanced toward the counter where a fresh batch of cookies sat cooling on a wire rack, Charlie's latest creation. The thought crossed her mind that, under the circumstances, some people might refuse to touch anything he had made. But they wouldn't know. And it wasn't like he had set out to poison anyone.

"I'll take some cookies with me," she added. "People let their guard down when they've got something sweet in hand."

Robyn's eyes shone with mischief. "Well, if anyone can get them to spill, it's you. Just be careful, ok?"

Sarah took a sip of her coffee, feeling the familiar comfort of the strong brew settle her nerves. "I promise. I'm just going to talk to a few people. Maybe someone saw something that can help Charlie."

Chapter 8

Intent on trying to find answers, Sarah was surprised to almost immediately bump into Maya sitting outside the Queen's Hotel, perched on a low stone wall, her gaze unfocused as she stared at the sea. Here was an opportunity to speak to at least one person that had set off mini alarm bells the day before.

Sarah approached carefully, not wanting to spook her. "Hey, Maya."

Maya blinked, as if startled out of her thoughts, before offering a half-hearted nod in greeting. Sarah took that as an invitation to sit beside her on the wall, taking a moment to glance out at the water. The waves rolled in steady and rhythmic, an odd contrast to the turmoil of the past day.

"Quite the day yesterday," Sarah murmured. "Must have been a bit scary for you, especially with all the chaos."

Maya let out a breathy laugh, but there was no humour in it. "Yeah. You could say that."

Sarah nodded, giving her a beat before continuing. "I just got here to see if I can support Charlie, see if there's anything I can do." She hesitated, then added, "You seemed a little ruffled yesterday, even before the competition started. Was something bothering you?"

Maya tensed slightly but didn't look away from the horizon. "I don't know. Just… nerves, I guess."

Sarah tilted her head, studying her carefully. "Are you sure that's all it was?"

Maya exhaled sharply and ran a hand through her hair. "I saw Eleanor acting weird before the competition," she admitted finally. "She was hovering around her own station, adjusting things, like she was checking something over and over. It didn't seem like a big deal at first, but... I don't know. It gave me a bad feeling."

Sarah kept her tone neutral. "Ah, that's why Gemma saw you at Eleanor's station?"

Maya flinched. "I wasn't messing with anything."

Sarah, wanting to press Maya further and recalling that Gemma had mentioned seeing her near Eleanor's equipment, asked, "Then why did she see you hunched over her machine?"

Maya's throat bobbed as she swallowed. "I…" She hesitated. "It wasn't what it looked like."

Sarah waited, keeping her expression calm, inviting her to continue. Maya sighed.

"I just wanted to see what she had been doing. I wasn't touching anything important, just looking."

"And you didn't think to mention this sooner?" Sarah pressed gently.

Maya rubbed her temples. "I thought I was being paranoid. And then when Roger collapsed, I panicked, I didn't want to be blamed for something I didn't do."

Sarah studied her carefully. Maya looked exhausted, sick, even. But whether it was nerves or guilt was still unclear.

"If you're lying, Maya…"

"I'm not." Her voice was barely above a whisper. "I swear."

For a moment, Sarah thought she might press her further, but something in Maya's expression shifted. Her shoulders tensed, and she hugged her bag tightly against her chest as if physically shielding herself from the conversation.

"I need to get going," Maya muttered, not meeting Sarah's eyes. Without another word, she shuffled off the wall, her movements stiff and uncertain, before turning on her heel and walking away in the direction of the shops.

Sarah watched her retreating figure, frowning. There was something off. Whether it was fear or guilt, she wasn't sure, but one thing was clear, Maya didn't want to talk.

Exhaling, Sarah straightened up. She had more people to try and speak to, and standing here watching Maya disappear into the distance wouldn't get her any closer to the truth. She turned and made her way back up the steps into the hotel's reception area, pushing open the canopied doors with a renewed sense of determination.

Inside the grand lobby of the Queen's Hotel, daily life carried on as though nothing had happened. Guests wheeled their suitcases across the polished floors, reception staff answered phone calls with professional smiles, and a porter hurried past with a stack of fresh towels. The catastrophe of the previous day was now nothing more than hushed whispers exchanged in passing.

Sarah adjusted the strap of her bag and took a steadying breath. Her conversation with Maya had left her with more questions than answers. There was something about the young woman's hesitation, the way she skirted around certain details, that put Sarah on edge. She wasn't satisfied yet. And then, as though fate was nudging her forward, her eyes landed on Gemma.

The waitress stood by the reception desk, adjusting a stack of menus and leaflets, her expression preoccupied. Sarah hesitated for only a second before making her way over, weaving through a group of newly arrived guests.

"Hello, Gemma," she said smoothly, keeping her tone light.

Gemma startled slightly before looking up, her lips parting in recognition. "Oh hi. Sarah, right?"

Sarah nodded. "Yes. We met yesterday." She paused, then added with an encouraging smile, "I was actually just talking to Maya."

Gemma's hands stilled over the stack of papers. "Maya?" she echoed, her voice guarded.

"Yes. She seemed… hesitant to talk about what she saw." Sarah watched Gemma closely, noting the flicker of something, anxiety? guilt? that flashed across her face. "I thought perhaps you might have noticed something she didn't mention."

Gemma hesitated, glancing around the lobby as though ensuring no one was listening. Then, lowering her voice, she said, "Maya's been on edge since the competition. She won't say why, but I know she was nervous about something. It seemed like to was more than just the judging."

Sarah leaned in slightly. "Did she say anything to you before the incident? Anything about Roger?"

Gemma exhaled through her nose, her fingers tightening around the menus. "Not directly. But I did see her talking to one of the porters. They were by the kitchen entrance, and he had a milk tray in his hands. She looked upset."

A milk tray. The same detail that had come up before. Sarah's pulse quickened. "Did you hear what they were saying?"

"No, but…" Gemma hesitated again, biting her lip. "It looked like she was warning him about something. She kept shaking her head. And after that, she barely spoke to anyone. She just… kept her head down."

A warning. Sarah's mind raced through the possibilities. Could Maya have known something dangerous was about to happen?

"What about Roger?" she pressed. "Did you see him talking to Maya before, before it happened?"

Gemma shook her head. "Not Maya, but…" She hesitated. "I did see him arguing with Eleanor Wren before the competition started."

Sarah's brows lifted in surprise. "Eleanor? What were they arguing about?"

"I don't know exactly. But it got pretty heated. She stormed off looking furious."

Eleanor had already come up in Sarah's investigation, but this was the first mention of a direct confrontation with Roger. The pieces of the puzzle were shifting again.

Before Sarah could push further, a voice called out from across the lobby. "Gemma! We need you in the restaurant."

Gemma shot Sarah an apologetic look. "I have to go."

Sarah nodded, stepping back. "Thanks, Gemma. You've been really helpful."

Gemma hesitated, then said under her breath, "Be careful, Sarah." And with that, she hurried off.

Sarah stood in the middle of the bustling lobby, her mind spinning. A nervous contestant, a warning whispered by the kitchen, a heated argument with Roger, all signs pointing to something deeper, something more tangled than she had originally suspected.

She turned slightly, eyes scanning the room as she processed what she had learned. That was when she spotted Teddy behind the bar, meticulously polishing glasses.

She made her way over to the bar, slipping into a seat as Teddy finished drying the last glass and set it down with a quiet clink.

"Hi, Teddy," she greeted.

He glanced up, flashing a quick smile. "Oh, hello. Sarah, right?"

"Yes," she confirmed. "I was just talking to Gemma. She mentioned something about one of the contestants talking to the kitchen staff. You were here yesterday too, weren't you?"

Teddy nodded, placing the last glass on the rack. "Yeah, I was. It's been a bit of a whirlwind, to be honest."

Sarah nodded sympathetically. "I can imagine. I'm just trying to piece together what might have happened. Anything you remember that seemed out of the ordinary?"

Teddy thought for a moment, his expression pensive. "Well, there was quite a bit of tension in the air. The contestants were all really on edge, more so than usual, I'd say. I did see Roger Alton speaking to Eleanor too, and it looked pretty heated. Something about her expression afterward... she seemed really upset."

Sarah's pulse quickened. So it wasn't just idle gossip, more than one person had noticed Eleanor's interactions with Roger. That made it harder to ignore. Harder to dismiss as coincidence. Something had passed between them, something people had seen, and if enough people had seen it, maybe someone knew exactly what it meant.

As Teddy glanced toward the far side of the lobby, Sarah followed his gaze. Two of the remaining contestants were making their way up the grand staircase, their voices carrying just enough for her to catch snippets of their conversation.

"I can't believe this is happening," one of them, a tall man with a deep voice, said. "It just doesn't make sense. Why would Charlie do something like that?"

"I don't think he did," the other replied, a petite woman with a strong Northern accent. "But people are talking, saying he might've had a motive. Some nonsense about wanting to win at all costs."

Sarah felt a pang of frustration. Whispers and rumours. They were like wildfire, spreading faster than truth. She knew Charlie was innocent, but convincing others was another matter entirely.

As she returned her focus to Teddy, he had begun wiping down the counter, but his expression was thoughtful. "You know," he said, lowering his voice slightly, "there's something else. I saw Eleanor slip out the back after the argument. She looked shaken. Not angry anymore, more like… scared."

Sarah's breath caught for a moment. Scared? That changed things. With each piece of information, Sarah's determination grew. There was more to Eleanor's interactions with Roger than met the eye, and more to Maya's reluctance than simple nerves.

She decided to take a moment to collect her thoughts, stepping out into the hotel's courtyard for some fresh air. As she leaned against the stone railing, the cool breeze helping to clear her head, her focus sharpened. The truth was buried somewhere within these walls, and she was going to find it.

As Sarah walked briskly down the steps of the Queen's Hotel, lost in thought about her next move, she collided with a solid figure coming up the stairs towards her. Startled, she looked up to find herself face-to-face with Inspector Stanley. The inspector's expression was unreadable, his sharp eyes assessing her with a mix of curiosity and caution.

"Mrs. Meadows," Stanley said, his tone formal but not unfriendly. "I didn't expect to see you here again so soon."

There was a pregnant pause, one where Sarah weighed her words carefully. She could feel the weight of his scrutiny. Normally, she would correct him, "That's Sarah to you," she might have said with an easy smile. But today, the words stuck in her throat.

She wasn't feeling particularly friendly toward him, and she wasn't sure if that was entirely fair. Stanley had always been professional with her, sometimes even patient, but right now, all she could see was the man leading an investigation that had placed a target on her son's back. A man who, despite all his so-called objectivity, seemed willing to entertain the idea that Charlie might be capable of something as monstrous as murder.

Rationally, she knew Stanley wasn't the enemy. He was just doing his job. But emotionally? Emotionally, she felt the simmering frustration bubbling beneath the surface, an irritation she couldn't quite suppress. So she let it go. Let the formality remain between them like a quiet wall.

She took a step back, trying to regain her composure. Her heart, which had been racing from the rush of information she'd gathered, now pounded for an entirely different reason. She had intended to leave quietly, unnoticed by the authorities, but now she found herself caught in the act.

"Inspector," she replied, offering a polite nod. "I just came back to... retrieve something I left behind."

Stanley arched an eyebrow, clearly sceptical. "And did you find what you were looking for?"

"I found some things," she answered vaguely, lifting her chin ever so slightly.

Stanley's eyes flickered with something, mild amusement? Suspicion?

For a moment, they simply stood there, the crisp morning air wrapping around them. Sarah wasn't sure if Stanley was going to press her further, ask what exactly she had found or why she had come back at all. She braced herself for it.

Instead, he shifted his stance slightly, his gaze fixed on her with unsettling calm. "Sarah," he said, her name landing more friendly, quieter, almost gentle. This time, though, her name came with a quiet warning threaded through it.

"I hope you're not thinking of turning this into a personal project."

Sarah's jaw tightened. He wasn't wrong. But hearing it from him, *hearing it in that voice*, the one that tried to be reasonable, tried to soothe, set her teeth on edge. It wasn't soothing. It was patronising.

"A thorough investigation?" she said, her voice rising slightly, arms folding across her chest like a shield. "Then why is Charlie the only one under a microscope?"

He flinched slightly at that, just a shift of the eyes, but it was enough to show she'd hit a nerve.

Stanley exhaled, rubbing the bridge of his nose. "Charlie's drink was the last one Alton tasted before his reaction. That makes him a focus, not a suspect."

Sarah stepped closer. "There were dozens of competitors, dozens of drinks. What if someone tampered with it after he made it?"

Stanley met her gaze, his expression unreadable. Then, softer: "Then I'll find out."

Sarah studied him for a beat longer. He meant it. But she also saw it, the nagging doubt in his eyes.

"See that you do," she muttered.

Stanley sighed, his face softening slightly as he met Sarah's gaze. "I understand your concern for Charlie, truly I do. But you must understand the boundaries here. Interfering with a police investigation is not only inadvisable, but it could also jeopardise the case."

Sarah bit her lip, her frustration mounting. The feeling of helplessness that had been gnawing at her since the incident reared its head again. She had never felt so powerless, and the thought that her actions might inadvertently harm Charlie's defence filled her with dread.

"But, Inspector," she protested, trying to keep her voice steady, "surely there must be more we can do. The evidence needs to be examined from every angle. What if there's something you've missed?"

Stanley regarded her for a long moment, his eyes searching hers. "I assure you, we are pursuing every lead and examining every piece of evidence. But the law is the law, and we must abide by its constraints. You have to trust the process."

Trust the process. The words echoed in Sarah's mind, mingling with her fear and uncertainty. Trust was a luxury she couldn't afford when her son's reputation and freedom were on the line. Her instincts screamed at her to push forward, to dig deeper, to uncover the truth that would exonerate Charlie.

But standing there, under the inspector's watchful gaze, she realized that she was walking a fine line between desperation and recklessness. Every move she made had to be calculated, every question she asked had to be measured. She couldn't afford any missteps, not now.

"I understand, Inspector," Sarah said finally, her voice resigned but firm. "I'll... try to stay within the lines. But please, keep me informed. Charlie doesn't deserve this shadow hanging over him."

Stanley nodded, a hint of sympathy in his expression. "I promise you, we're doing everything we can to find the truth. But give us time, and please, for Charlie's sake, let us handle the investigation."

With a final nod of agreement, albeit reluctant, Sarah turned away, her mind racing with thoughts of what to do next. As she walked down the steps and into the bustling street, the reality of the situation settled heavily on her shoulders.

The inspector's words rang true, but they did little to quell the storm of emotions within her. Every instinct screamed at her to keep digging, to keep asking questions, to protect Charlie at all costs. She knew she had to be careful, to balance her determination with caution.

The battle for her son's future had only just begun, and Sarah was ready to fight. But she knew she had to be smart, to think like the detectives she'd always admired in books and stories, using her own skills and intuition to find the missing pieces of this puzzle.

And as she walked, the bustling streets of Southsea around her, Sarah's resolve strengthened. She would find the truth, and she would do it her way, all while keeping one step ahead of the law.

The dim light from the desk lamp cast long shadows across Inspector Stanley's office, illuminating the scattered papers and open files that cluttered his desk. Stanley sat in his chair, leaning forward with his elbows on the desk, rubbing his temples in frustration. The initial interviews with the competitors had given him plenty of information, but very little clarity. The more he tried to piece it together, the more tangled the web seemed to become.

He sighed, pushing his chair back slightly and staring down at the notes in front of him. Each sheet held the hurried scrawl of his interview notes, fragments of conversations, observations, and small details that had seemed irrelevant at the time but now nagged at him. There was something here, something he was missing, but what?

His eyes fell on the names of the competitors: Charlie Meadows, Eleanor Wren, Martin Acton, Maya Patel,

Victor Chan, Olivia Green. The evidence, or lack thereof, was leading nowhere. He couldn't shake the feeling that the truth was just out of reach, hidden behind a veil of lies and half-truths.

Stanley leaned forward again, tapping his pen against the desk, and muttered to himself, "There's no way around it, I need to speak to them all again. Something doesn't add up."

He picked up the phone and dialled the front desk. When the line connected, he spoke with calm authority, "This is Inspector Stanley. I need you to contact each of the competitors from the Queen's Hotel competition and request that they come to the station tomorrow for further questioning. Set the appointments up at one-hour intervals, starting at 9 AM."

There was a brief pause on the other end as the receptionist processed the request. "Yes, Inspector. I'll make the calls right away."

"Thank you," Stanley replied, hanging up the phone.

As he leaned back in his chair, Stanley allowed himself a moment to think. The next round of interviews would need to be more focused, more probing. He had to get to the heart of each competitor's story, to find the inconsistencies that would crack the case wide open. There were still too many loose ends: Martin Acton's strange interaction with Roger, Eleanor Wren's suspicious behaviour with the milk, Olivia Green's frustration with Roger's bias.

He opened the file containing the competitors' backgrounds, flipping through the pages with a critical eye.

There was a pattern here, he was sure of it. Roger Alton hadn't just been a judge, he had been a key player in each of their lives, for better or worse. Now, with his death, the true nature of their relationships with him was beginning to surface.

Stanley paused, his gaze lingering on Eleanor Wren's file. There was something about her that bothered him, her ambition, her ruthlessness, the way she had talked about the competition as if it were a battlefield. She was one to watch, certainly, but was she the key?

He scribbled a few notes in the margin and moved on to Victor Chan's file. Chan had been polite, almost too polite, during the initial interview. He had spoken highly of Roger, but there had been an undercurrent of tension in his words. Was it respect, or was it something else?

Stanley sighed and closed the file, his thoughts whirling. He needed to hear their stories again, to dig deeper and see what new details might emerge. Tomorrow would be a long day, but it was necessary. One of them was hiding something, and he intended to find out who it was.

As he gathered the files and placed them neatly in a pile on his desk, Stanley's resolve hardened. He told himself he was just doing his job, following the facts, the evidence, the process. That's what mattered. That's what always mattered.

But even as he tried to maintain that professional detachment, the memory of Robyn's anger and Sarah's frustration lingered like smoke in the back of his mind. Robyn's sharp words, thrown at him like darts, and Sarah's cool, disappointed stare, both had stung more than he cared to admit.

He liked them. Both of them. More than was professionally convenient. And the truth was, he didn't want to lose their respect. He'd worked too hard, for too long, to be dismissed as just another blunt instrument of the law. He needed to get to the bottom of this, not just to close a case, but to prove, to them and to himself, that he still deserved to be trusted.

With that thought, he reached for his coat, switched off the desk lamp, and left the office, the click of the door echoing in the empty hallway behind him. Tomorrow would bring answers, or at the very least, more pieces to the puzzle.

Chapter 9

Inspector Stanley leaned back in his chair, his eyes narrowing as he observed Martin Acton across the table. The atmosphere in the small interrogation room was tense, the air thick with unspoken words. Stanley's notepad lay open before him, but he hadn't written anything down in the last few minutes, waiting for Martin to break the silence.

Finally, Martin sighed, rubbing the back of his neck with a weary hand. "All right, Inspector. I'll admit it, we did have a heated argument. But it wasn't what you think."

Stanley leaned forward slightly, his interest piqued. "Go on."

Martin hesitated, his gaze flickering to the door as if contemplating an escape. But there was no way out, not now. He sighed again, his shoulders sagging as he finally spoke. "It was about sponsorship deals. Roger and I... well, we didn't exactly see eye to eye."

Stanley raised an eyebrow. "Sponsorship deals? You mean you wanted Roger to sponsor you?"

"Oh no, quite the opposite," Martin replied quickly, shaking his head. "Roger wanted to sponsor me. He thought his brand could give my career a boost, and he was very persistent about it. But I really didn't want anything to do with him."

Stanley's eyes narrowed. "That's an unusual stance. Most competitors would jump at the chance for financial backing, especially from someone as influential as Roger."

Martin gave a bitter laugh, leaning back in his chair. "You've seen what people thought of him. Roger was... divisive, to say the least. Sure, he had money and connections, but his reputation wasn't exactly sterling. Did I really want to be associated with that? With someone who could ruin my credibility just by being in my corner? No, Inspector, I didn't."

Stanley nodded slowly, considering Martin's words. "So you turned him down, and that led to the argument?"

Martin grimaced, his expression tightening with the memory. "Yes. He didn't take it well. He was used to getting what he wanted, and he couldn't stand the idea that someone would refuse his 'generosity.' He accused me of being ungrateful, short-sighted, even arrogant. Things got heated. But I swear, that's all there was to it."

Stanley tapped his pen against the notepad, his mind turning over this new information. "I can see how that might ruffle some feathers," he said thoughtfully. "But it also raises some questions. You must have known that rejecting Roger could have consequences, especially given his influence in the industry."

Martin nodded, his face solemn. "I did. But I wasn't willing to compromise my integrity. I wanted to make it on my own terms, without someone like Roger pulling the strings."

The inspector studied Martin for a long moment, his expression unreadable. "It's a noble stance, Mr. Acton, but it doesn't change the fact that you had a motive to dislike Roger. And in a competition like this, tensions run high."

Martin met his gaze steadily. "I won't deny that Roger wasn't my favourite person, Inspector. But I had no reason to want him dead. Whatever happened to him, I had nothing to do with it."

Stanley remained silent, his mind working through the implications. Martin's reluctance to accept Roger's sponsorship painted a different picture, one that hinted at deeper divisions and hidden motivations. But whether it pointed to guilt or just another layer of the complex web surrounding Roger's death, he wasn't sure yet.

After another moment of silence, Stanley decided to probe further, his gaze sharpening as he formulated his next question.

"Mr. Acton," Stanley began, his tone steady but probing, "before you go, there's one more aspect of the competition I'd like to discuss, something that might seem insignificant but could be crucial to understanding what happened."

Martin turned back to face the inspector, a flicker of apprehension in his eyes. "What is it, Inspector?"

Stanley leaned forward, his elbows resting on the table, fingers steepled in front of him. "I'm talking about the milk you used in the competition. You see, we've been hearing some rather curious things about the milk bottles. There are reports of competitors inspecting them more closely than usual, almost as if they were looking for something, or perhaps worried that something wasn't quite right."

Martin frowned, confusion and concern mingling on his face. "The milk? I don't see how that could be relevant. Everyone used the same brand, didn't they?"

The inspector's gaze didn't waver. "Not necessarily. We've learned that some competitors might have had particular preferences or dietary restrictions, which could have led them to use different ingredients. I'm wondering, Mr. Acton, whether you were one of those competitors. Did you use the provided milk, or did you bring your own?"

Martin's expression softened slightly, a hint of pride seeping into his voice as he replied. "Actually, Inspector, I'm vegan. I've been vegan since I was young, and I'm very particular about what I use in my cooking. I wouldn't touch regular milk. I brought my own soya milk for the competition."

Stanley nodded slowly, noting this down in his mind. "I see. So, you didn't use the milk provided by the organizers at all?"

"Correct," Martin affirmed, his tone firm. "I've always been very protective of my ingredients. I make sure to bring everything I need with me, especially when it comes to something as important as the type of milk I use. I even double-check that it's stored properly and not mixed up with anyone else's. My soya milk is non-negotiable."

The inspector considered this for a moment. "And there's no chance that your soya milk could have been swapped with someone else's ingredients, or that someone could have tampered with it?"

Martin shook his head confidently. "No chance, Inspector. Like I said, I'm very careful. I store my ingredients separately, and I never let them out of my sight. I even label everything clearly, so there's no room for confusion. Besides, the other competitors knew I was vegan, it's not exactly a secret. They wouldn't have any reason to mess with my stuff."

Stanley leaned back in his chair, tapping his pen thoughtfully against the notepad. "That's good to know, Mr. Acton. But tell me, did you notice anything unusual with the other competitors' milk? Anything that seemed out of place?"

Martin paused, thinking back to the competition. "Now that you mention it… I did see something strange. There was a moment when Olivia was inspecting one of the milk bottles rather closely. At the time, I thought she was just being cautious, but now I wonder if she was checking for something specific. It seemed odd, but I didn't think much of it."

Stanley's interest piqued. "Olivia you say? Interesting. Did she say anything about why she was inspecting the bottle?"

Martin shook his head. "No, she didn't. She just looked at it for a few seconds and then moved on. It struck me as strange, but I was too focused on my own preparation to ask her about it."

The inspector made a mental note of this new piece of information, adding it to the growing list of details surrounding the mysterious milk bottles.

"Thank you, Mr. Acton. That's very helpful." Stanley paused for a moment, his tone shifting into something more conversational, but with a careful undertone. "Just one last thing. If someone had wanted to interfere with one of the milk bottles… during the event itself, say… do you think it would've been noticeable?"

Martin frowned slightly, clearly choosing his words. "I mean… I guess it's possible. We were all really focused on our own stations, our routines. Tunnel vision, you know? But we weren't blind. If someone was messing around where they shouldn't have been, especially near someone else's setup, I think someone would've noticed."

Stanley nodded slowly. "So it would've had to be subtle. Quiet."

Martin gave a non-committal shrug. "If it happened at all."

"Thank you for your honesty, Mr. Acton," Stanley said, tone smooth but unreadable. "We'll be in touch if we have any further questions."

Martin nodded and stood, a flicker of relief crossing his face as he made for the door. But just as his hand touched the handle, Stanley spoke again.

"Oh, and Mr. Acton? If anything else comes to mind… anything at all… I'd appreciate a call."

Martin gave a tight smile over his shoulder. "Of course."

As the door closed behind him, Stanley remained seated, staring at the space Martin had occupied. He exhaled slowly, running a hand through his hair as the full weight of the investigation's challenges settled on his shoulders. The coffee competition case was proving to be frustratingly complex, like trying to solve a puzzle where the pieces kept changing shape.

He flipped through his notes, the pages filled with witness statements, timelines, and observations. The central problem remained unchanged: everyone had the same alibi. When Roger collapsed, all the competitors, judges, and most of the staff had been present in the main hall, surrounded by dozens of witnesses and several cameras. Yet Roger had died, and someone in that room was responsible.

"It had to be premeditated," Stanley murmured to himself, tapping his pen against the notepad. "Something set up before the event began."

The timing suggested that Roger had been poisoned, the toxicology results would confirm that soon enough, but the how and when remained elusive. Had someone tampered with his food? His coffee? Or perhaps his equipment? Stanley made a note to check if Roger had consumed anything that morning that others hadn't.

And then there was the milk question. Why were competitors so interested in the milk bottles? Martin's revelation about Olivia's behaviour added another layer to consider. Had she noticed something amiss? Or was she checking to ensure her own milk hadn't been tampered with?

Stanley leaned back, stretching his neck as he considered the tangle of motives emerging from his interviews. Everyone, it seemed, had reason to dislike Roger Alton. The man had made a career of creating enemies, competitors he'd humiliated, businesses he'd undercut, people whose careers he'd sidelined. The challenge wasn't finding someone with motive; it was narrowing down the field of suspects who all seemed equally justified in their animosity.

"Too many suspects, not enough evidence," Stanley muttered to himself.

Back at home and curled up on the sofa with her laptop, Sarah felt a mixture of exhaustion and determination. The cosy living room, usually a sanctuary of peace, was now her makeshift war room. The soft glow of the screen illuminated her focused expression as she plunged into a sea of information about nut allergies.

She typed furiously, scanning medical articles and journal entries, trying to understand how even trace amounts of nut proteins could cause anaphylaxis. One article in particular caught her attention, an in-depth study explaining how even a microscopic quantity could trigger a fatal reaction in someone highly sensitive.

Sarah's breath caught. If someone had deliberately tampered with the milk, ensuring that even a sliver of almond residue made it into Roger's drink, it could've killed him. And no one would have needed a large dose. Just the right moment. Just the right cup.

She bookmarked the article, made a few scribbled notes in the margin of her planner, and turned back to her main goal, finding anyone with motive. The discovery she'd made earlier about Roger's potential investment in a rival coffee chain had only sharpened her suspicions, but she needed more. She needed something personal. Concrete.

Scrolling through old industry news, her eyes caught on a headline from a few years back:

Bitter Brew: Legal Dispute Over Coffee Trade Secrets Heats Up Between Roger Alton and Local Barista

Sarah sat up straighter, her pulse quickening as she clicked the link. The article detailed a legal conflict between Roger and a rising local figure, **Olivia Green**, a celebrated new coffee entrepreneur known for her inventive flavour profiles and single-origin blends. According to the report, Olivia had accused Roger of stealing the formula for a proprietary roast she'd developed during her early career. The blend had become a best-seller in Roger's cafés. Olivia, meanwhile, had faded into near-obscurity, her brand tainted by the controversy.

Sarah kept reading, heart sinking with each line. The case had never gone to court, settled privately, the article said, though not before serious damage had been done to Olivia's reputation. Sponsors pulled out. Investors backed away. Her dream café shuttered within the year.

And now here she was, years later, resurfacing at the South Coast Latte Art competition. Competing. Smiling for cameras. Holding herself with poise and precision.

Sarah opened Olivia's social media profiles, curious to see what time, and bitterness, might have done.

There were the usual things: slick coffee reels, motivational posts, filtered latte art. But in between, Sarah noticed a different tone. Pinned beneath curated flat lays and brand partnerships were captions that brimmed with something darker. Subtle, but present.

"People say karma takes time. That's fine—I've always had patience."

"Success tastes even better when you've had to claw it back."

But one post, dated just a few weeks before the competition, made Sarah's stomach tighten.

"Sometimes, to move forward, you've got to bury the past properly. #NoMoreLooseEnds"

Her fingers trembled slightly as she copied the quote into her notes. Was it just bluster? A general comment on resilience? Or something more targeted?

She searched again, this time more deliberately looking for threads connecting Olivia and Roger beyond the headline. And there they were. More mentions. A photo from a panel discussion five years back, where Olivia sat at the end of a row, stiff-faced, while Roger grinned in the centre.

An older interview surfaced where she refused to name names but spoke openly about the betrayal she'd experienced early in her career. How she'd learned not to trust mentors. How losing everything had "forced her to sharpen her instincts and start over alone."

Sarah leaned back slowly. It all fit, the quiet resentment, the need for a comeback, the opportunity. If anyone had motive to see Roger humiliated, or worse, Olivia did.

She clicked open another tab and began digging through competition footage and behind-the-scenes photos. She wasn't sure what she was looking for anymore. A glimpse of tension? Olivia watching Roger a moment too long? Her hovering by the milk fridge?

Time slipped by unnoticed. The only sounds were the occasional click of her keyboard and the quiet crackle of Missy shifting in her sleep by the fireplace. The usual warmth of the room felt distant tonight, the shadows deeper, as if even the house could sense that something was off.

Finally, Sarah shut the laptop and rubbed her eyes. It was well past midnight, but she didn't feel ready for sleep. Her thoughts were a tangled web of motive, access, timing, and a growing sense that she was closer to something, even if she couldn't yet name it.

Before heading upstairs, she scribbled a note to herself:

Call allergy specialist. Compile Olivia's past statements. Recheck competition footage.

She paused, pen hovering, then underlined Olivia's name, twice.

Curling up under her duvet, Sarah allowed herself one deep breath. Tomorrow, she would start making calls. She would keep digging. Because something told her that Olivia hadn't come to Southsea just to win a trophy. And the past Roger had buried might finally have come back to haunt him

Chapter 10

As Sarah finally succumbed to sleep, her body sinking deeper into the comfort of her bed, the soft hum of her phone vibrating on the bedside table broke the silence of the night. The screen lit up in the dim room, casting a faint glow that flickered against the walls. A message had just come through from an unknown number.

The gentle buzzing continued for a few seconds, persistent enough to stir Sarah from her fragile slumber. Groggily, she reached for her phone, squinting at the bright screen. Her heart skipped a beat as she read the message that had flashed onto the display:

"Stop digging. You're getting too close. This isn't a game, and you won't like what happens if you keep pushing."

The words seemed to pulse ominously on the screen, and a cold shiver ran down Sarah's spine. Sleep was now a distant memory, her mind jolted back into full alertness by the sharp, threatening tone of the message. She stared at the unfamiliar number, her thoughts racing.

Who could have sent this? Was it connected to what she had been investigating? The warning was clear, someone didn't want her to continue her search for answers. But who? And why?

A knot of fear tightened in her chest as she considered the possibilities. The message was chillingly direct, and its arrival just after she had spent hours researching Roger's death only heightened her anxiety. Whoever had sent it knew what she was doing, and they were watching her.

But beneath the fear, Sarah felt a surge of defiance. If anything, this message only solidified her resolve. She had been right, there was more to this than met the eye, and someone was trying to cover their tracks.

Still, the threat was real, and the danger to herself and Charlie was undeniable. Sarah knew she had to be more careful, more strategic in her approach. She couldn't let her emotions cloud her judgment or lead her into reckless actions.

She quickly saved a screenshot of the message and added the number to her contacts under "Unknown Threat." Then, taking a deep breath, she locked her phone and placed it back on the coffee table, her mind whirring with new questions.

Her fingers hovered over her phone again. Part of her wanted to call Stanley right there and then, to hand it all over and let the professionals deal with it. But his voice echoed in her mind, calm, measured, but unmistakably firm: *"Let me handle this, Sarah. You need to step back."*

Step back. Stay out of it. Except she hadn't. Not really. Not at all.

If she told him now, she'd be tipping him off to the fact that she'd been digging, again, ignoring his warning and continuing to pursue leads on her own. And what if this message wasn't a real threat? What if it was just someone trying to shake her, to scare her off? She didn't want to give them that satisfaction, or risk Stanley clamping down harder, especially if it meant keeping her away from Charlie's case.

She stared at the dark screen in her lap for another long moment before finally setting it aside.

No. Not yet. She'd keep this to herself, for now. But she made another note in her journal, just in case. If someone *was* trying to silence her, they'd picked the wrong mother.

The room felt colder now, the quiet darkness pressing in on her as she sat there, wide awake and grappling with what to do next. She had to think carefully, to weigh her options.

She pulled the blanket tighter around herself, trying to shake off the lingering unease. There was no way she could sleep now, not with the ominous warning hanging over her. The unsettling message had jolted her wide awake, and every nerve in her body was on edge. The room was steeped in darkness, the only light coming from the faint glow of her phone screen, which she quickly dimmed as low as it would go.

Sarah glanced at Mike as he lay beside her, his face relaxed in the grip of deep sleep, oblivious to the turmoil that was now coursing through her. She didn't want to disturb him, he needed his rest. He didn't need to carry the weight of her worries as well, not tonight.

Carefully, or as carefully as she could manage, Sarah slipped out of bed, only to immediately stub her toe on the leg of the bedside table. She bit back a curse, hissing under her breath as she clutched her foot. The wooden floor was cool under her feet as she shuffled forward, bumping into the dresser next, then nearly knocking over a stack of books on the floor.

She winced and glanced back at Mike, holding her breath. He shifted slightly in his sleep, mumbling something incoherent before settling again. At least she hadn't woken him.

The only one she had disturbed was Missy, who had been draped over Mike's feet at the end of the bed. The chocolate labrador lifted her head, blinking sleepily at Sarah before stretching and hopping off the bed with an eager thud. Never one to miss an opportunity if a midnight snack was up for grabs, Missy trotted ahead, tail wagging as she padded through the darkness, becoming yet another obstacle for Sarah to avoid.

Grumbling under her breath as she inched towards the small desk in the corner of their bedroom, she tried not to trip over the dog. She eased into the chair, her fingers hovering over the laptop, hesitating for just a moment as she debated whether she had the energy for whatever thoughts had driven her awake in the first place.

Sarah opened her laptop, the soft click of the keys almost too loud in the otherwise silent room. She angled the screen so that the light wouldn't spill across the room and disturb Mike, the brightness adjusted to a dim glow that barely illuminated her face. Her heart was still pounding from the message, but she forced herself to focus, to channel that nervous energy into something productive.

Every so often, she glanced over at Mike, making sure he was still peacefully asleep. She was grateful for his presence, for the solid, reassuring comfort he provided, even when he was unaware of her turmoil. But this was something she needed to do alone, at least for now. The less he knew about the threatening message, the better.

As the minutes turned into hours, Sarah's notes grew longer, more detailed. She made a list of possible leads, people she needed to talk to, connections she needed to explore. The pieces of the puzzle were beginning to take shape, but there were still so many gaps, so many unknowns. The warning she had received only confirmed her suspicions that there was something more sinister at play, something that went beyond a simple accident.

The night stretched on, but Sarah hardly noticed. Her focus was absolute, her determination unwavering. She could feel the tension in her neck and shoulders, but she pushed through, ignoring the fatigue that was starting to creep in. This wasn't just about clearing Charlie's name anymore, it was about uncovering the truth, no matter how deep she had to dig.

By the time the first light of dawn began to seep through the curtains, Sarah had compiled a comprehensive list of questions and avenues to pursue. She knew it wasn't enough to solve the mystery, not yet, but it was a start. And it was more than she had before.

She finally closed her laptop, her eyes gritty from staring at the screen for so long. As she rose from the chair, stretching her stiff limbs, she glanced over at Mike one last time. He was still sound asleep, blissfully unaware of the chaos that had unfolded in the past few hours.

Sarah crept back to bed, careful not to wake him as she slid under the covers. She lay there, staring at the ceiling, her mind still buzzing with everything she had uncovered. The warning had shaken her, but it had also steeled her resolve. Whoever was behind this wanted her to stop digging, but all they had done was push her to dig deeper.

As she finally closed her eyes, Sarah knew that the road ahead would be treacherous. But she was ready for it. She would protect her son, uncover the truth, and ensure that justice was served. No matter what it took.

The early morning light filtered through the window of Sarah's small office, casting long shadows across the room. The space was usually reserved for the quieter tasks of running *Sarah's Secrets*, stock checks, invoice filing, rotas, but today it had taken on the chaotic energy of an amateur detective's lair. The desk was strewn with competition brochures, scribbled notes in several different colours of ink, old receipts, and at least three half-drunk cups of coffee, evidence of Sarah's sleepless night and increasingly tangled thoughts.

She sat back in her chair and let out a long breath, dragging her hands through her hair in frustration. "I can't see the bloody thing for all the clutter," she muttered aloud. Her notes had started to blur into one long, caffeine-fuelled scrawl. There were connections in there, she was sure of it, but somewhere between the allergy research, old social media posts, and whispered rivalries, she'd lost the thread.

Pushing her chair back with a scrape against the wooden floor, Sarah stood abruptly. She needed a clearer way to think, something visual, something she could move around, shift, reorganise. Her eyes flicked to the overflowing corkboard on the wall, then past it to the door that led into the main part of the coffee shop.

An idea sparked.

Sarah walked out to the centre of the coffee shop, staring up at the large chalk display board mounted on the wall. She had used it for promotional displays in the coffee shop, but now it would serve a much more critical purpose. She needed to organise her thoughts, to create a timeline of events that would help her see the bigger picture. This wasn't about coffee shop decor anymore. This was her case board now. But first, she had to get the board down. Dragging a chair across with her, she climbed up carefully.

Balancing precariously on the edge of the wobbly chair, Sarah reached up, stretching as far as she could to unhook the board. Her fingers brushed the top, but she was still a few inches short. She sighed, muttering to herself about how she really should have asked Mike to help with this before he left for work. Determination sparked in her eyes as she stood on her tiptoes, trying to gain just a little more height.

That's when Robyn walked in.

"Auntie Sarah!" Robyn's voice was a mix of amusement and concern as she took in the scene. Sarah, teetering on the chair, was not a sight for the faint-hearted, especially knowing her aunt's notorious clumsiness.

"Hey, Robyn!" Sarah replied, a little breathless. "I just need to get this board down so I can start putting everything together. Could you…"

Robyn was already moving towards her, her hands reaching out to steady the chair. "You're going to give me a heart attack one of these days," she joked, gripping the wobbly chair legs. "Let me hold this before you break your neck."

Sarah chuckled, though her laugh was tinged with nerves as she tried to maintain her balance. "I've got it, I've got it… just a little… almost…" She stretched again, finally managing to unhook the board from the wall.

"Careful now," Robyn cautioned, her tone softening as she watched Sarah struggle to lower the board without toppling over. "Here, let me help."

Sarah hesitated for a moment, then nodded, letting Robyn take the other end of the board as she carefully climbed down from the chair. The board was heavier than she remembered, and the two women manoeuvred it down with a mix of awkward laughter and tense concentration.

"Thanks," Sarah said, finally standing safely on solid ground. She set the board against the wall, leaning it at an angle while she caught her breath. "I don't know what I was thinking, trying to do that by myself."

Robyn shook her head, a fond smile playing on her lips. "You were thinking that you needed to solve this case and save Charlie, and you're willing to do whatever it takes to make that happen, even if that includes breaking your neck!"

Sarah sighed, her shoulders slumping as the weight of everything she'd been through settled back on her. "I just... I don't know where to start, Robyn. There's so much to piece together, and I feel like I'm running out of time."

Robyn placed a comforting hand on Sarah's arm. "We'll figure it out. You've got all this information swirling around in your head, now we just need to lay it out where we can see it. That's what this board is for, right?"

Sarah nodded, her resolve firming as she glanced at the blank chalkboard. "Right. If I can see the timeline of events, maybe something will jump out at me. Something that everyone else has missed."

Sarah stood in front of the chalkboard, her hand hovering over the surface as she mentally prepared to start mapping out the puzzle pieces. She could feel Robyn's supportive gaze on her, grounding her amidst the chaos that had engulfed their lives. Taking a deep breath, she finally put the chalk to the board and wrote, "What We Know."

Robyn, ever the practical one, pulled a chair closer and sat down, organising the various notes, flyers, and scraps of paper that they had accumulated over the past few days. "Ok then, what do we already know?" she prompted, her tone encouraging.

Sarah nodded, appreciating Robyn's methodical approach. "First, we know that Roger was severely allergic to nut milk. That's a fact. And it's crucial because it ties directly to how he died, his allergic reaction was triggered during the competition."

She started a list on the chalkboard, writing "Roger's nut allergy" at the top.

Robyn leaned forward, handing Sarah a piece of paper. "Right, and Gemma and Teddy both confirmed that they saw one of the competitors, the one you mentioned earlier, in the doorway of the kitchen. They were with a kitchen porter who was responsible for bringing out the milk trays to the competition room. That's suspicious."

Sarah added to the list, "Competitor seen with kitchen porter (milk trays)."

"And don't forget," Robyn continued, her voice thoughtful, "there were mutterings in the audience about Roger scoring unfairly. People thought he was showing favouritism."

Sarah paused, chalk poised in midair. "Yes, that's right. But why would that matter? Why would someone care so much about Roger's scoring that they'd go to such lengths?"

Robyn tapped her fingers on the table, her brow furrowing. "Well, there's prize money involved. It's not just about the title, there's a significant cash prize. Maybe someone was desperate to win."

Sarah scribbled "Potential motive: Prize money" on the board, then stepped back to look at the emerging picture. "So, we have a few key points. Roger's allergy, a competitor in the kitchen, possible favouritism in scoring, and the motive of prize money. But how do these connect? And where do we go from here?"

Robyn stood up, moving closer to the board to study it alongside Sarah. "I think the next steps should be to dig deeper into the competitor who was seen in the kitchen. We need to find out if they had any history with Roger, maybe they had a reason to believe he was scoring unfairly."

Sarah nodded, writing "Investigate competitor" as the first of their next steps. "And we should also look into the kitchen porter. If they were helping with the milk, they might have more information about what happened behind the scenes."

Robyn added, "We should also track down those people in the audience who were muttering about the favouritism. Maybe they saw or heard something more specific."

She looked at the board, feeling a mixture of anxiety and determination. "It's a start," she said, more to herself than to Robyn.

Robyn placed a comforting hand on Sarah's shoulder. "It is. And remember, we're in this together. We'll figure it out, one step at a time."

Sarah managed a small smile, her spirits bolstered by Robyn's unwavering support. "Thanks, Robyn. I don't know what I'd do without you."

Robyn grinned. "Well, you're stuck with me, so no need to find out. Now, let's start with the competitor. Do you think we can get some more information on them?"

Sarah glanced at the clock on the wall. Time was ticking, and they needed to act fast. "We need to split up if we're going to get to the bottom of this before Charlie's situation gets any worse."

Robyn agreed, her determination mirroring Sarah's. "I'll head over to the hotel and see if I can have a word with Gemma, Teddy, and the kitchen porter. Maybe they'll be more open with me since I'm closer to their age. Plus, I can come across as just another curious young person, not someone who's too invested."

"That's a good idea," Sarah said, nodding approvingly. "If I go back, it might look like I'm pestering them, and we don't want them to clam up. Just be casual about it, but see if you can get anything more out of them, especially the kitchen porter. He could be the key to all this."

Robyn grabbed her coat and slung her bag over her shoulder, ready to head out. "What about you, Auntie Sarah? What's your next move?"

Sarah straightened up, glancing at the list they had compiled on the chalkboard. "I'm going to follow up on that muttering we heard in the audience, about Roger possibly showing favouritism. There's got to be a reason people were suspicious of his scoring. I'll head to a couple of the cafes where I know some of the other competitors hang out and see if anyone's talking."

Robyn smiled, her eyes gleaming with the thrill of the investigation. "Sounds like a plan. I'll let you know as soon as I have anything."

"Be careful," Sarah added, her voice softening with concern. "We're getting closer to something, I can feel it. But that also means we're probably ruffling some feathers."

Robyn gave her a reassuring smile. "Don't worry, I'll keep my head down. I'll be back soon with whatever I can find."

As Robyn left the coffee shop, Sarah turned back to the chalkboard, reviewing what they had so far. The pieces were slowly coming together, but there were still so many gaps. She felt a pang of worry for Charlie, who was back at the hotel where several competitors had stayed overnight. He'd been reluctant to venture out in public since everything happened, understandably so.

She'd told him earlier not to worry, to take his time and come to Sarah's Secrets later in the day if he felt up to it. She glanced at her watch, making a quick calculation. With both her and Robyn heading off in different directions, she'd have to close the shop for a couple of hours. A twinge of guilt about the lost business passed through her mind, but she brushed it aside. If shutting down temporarily meant helping Charlie, it was worth it.

Sarah grabbed her own coat and prepared to head out, flipping the "Open" sign to "Closed" and jotting down a quick note about when she'd return. In the back of her mind, the anonymous warning still lingered, a dark cloud over her thoughts. She knew she was treading dangerous waters, but for Charlie's sake, she would keep going. She had to believe that the truth was within her grasp, she just had to reach out and seize it.

Southsea was never short on coffee spots. Independent cafés lined the streets like punctuation marks, each with its own loyal following, house blend, and quirky charm. On any other day, Sarah might have enjoyed the leisurely stroll, ducking into one or two to sample something new or chat with a fellow coffee lover. But today, her walk had a purpose. And as she passed her fourth café in twenty minutes, she was beginning to feel like she was chasing a shadow.

It could've been like finding a needle in a haystack. The city's baristas and coffee obsessives were scattered across dozens of little venues, any one of them a potential hiding place for the people she wanted to see. She'd tried not to get her hopes up, just letting instinct guide her, glancing briefly through the windows of each café she passed.

And then, some good luck. Through the large front window of a charming little spot tucked along a quieter side street, she caught sight of two familiar faces. Victor Chan and Eleanor Wren. Seated near the back, half-hidden behind a hanging plant and a shelf of donated books, they looked relaxed, deep in conversation with a small group of other coffee folk.

Sarah's pulse quickened, not with nerves, but with the sudden buzz of possibility. She had found them.

She stepped inside, the warm scent of ground beans and steamed milk wrapping around her like a blanket. The café was bustling, groups clustered around small tables, the hiss of espresso machines underscoring a soft indie soundtrack. It was the kind of place where Southsea's coffee crowd liked to gather, to trade notes and gossip, to talk shop without the pressure of competition. Perfect.

She approached the counter first, ordering a flat white and a small box of pastries to go. Then, casually, she added a request to speak with the owner about sourcing new products for *Sarah's Secrets*. It wasn't exactly a lie, she was always keeping her eye out for new flavours or suppliers, but today, her focus was elsewhere. Her gaze flicked again to the back table.

Victor and Eleanor were laughing at something, a shared grin between them that suggested ease, familiarity. But Sarah couldn't shake the feeling that behind the smiles, there might still be secrets worth uncovering.

As she waited for her order, Sarah positioned herself at a nearby table, close enough to overhear Victor and Eleanor's conversation without drawing attention to herself. She kept her posture relaxed, her expression neutral, but her ears were sharp.

"…I'm just saying, the judging felt off," Victor was saying, his voice low but animated. "I've competed in a fair few of these over the years, and I don't think I've ever seen scores shift so much between rounds. I mean, Roger was… unpredictable."

Eleanor snorted into her cup. "Unpredictable is one word for it."

Victor gave a little laugh, clearly trying to keep the conversation light. "Don't get me wrong, I'm not saying there was anything deliberate, but…"

"Oh, it was deliberate," Eleanor cut in, her voice sharp. "Come on, Victor. You saw the way he was looking at certain people's drinks like they were spun gold. Martin, in particular. That pour wasn't even that clean, and Roger was practically drooling over it."

Victor hesitated. "Well... I mean, Martin's been around for a while. He's got a good reputation."

Eleanor rolled her eyes. "Please. Reputation or not, that latte art was nothing special. It was who made it that mattered."

Victor leaned in slightly, a frown forming. "You think he was biased?"

"I *know* he was biased," Eleanor replied, setting her cup down with a quiet clink. "And not just professionally. There was something else going on, did you see the way they spoke to each other? All low voices and private smiles. You don't talk like that to just anyone."

Victor blinked. "You mean... like, *personal* personal?"

Eleanor gave a shrug, but it was theatrical, dripping with implication. "Wouldn't surprise me. A little behind-the-scenes favouritism. Special treatment. That would certainly explain why someone with an average pour and a basic roast was suddenly golden boy of the event."

Victor shifted uncomfortably. "That's a big assumption."

"Is it?" Eleanor leaned back, her gaze drifting towards the window, voice low and tight. "People like Roger think they're untouchable. They step on everyone else to get where they are, and then act surprised when someone finally snaps."

Victor looked at her, caught off guard by the bite in her tone. "Eleanor..."

But she wasn't done. "You can only push people down for so long before someone decides to push back. Hard."

There was a beat of silence. Victor stared at her, brow furrowed. He opened his mouth, then closed it again.

Eleanor sipped her coffee like nothing had happened.

Sarah, meanwhile, sat perfectly still, the words ringing in her ears.

At that moment, the barista called her name. She stood and made her way to the counter, forcing herself to breathe normally, to move casually. She accepted her order with a quiet thank you and approached the owner, launching into a brief discussion about potential product partnerships. All the while, her attention stayed on the conversation at the back table.

As she wrapped up the conversation, Eleanor's voice drifted clearly across the room once more.

"...and don't even get me started on the scoring system," she was saying. "It was designed to reward whoever Roger had already decided was going to win. It wasn't about skill, it was about who had his ear."

Victor sounded uneasy. "I mean... maybe it was just poor judging, not, like... sabotage."

Eleanor's laugh was bitter. "You're sweet, Victor. But no one sabotages things quite like the powerful protecting their own."

Victor didn't respond right away. When Sarah glanced over, she saw him giving Eleanor a wary look, like he wasn't sure whether to agree, or be concerned.

Sarah stepped out of the café a moment later, her coffee forgotten in her hand. Her thoughts buzzed with the implications of what she'd heard. Eleanor's bitterness, the suggestion of a deeper connection between Roger and Martin, and that final, chilling line: *push back, hard*.

If there was someone in the competition with motive and opportunity, Eleanor was quickly climbing to the top of that list.

She paused at the corner, pulling out her phone to jot down every word she could remember, every tone, every pause. For the first time, the anger in Eleanor's voice didn't just sound like wounded pride.

It sounded like a warning.

Chapter 11

Robyn approached the Queen's Hotel with a mix of nerves and determination. Not more than thirty six hours ago, she'd been pottering around the shop, excited at the prospect of coming here to watch Charlie compete, but now the grand building loomed before her, its elegant facade belying the tension that still lingered from the events of the weekend. She took a deep breath, reminding herself that this was for Charlie. If there was even a chance she could uncover something useful she had to try.

Inside, the atmosphere was subdued, a stark contrast to the lively competition that had taken place just a day before. Robyn headed towards the reception desk, hoping to catch sight of Gemma or Teddy. She had rehearsed her story on the way over, planning to ask about any job opportunities that might be available, as a way to start a conversation.

Robyn hovered near the counter, scanning the notice board with mild interest before leaning over to ask the barista about any job vacancies.

Gemma, who had been wiping down the end of the bar, looked up at the word *vacancies* and stepped closer with a friendly smile.

"Oh, sorry, I couldn't help overhearing. You're asking about jobs?"

Robyn turned, a little surprised but smiled. "Yeah, just curious if you're hiring."

Gemma glanced toward the back of the café, then nodded. "I'm not sure, but I can ask the manager for you if you want. I only started a few weeks ago myself, so I don't know the full ropes yet."

Robyn perked up. "Oh, you're new too?"

Gemma gave a small laugh, brushing a loose strand of hair behind her ear. "Very. Just got thrown into the deep end, really. Especially with… everything that's been going on. Not exactly your typical training week."

Robyn's smile grew, sensing an opportunity. "No kidding. I can't even imagine how shocking it must have been. Everyone must be so on edge. Did you… see anything unusual before it all happened?"

Gemma hesitated for a moment, as if weighing her words. "Well, not really… everything seemed pretty normal at first. But then again, I'm still getting to know how things work around here."

Robyn leaned in slightly, lowering her voice to make the conversation feel more personal. "I heard that someone might have tampered with the milk. Did you notice anything strange about the bottles, or see anyone doing something they shouldn't have?"

Gemma bit her lip, clearly unsure if she should say more. "I didn't think it was possible," she began slowly. "All the bottles were sealed, so I didn't really think twice about it."

Robyn nodded, encouraging her to continue. "But…?"

Gemma sighed, glancing around to make sure no one was listening. "Well, now that you mention it… I did see Eleanor Wren holding one of the milk bottles for a bit longer than usual. She was lifting it up, turning it around like she was inspecting it or something. I thought it was odd, but then again, she could have just been checking the label."

Robyn's pulse quickened. "Did it seem like she was looking for something specific?"

Gemma frowned, as if trying to recall the moment. "It almost seemed that way, yes. Like she was trying to see if it was the right one. But it was so quick, and then she passed it on to the next person. I didn't think much of it at the time."

Robyn thanked her, making a mental note to dig deeper into Eleanor's actions. She had another question, something that had been nagging at her since Sarah mentioned it. "Did you see Roger interacting with anyone else… besides Charlie, I mean?"

Gemma's expression darkened slightly. "I did, actually. He had a tense conversation with Olivia Green, one of the other competitors. It looked like they were arguing about something, but I was too far away to hear what it was about."

Robyn's curiosity piqued. "Do you know what it was about?"

Gemma shook her head. "No, but Olivia looked upset afterward. She's known for being creative with her techniques, really pushing boundaries. Maybe Roger didn't like that."

Robyn pressed gently, "Why would that be a problem?"

Gemma shrugged. "Maybe he thought she was too experimental, not traditional enough. Some people say that's why she hasn't won more competitions. Roger might have been biased against her."

Robyn hesitated, her brain scrambling for another question that wouldn't come across as too obvious. "And… I suppose you didn't hear anything else? People chatting in the staff areas, or maybe the competitors talking when they thought no one was listening?"

She smiled, trying to keep her tone light, casual, as if this was just idle curiosity rather than a calculated line of questioning. But even as the words left her mouth, she could feel how close she was skirting to outright interrogation.

Gemma's expression flickered. She didn't look upset, just suddenly aware. Her eyes darted over Robyn's shoulder, and her smile faltered slightly.

Robyn followed her gaze and spotted a man in a waistcoat watching from behind the reception desk. He wasn't glaring exactly, but the look he gave Gemma was enough to make her straighten her posture and tuck her cleaning cloth neatly under one arm.

"I probably shouldn't be hanging around gossiping," Gemma said, her voice quieter now, apologetic. "The manager doesn't love it when we're too chatty on shift."

"Oh, of course," Robyn said quickly, stepping back. "I didn't mean to…"

"No, it's fine," Gemma said with a small smile. "I hope some of that helped."

"It really did," Robyn said, meaning it. "Thanks again."

With a polite nod, Gemma slipped away behind the counter, her movements brisk and purposeful now.

Left alone in the reception area, Robyn took a slow breath and glanced around. No one was paying her any attention. She still had a little time. Maybe enough to do a bit of wandering… and see what else the Queen's Hotel had to offer, quietly, of course.

With that, she turned and began to make her way deeper into the building, her steps light, her curiosity very much awake.

As Robyn wandered through the quieter corridors of the Queen's Hotel, she let her steps slow, curiosity tugging her along more than any clear plan. She passed a small sitting area where an elderly couple read the paper in silence, then a hallway lined with black-and-white photographs of the hotel in its Edwardian heyday. Just as she was about to circle back to the reception, a discreet sign caught her eye: The Duke's Bar.

She hesitated, then pushed the door open just enough to peer inside. The room was quiet and dimly lit, the kind of old-world elegance that whispered of cigar smoke and brandy rather than flat whites and frothy lattes. There was no one at the bar, but in the far corner, seated at a small table with a neat stack of papers and a leather-bound diary, was Helen Williams.

Robyn froze, just inside the doorway. Helen hadn't noticed her. The assistant was completely absorbed in her work, brow furrowed as she scanned a document, her pen moving in swift, confident strokes. Every so often she paused, double-checked something in the diary, and made another note in the margin of the page she was reading.

There was a meticulousness to her movements that immediately caught Robyn's attention. This wasn't idle admin work. It looked important. Intentional.

Just as Robyn was about to turn away, the assistant's mobile phone rang, causing her to jump slightly. She answered it with a hint of irritation in her voice, clearly agitated by whoever was on the other end of the line. With a sharp sigh she got up and walked briskly toward the front door of the hotel, her free hand gesturing in frustration as she spoke.

Robyn hesitated, her heart racing. She knew it wasn't right to snoop, but something inside her urged her forward. It was as if a magnetic pull was drawing her to that desk, to those papers. Before she could second-guess herself, Robyn found herself moving quickly across the lobby, her eyes darting to the assistant's retreating figure as she stepped outside to vape and pace while continuing her tense phone conversation.

Once Robyn reached the desk, she glanced down at the paperwork spread out in front of her. Her breath caught in her throat as she realised what she was looking at, Roger's scoring sheets. The same sheets he had been using during the competition to note down his thoughts and assign scores to each of the contestants. This was it. This could be the key to understanding what had really been going on behind the scenes.

Robyn cast a quick glance toward the glass doors of the hotel. The assistant was still outside, her back to the lobby, the vape releasing small clouds of smoke as she gestured animatedly into her phone. Knowing she didn't have much time, Robyn pulled out her phone with trembling hands. She opened the camera app and quickly snapped a photo of the first sheet, trying to keep her movements as discreet as possible.

She flipped to the next page, snapping another photo, and then another. Her pulse quickened as she worked, her mind racing with the implications of what she was capturing. Each page revealed more of Roger's thoughts, his scores, and the detailed comments he had made about each contestant's performance. Some of the notes seemed to align with what Sarah had told her, but others were more cryptic, hinting at a bias that wasn't immediately obvious.

As Robyn reached the last page, she took one final photo, her heart pounding in her chest. She quickly slipped her phone back into her bag and turned to leave, but as she did, she caught sight of the hotel receptionist watching her with a curious expression. Robyn forced a casual smile, her mind racing for an excuse. She nodded politely to the receptionist and hurried out of the hotel, her head down, doing her best to appear unbothered.

Once outside, she took a deep breath, trying to steady her nerves. The weight of what she had just done hit her all at once. She had crossed a line, but deep down, she knew it was worth it. This information could be exactly what they needed to clear Charlie's name.

Robyn made a quick call to Sarah, her voice barely containing her excitement. "Sarah, you won't believe what I've just found," she said, breathless. "I managed to get a look at Roger's scoring sheets. I took photos of everything."

Sarah's voice came through the phone, filled with equal parts surprise and urgency. "You did what? Robyn, that's incredible! We need to go through those as soon as possible. This could be exactly what we need to shift the focus away from Charlie."

As Robyn filled her in on the details, Sarah's mind was already working to connect the dots. There were so many moving parts to this investigation, so many secrets and lies tangled together. But with these new pieces of information, they were getting closer to the truth. Piece by piece, the puzzle was coming together.

But as Sarah and Robyn both knew, the closer they got to the truth, the more dangerous the situation became. They were venturing into territory that others would rather keep hidden, and the consequences of their investigation could be more severe than they ever anticipated. But for Charlie's sake, they were willing to take the risk.

Sarah ended the call with a renewed sense of determination. They were onto something big, something that could expose the truth behind Roger's death. But they had to be careful. The deeper they dug, the more enemies they could potentially make. And as they'd both learned, some stones were better left unturned.

As Robyn walked away from the hotel, she couldn't shake the feeling that she was being watched. She quickened her pace, her thoughts racing with everything she had just uncovered. There was no turning back now. The game was on, and they were playing for keeps.

Sarah stepped out of the coffee shop, tugging her scarf a little tighter against the coastal breeze that whipped through the narrow lanes of Southsea. The bell above the door gave its usual cheerful chime as it closed behind her, but the warmth and comfort of the shop felt a world away from the unease still simmering in her chest.

She needed air. Movement. Something to shake the static from her thoughts.

The little shopping precinct just around the corner was bustling with Saturday morning life. A pop-up farmers' market had taken over the square, stalls stretching out in neat rows beneath colourful bunting that flapped in the wind. The scent of fresh herbs and sourdough mingled with the salt of the sea, and the air was filled with the chatter of shoppers, children tugging at parents' hands, and the soft clatter of crates being unloaded.

Sarah weaved her way through the crowd, absently scanning displays of glossy tomatoes, jars of local honey, and homemade chutneys. She paused to pick up a punnet of strawberries, turning one over in her fingers before placing it gently back down. Her mind wasn't on shopping. It was still tangled in timelines, motives, and the lingering shadow of Roger Alton.

She moved on, passing a stall with baskets of artisanal soaps, another displaying chunky knit scarves. She wasn't really drawn in, just walking, letting her feet carry her while her brain quietly whirred in the background. And then she heard it.

"I'm telling you, if Roger had gone through with that investment, it would've shaken things up for everyone around here," one of the local business owners was saying in a low voice.

Sarah stopped mid-step, her head snapping instinctively toward the sound. A pair of women stood just to the side of a handmade jewellery stall, their backs turned, one of them cradling a paper cup of coffee in gloved hands. They didn't notice Sarah, or if they did, they didn't care. The conversation was clearly too good to interrupt.

Sarah shifted slightly closer, her body angled just enough to look like she was admiring a tray of enamel earrings. But her ears were tuned entirely to the words drifting over.

"Right," agreed her companion, a middle-aged woman with sharp features, who Sarah knew owned the bakery on the next street. "A new coffee shop, with Roger's backing no less, would've drawn a lot of business away. It could've put the rest of us in a tight spot."

Sarah's interest was piqued. Roger investing in a rival coffee shop? She hadn't heard anything about that before. She pretended to inspect a nearby stall, straining to hear more.

"Well, not anymore," she muttered, shaking her head. "With him gone, that plan's dead in the water. But it makes you wonder, doesn't it? Who would have benefitted the most from him not going through with it?"

The woman nodded, her eyes narrowing as she considered it. "A lot of people, I reckon. Whoever was worried about losing business, for one. Or maybe someone who didn't want him to pull out of a different deal. I'm just glad it's not my problem anymore."

Sarah's heart raced as she quickly moved on, careful not to draw attention to herself. This was a significant piece of the puzzle, if Roger had been planning to invest in a rival coffee shop, it could explain a lot about the tensions in the competition, and even provide a motive for his murder.

But as she rounded the corner near the flower stall, her thoughts were interrupted by a figure stepping out from the shadows. The person, a man wearing a dark coat and a flat cap pulled low over his face, moved directly into her path, forcing her to stop abruptly.

"Mrs. Meadows," he said quietly, his voice barely above a whisper. "A word of advice, some stones are better left unturned."

Sarah's breath caught in her throat. The market around her seemed to fade into the background as she focused on the man's words. There was an unmistakable edge to his tone, one that sent a chill down her spine.

"Who are you?" Sarah demanded, trying to keep her voice steady. "What do you want?"

The man gave a small, almost apologetic shrug. "Just a concerned party. You've been asking a lot of questions lately. Not everyone likes that."

Before she could respond, the man tipped his hat slightly and disappeared into the crowd, leaving Sarah standing there, stunned. Her heart pounded in her chest as she replayed his words in her mind. The warning was clear, someone was watching her, someone who didn't want her to dig any deeper.

As she slowly began to move again, the bustling market felt different. The familiar faces and friendly chatter now seemed tinged with suspicion, as if everyone around her could be hiding secrets. The cheerful atmosphere did little to dispel the unease that settled over her like a dark cloud.

With a determined set to her jaw, Sarah quickened her pace, heading back to the coffee shop. This warning, however unsettling, had only strengthened her resolve. Whoever was behind this was getting nervous, nervous enough to try and scare her off. And that meant she was on the right track.

But as she walked, Sarah couldn't help but feel a creeping sense of dread. This wasn't just about clearing

Charlie's name anymore. The stakes were higher than she had imagined, and the danger was becoming all too real.

Chapter 12

Charlie was behind the counter at *Sarah's Secrets*, methodically wiping down the espresso machine for the second time in half an hour. The usual precision of his movements was there, but none of the usual flair. No humming. No idle chat with customers. Just silence and a kind of mechanical stillness.

Sarah watched him from across the room, her heart quietly breaking. This weekend should've been his moment, his celebration. Instead, it had hollowed him out.

She didn't say anything. There was nothing she could say that would pull him back to himself.

Instead, she turned her attention to the stack of printouts Robyn had handed her earlier: scanned copies of the judges' scoring sheets. The competition's official documents, complete with Roger Alton's notes and numbers. Sarah spread them across the long wooden table in the back room, smoothing the pages down, already recognising the pattern they all feared.

Roger had played favourites. That much had become increasingly clear over the last twenty-four hours. But Sarah wasn't here to prove bias anymore, she was looking for something else. Something new.

As her eyes moved down the columns of numbers, a flash of handwriting in the margin caught her attention. A note, one that didn't match Roger's tidy cursive. It was scrawled in blue ink, different from the rest of the black biro on the page. "Ask re: list change. Timing issue?"

It was next to Charlie's final-round entry. Sarah squinted. She flipped through the stack, found another similar scrawl, this one near Martin's score sheet: "Approved late – confirm?"

She stared at the notes, her breath catching. These weren't part of the official judging rubric. They weren't feedback. These were side notes, administrative, maybe, but why scribbled on scoring sheets?

Sarah had seen that handwriting before. In a meeting agenda for the competition, stuck to the fridge in the staff area. That neat-but-rushed script belonged to Roger's assistant.

Why had Helen been making notes on the score sheets? And what list change? What needed approval after the round had begun?

She flipped to another sheet, and this time her heart quickened even more sharply. Another scribble from Helen, partially smudged, caught her eye: "Check Roger's business storage, inventory list?"

Roger had a business storage facility? Sarah frowned deeply, a dozen new questions flooding her mind. What was Helen checking for, and why was it important enough to scribble onto competition notes?

She took out her phone and snapped quick photos of the margins, carefully cropping the images. A seed of unease grew in her chest. There was something here, something they'd missed because they were focused on bias and scores.

As Sarah shuffled through the stack of competition paperwork, her phone buzzed quietly. She glanced briefly at the screen: Message from Amy, 'Need a quick chat about something exciting!' Sarah sighed and put the phone aside; whatever Amy's latest idea was, it would have to wait. Right now, Charlie's problem consumed her attention entirely.

Charlie entered quietly and placed a fresh cup of tea next to her elbow.

"Thanks, love," Sarah said softly.

He nodded but didn't speak. He lingered for a second, then returned to the counter, where he resumed polishing a stack of cups that didn't need polishing.

Robyn slipped through the door a moment later, breathless and wind-flushed from walking over. "Anything?"

Sarah gestured to the sheets. "Helen wrote these."

Robyn leaned in. "Is that…?"

"Look," Sarah said, pointing to the first scribble. "She mentions a 'list change' and 'timing.' Something was altered. 'Approved late'. Doesn't that sound odd?"

Robyn frowned. "Could be competitor order? Presentation schedule?"

"Or the milk rotation," Sarah added grimly. She pointed to the newly discovered note. "And Helen also mentions Roger's business storage. What if the milk was swapped out with something Roger himself had stocked away?"

Robyn pulled out her phone. "We need to ask her."

Sarah shook her head. "No. Not yet. Not until we know what these notes actually mean."

Charlie's quiet voice broke the moment. "It won't matter."

They both turned. He was leaning against the counter now, arms crossed, eyes dark with something like resignation.

"They've already made up their minds," he said quietly. "Stanley barely looked at me during the last interview. He's not listening."

"He's just being thorough," Sarah said, rising from her chair.

Charlie gave a dry laugh. "Is that what this is?"

His voice cracked slightly at the end, and Sarah saw the weight of it settle deeper on his shoulders.

"Sweetheart," she said gently, moving toward him. "We're getting somewhere. We're close."

Charlie just shook his head and walked into the back, the bell on the stockroom door jingling softly behind him.

Robyn and Sarah exchanged a look.

"He's broken," Robyn said. "And who could blame him?"

Sarah's jaw tightened. "Then we keep going."

Robyn sat at the back table, scrolling through notes. Sarah stood behind the counter, staring into space until her gaze landed again on the score sheets.

She pulled one toward her. Helen's note: Approved late. Check Roger's business storage. Sarah's heart thudded. What if the change Helen noted had nothing to do with scheduling, and everything to do with the ingredients stored at Roger's facility?

She grabbed her phone. "I'm going back to the hotel."

Robyn looked up. "Now?"

"I need to see that prep list. The original one. Before anyone had the chance to 'approve' anything." Sarah stood in the centre of the quiet café, the score sheet still in her hand, her pulse ticking faster now. The prep list. The milk switch. Helen's notes. Roger's business storage. It was all beginning to feel like more than just favouritism, it was sabotage. Or, at the very least, manipulation.

She tapped her phone against her palm, thinking.

She needed that original prep list from the Queen's Hotel. But getting her hands on it wouldn't be easy, not without alerting someone, especially if Stanley or his team were still doing follow-up interviews. She couldn't just march in and demand access. Not yet.

No, she'd need to be subtle. Play it like she was just tying up loose ends. Maybe chat to the kitchen staff, Gemma, if she was around. Get a look at the morning logs, the deliveries, maybe even the CCTV if she could figure out a reason. But that could wait another hour.

In the meantime, Sarah turned to Robyn, who was still poring over screenshots and scribbled notes like a woman possessed. "I'm heading out."

Robyn looked up. "Be careful at the hotel?"

"I'll head over there in a bit," Sarah said. "I want to talk to a few of the other competitors first. If something shady happened with the prep list, maybe someone else noticed something weird, if not at the time, then in hindsight. And I want to start with Olivia."

Robyn raised an eyebrow. "You think she'll talk?"

Sarah shrugged. "If I ask the right questions." She pulled on her coat, tucking her phone into her pocket and wrapping her scarf tight. The late afternoon was already dimming, the light slanting gold and tired through the windows.

As she stepped outside, a sudden gust of cold air bit at her cheeks. With a small smile, Sarah pulled out her headphones and slipped them over her ears. They were big, bulky, and made her feel a bit like a middle-aged Cyberman, but they helped block out the world and gave her the focus she needed. As she made her way toward the seafront, she queued up one of her guilty pleasures, a murder mystery podcast. The familiar intro music started playing, and Sarah chuckled to herself at the irony of indulging in fictional mysteries while navigating one of her own.

With a final deep breath, she pulled off her headphones and tucked them into her bag. She smoothed her hair, plastered on her best polite-customer expression, and stepped through the door into Olivia's brew house, determined to uncover what Olivia remembered, and perhaps, quietly, to learn more about Roger's mysterious storage facility.

The coffee brew house at the end of the road had a warm, inviting atmosphere that greeted Sarah the moment she stepped through the door. The scent of freshly roasted beans mingled with the salty breeze from the nearby seafront, creating a unique charm. The place was cosy yet industrial, with sacks of beans stacked neatly in the corner, a sleek roasting machine whirring softly, and an array of polished equipment glinting under warm lights.

Olivia Green, the owner, looked up from behind the counter, her face lighting up. "Hey there, Charlie's mum, isn't it? What brings you in today?"

Sarah smiled, her eyes sweeping the space with appreciation. "I'm looking to pick up some local coffee for *Sarah's Secrets*, something seasonal. Thought it might be a nice addition to the menu."

Olivia's eyes brightened with interest. "Well, you're in luck. I've been testing a few new blends that could be just what you're after."

As Olivia moved to gather samples, describing flavour profiles and roasting methods, Sarah wandered closer to the roasting machine in the back. Its smooth design and gentle hum gave it a quiet authority in the room.

"Charlie would love something like this," Sarah said, gesturing toward it. "He keeps talking about roasting our own beans one day, but it still feels a bit out of reach."

Olivia chuckled, glancing over her shoulder. "Honestly, it's not as intimidating as it looks. Once you get the basics down, it's just about practice, and a bit of patience."

She hesitated for a beat, then added more quietly, "Though I'd be lying if I said the market isn't already crowded. Every new roaster shifts the balance a bit."

Sarah caught the undercurrent in her voice. "It must be hard, staying ahead in such a competitive space."

Olivia gave a small shrug, her smile tinged with something harder to define. "There's always someone who thinks they know better. Or someone who's been around long enough to think they get to set the rules."

"Like Roger?" Sarah asked gently.

Olivia paused, eyes flicking to Sarah's with a guarded expression before she turned back to the counter. "He had strong opinions. Liked things a certain way."

Sarah leaned slightly closer, sensing more beneath the surface. "Did you two clash?"

A soft laugh escaped Olivia. "I suppose you could call it that. I've always believed in pushing boundaries, trying new things. Roger... not so much. He valued tradition, structure. Said it kept the craft pure." She ran her fingers along the edge of the counter, her voice thoughtful. "There's something admirable about that, I guess. But it didn't leave much room for people like me."

Sarah tilted her head. "People like you?"

Olivia looked up, eyes meeting Sarah's with quiet intensity. "New ideas. New voices. Especially if those voices didn't sound quite like his." She gave a small, almost self-deprecating smile. "It wasn't always easy being taken seriously."

"But you've built something incredible here," Sarah said.

Olivia nodded, her gaze drifting across the café. "I've tried. I wanted a place that felt different, personal, meaningful. Not just another coffee shop." She hesitated again. "Sometimes it felt like Roger didn't really see that. Or maybe he did... and didn't like it."

There was a moment of silence before she added, more softly, "He had a lot of influence. And he wasn't shy about using it."

Sarah sensed the edge in her tone but also restraint. Olivia wasn't venting; she was choosing her words carefully.

"I'm sorry," Olivia said after a moment, shaking her head. "Didn't mean to go on like that. It's just... complicated, I guess."

"No need to apologise," Sarah said gently. "I get it. Sometimes people hold more power than they should."

Olivia offered a small, wry smile. "And sometimes we let them."

As Sarah reached for the coffee blends Olivia had set aside, something on the shelf caught her attention, a row of vibrantly coloured bottles, lined up with care.

"What are those?" she asked, stepping closer.

Olivia followed her gaze and smiled. "That's my latest experiment, kombucha. I've been brewing small batches, testing flavours. Ginger, hibiscus, a lavender one I'm still perfecting."

"Kombucha? That's a bold move," Sarah said, picking up a bottle. "You're really branching out."

Olivia nodded. "Well, I figured why not? The market's changing fast. You have to adapt, or risk falling behind."

Sarah studied the label thoughtfully. "It's impressive. But... doesn't it feel like a lot to take on?"

There was a flicker of something unreadable in Olivia's expression. "Maybe. But I've got to keep pushing forward. I don't want to stay in one lane just because that's what's expected. That was always Roger's philosophy, stick to what you know."

Her tone wasn't bitter, exactly. More... reflective. As if she were still deciding how she felt.

Sarah placed the bottle back gently. "Sounds like you've got big plans."

Olivia gave a slow nod. "I do. Or at least, I *did*. Sometimes it's hard to know if those plans still make sense, or if I'm chasing something that's already moved on without me."

Sarah watched her, seeing now not just the ambition but also the fatigue that came with constantly trying to prove yourself. Olivia wasn't consumed by resentment, but by something quieter, disappointment, perhaps, or a longing to be seen for what she was capable of.

"Well," Olivia said after a pause, forcing a smile, "whatever comes next, it won't be decided by someone else. I've learned that much."

Sarah nodded slowly, the mood lingering with her as she gathered her things. Olivia's words weren't a confession, but they painted a portrait of someone who had spent years pushing against walls built by others, Roger among them.

Whether that made her dangerous... or just determined... Sarah wasn't quite sure.

As Sarah's mind swirled with these questions, Olivia was completely oblivious to the weight her words carried. She didn't seem to notice the shift in Sarah's expression or the tension that had crept into the conversation. Instead, Olivia smiled brightly and launched into a completely different topic, her tone upbeat.

Sarah was listening, or at least trying to, but her attention had started to fray. Her mind kept drifting back to the notes, the altered list, the milk switch. She needed to get to the Queen's Hotel. Soon.

Her phone buzzed in her coat pocket. She ignored it, offering a polite smile as Olivia launched into a description of her flavour notes. Nutmeg. Dried fig. Something about mouthfeel. Another buzz. Then a pause.

Sarah shifted slightly in her seat, forcing herself to nod along. One call could wait. The phone buzzed again. Then again, insistently, two more times in quick succession. Her stomach sank.

"I'm so sorry," she said quickly, already rising to her feet. "I just need to take this. I really appreciate you talking with me."

Olivia gave a half-nod, slightly wary now. "Sure. Let me know if you want the contact info for my roaster?"

"I will," Sarah said, already halfway toward the door.

She fished the phone from her pocket, her fingers fumbling slightly as she pushed through the door and out into the sharp afternoon air. She barely registered the person she nearly collided with as she stepped out onto the pavement.

"Sorry, sorry," she muttered, sidestepping them without meeting their eyes. She jabbed the green button on her screen.

"Robyn?"

Her niece's voice came through in a rush. "Sarah, you need to get back. It's Charlie. Stanley just arrested him."

Sarah froze. "What?"

"They said they needed to question him further. But they put him in a car, Sarah, he's gone. They didn't even explain properly. I think they're going to charge him."

Sarah's heart slammed against her ribs. "I'm on my way."

Chapter 13

As Sarah burst through the heavy glass doors of the police station, her heart pounded with a mixture of fear and determination. The bright, sterile lighting of the station was a stark contrast to the warmth of the coffee shop she had just left, and the cold, institutional atmosphere only intensified her anxiety. She quickly scanned the room, her eyes locking onto the front desk where a uniformed officer sat, his expression one of practiced indifference.

"Excuse me," Sarah said urgently as she approached the desk, her voice trembling slightly despite her efforts to stay composed. "I need to see Charlie, Charlie, my son, he's been brought in for questioning. Please, I need to see him right away."

The desk sergeant, a grizzled man with a weathered face and tired eyes, looked up from his paperwork. He took in the sight of Sarah, her agitation clear from the way she was clutching her bag and the desperate look in her eyes. He put down his pen and offered her a measured, calm response.

"Ma'am, I understand you're concerned, but you need to calm down," he said in a steady tone, his hands raised slightly as if to placate her. "Charlie's in with Inspector Stanley right now. I'm afraid you'll have to wait until they're finished. Why don't you take a seat, and I'll see what I can find out for you?"

Sarah wanted to argue, to demand that they let her see Charlie immediately, but she knew it wouldn't help. She nodded reluctantly, her breath shaky, and turned toward the row of plastic chairs along the wall. She sat down, her body tense, her fingers tapping restlessly against her thigh. The minutes dragged on, each one feeling like an eternity as she fought to keep her emotions in check.

Her mind raced with questions and fears. What new evidence could they possibly have found? Why had they brought Charlie in like this, and what were they accusing him of now? Every worst-case scenario played out in her head, making it impossible to sit still. She shifted in her seat, crossing and uncrossing her legs, her fingers now gripping the edge of the chair.

The station buzzed with the quiet hum of activity, phones ringing, officers moving about, the occasional murmur of conversation, but to Sarah, it all felt distant and unreal. The only thing that mattered was getting to Charlie, understanding what was happening, and finding a way to fix it.

Finally, after what felt like an eternity, she saw Inspector Stanley emerge from a hallway to her left. He was a tall man with sharp features and an air of authority, his dark suit immaculate as always. As soon as their eyes met, he gestured for her to follow him. Sarah jumped up from her seat, her heart pounding as she hurried over to him.

"Mrs. Meadows, Sarah," Stanley said, his voice professional but with a touch of sympathy. "Please, come with me. I wouldn't normally allow this, but given the circumstances, I'll try to let you know what's happening."

He led her into a small side room, the kind used for private conversations away from the main bustle of the station. The room was sparsely furnished, just a table and a few chairs, but it felt slightly more personal, less intimidating than the rest of the station.

Stanley closed the door behind them and motioned for Sarah to sit down. She did so, but her posture remained rigid, her eyes wide with anticipation and dread. Stanley took a seat opposite her, his demeanour calm and measured.

"I know you're worried, and I'll do my best to explain what's going on," he began, folding his hands on the table. "Charlie has been brought in for further questioning because some new evidence has come to light. We have to follow protocol, and that means taking him into custody for now."

Sarah's heart skipped a beat, and she leaned forward, her voice laced with desperation. "What evidence? What have you found? I swear, Charlie had nothing to do with Roger's death. He's innocent, Inspector, you have to believe me."

Stanley's expression softened slightly, a rare glimpse of compassion breaking through his professional facade. "Sarah, I've known Charlie for a while now. In my heart, I don't believe the Charlie I know would ever do something like this. But I can't just ignore the evidence, even when it involves friends. I have a job to do, and that means I need to treat this case with the same seriousness as any other."

Sarah felt a lump rise in her throat at his words, but there was something in what he said that caught her off guard. "Oh," she murmured, trying to keep her voice steady, "so you do think of us as friends?"

Stanley hesitated for a brief moment, his demeanour softening further. "Well," he said with a small, almost shy smile, "I like to think that we are."

The unexpected warmth in his response gave Sarah a brief moment of solace in the midst of her turmoil. But the reality of the situation quickly pressed back in, and her anxiety returned.

Stanley continued, his tone gentle but firm. "I understand how difficult this must be for you, but we have to look at all the evidence objectively. There's a new witness who has come forward, claiming to have seen Charlie near the scene at a critical time. It's not definitive, but between that and the fact that Roger reacted right after Charlie's latte, it's enough to warrant further investigation."

Sarah felt a chill run down her spine. "But that doesn't mean he's guilty! Charlie was just trying to help, to figure out what happened. He would never hurt anyone."

Stanley nodded, his gaze steady. "I believe you, Sarah, but we need to question Charlie thoroughly and see how this new information fits with everything else we've gathered. That's why he's here."

Sarah's hands trembled as she tried to absorb the news. The thought of Charlie alone in one of those interview rooms, accused of something so terrible, made her feel physically sick. She had to trust that the truth would come out, that Charlie's innocence would be proven, but the fear gnawed at her relentlessly.

"Can I see him?" she asked, her voice barely above a whisper, all her previous resolve crumbling under the weight of her worry.

Stanley hesitated, then shook his head. "Not right now. We need to finish the questioning first. But I promise you, Sarah, we're not going to make any hasty decisions. We're looking for the truth, just like you are."

Sarah nodded, swallowing hard to keep the tears at bay. "Please, just... take care of him."

Stanley's expression remained serious, but there was a flicker of understanding in his eyes. "We'll do everything by the book, Sarah. I'll keep you informed as best as I can."

With that, he stood, indicating that their conversation was over. Sarah rose to her feet as well, feeling more exhausted than she had in a long time. As Stanley led her back to the main area of the station, she couldn't shake the feeling that all she could do now was wait, and hope that the truth would be enough to bring Charlie back home.

Stepping out of the police station, the bright midday sun did little to lift the heavy weight pressing down on her chest. The world outside was vibrant and bustling, but to her, it all felt distant, muffled, as though she were trapped in a bubble of despair that kept her separated from everything around her. She moved down the steps slowly, her feet dragging as if each step required a monumental effort.

Her mind was a swirl of emotions, fear, anxiety, frustration, and a deep, gnawing helplessness. Charlie's face flashed in her mind, his smile, his reassuring words whenever she had been the one in trouble. But now he was the one in the lion's den, and there was nothing she could do to reach him, nothing that could break through the cold walls of the police station that had swallowed him whole.

She reached the pavement and paused, unsure of what to do next. People passed by, going about their lives, unaware of the turmoil raging inside her. She felt like a ship adrift in a stormy sea, no anchor, no compass, just the endless, pounding waves of uncertainty. Sarah looked around, hoping for some sign, some direction that would tell her where to go, what to do. But there was nothing, just the cold, hard reality that her son was in custody, and she was powerless to help him.

Yet, as the despair threatened to overwhelm her, a small spark of determination began to flicker in her chest. It was faint, almost drowned out by the darkness, but it was there. She couldn't just walk away and leave Charlie's fate entirely in the hands of Inspector Stanley, no matter how competent he was. She knew Stanley was good at his job, in fact, she owed her life to his detective work. He had saved her once, when she was almost the second victim of a woman driven by revenge. But even though she trusted him, she couldn't ignore the voice in her heart that told her she needed to do more, to fight for Charlie in every way she could.

Sarah straightened up, wiping a stray tear from her cheek. She couldn't just sit back and wait for news. She couldn't be passive, hoping that everything would turn out all right. Charlie needed her, and she wasn't going to let him down. She had to keep pushing, keep searching for the truth, keep questioning until she had exhausted every possible lead.

She pulled out her phone, staring at the screen as she considered her next move. She needed to reach out to Robyn, to share what had happened and figure out what they could do next. But even more than that, she needed to follow her instincts, the same instincts that had saved her life before. There were still too many unanswered questions, too many loose ends that needed tying up. She wasn't a detective, but she was a mother, a mother who would stop at nothing to protect her child.

With a renewed sense of purpose, Sarah began to walk, her pace quickening as she made her way back toward her car. There were people she needed to talk to, things she needed to investigate. She couldn't let fear paralyse her. She couldn't let the uncertainty win.

As she drove through the familiar streets of Southsea, her mind was already forming a plan. She would start by revisiting the events of the competition, talking to anyone who might have seen something or heard something that could clear Charlie's name. She would dig deeper into Roger's life, his connections, and his enemies. And she would keep pushing, keep fighting, until she found the piece of evidence that would exonerate her son.

Sarah parked a little haphazardly along the seafront, her hands still trembling slightly from the meeting at the station. The wind had picked up, carrying the briny scent of the Solent and the sharp, metallic edge of something unsettled. She climbed out of the car and slammed the door with more force than necessary, shoving her keys into her coat pocket.

She needed air. Space. Something to still the thoughts ricocheting inside her skull. The tide was out, revealing the gritty stretch of stony beach that curved along the coast. She made her way across the uneven pavement, her boots crunching against scattered pebbles and driftwood, head down, arms wrapped around herself. Just five minutes. Just enough time to pull herself together.

She'd barely reached the edge of the promenade when a figure stepped into her path. Maya. She was walking quickly, head down, as though hoping not to be seen, but as soon as she spotted Sarah, her steps faltered.

Sarah's heart kicked up. "Maya."

Maya glanced sideways, as if considering flight, but Sarah had already stepped toward her.

"You need to tell me the truth."

Maya hesitated, then sighed, her shoulders sagging. The wind tossed her hair across her face, and she didn't bother to push it away. Her eyes looked tired, wary, but something in her expression softened.

"I know what it looks like," she said quietly. "But I wasn't trying to sabotage Eleanor. Or anyone else. I just… I got in too deep before I realised what I was doing."

Sarah didn't look away. "Then tell me what you were doing."

Maya rubbed her hands together like she was trying to warm them. "I got to the hotel early. Earlier than I told the organisers."

"That's not what you said before."

"I know." Her voice cracked a little. "I panicked. I didn't want anyone thinking I was sneaking around."

Sarah said nothing.

Maya pressed on, the words tumbling out now. "When I arrived, there was someone at their station. One of the competitors. They were… acting odd. Checking and re-checking everything, like they were looking for something. Or making sure something was exactly how they left it."

Sarah frowned. "Who?"

Maya looked away. "I'm not saying. I didn't see anything criminal, I just had a bad feeling. Something about the way they kept fiddling with things… it felt off. And then when they left, I couldn't shake it. I went over. I didn't touch anything, I swear. Just looked."

"Why?"

"Because the setup felt different. I don't know how else to explain it. I'd seen it before, earlier in the week. It wasn't the same. Something had changed."

Sarah took a slow breath, trying to keep her voice steady. "So that's why you were late to check in?"

Maya nodded. "I got caught up. Watching them. Checking the station. Making sure no one saw me. I didn't think anyone had."

Sarah narrowed her eyes. "Gemma said she saw you at Eleanor's station."

Maya groaned softly, burying her face in her hands. "I wasn't messing with it. But I can see how it looked. I was just trying to figure out what was going on. But after everything... after Roger... I knew how it would sound."

"Then why didn't you come forward?"

"Because I'd be next. On the list of suspects. You've met Stanley. He'd have me in cuffs before I finished explaining."

She pulled her coat tighter, shivering. "I know how these things go. People panic. They start pointing fingers. I thought if I kept quiet, it would blow over."

"It hasn't."

"I noticed."

Sarah took a half-step closer. "You had a bad feeling and ignored it. But you still won't say who you saw."

"Because I don't know if it meant anything," Maya said. "Maybe they were just nervous. Maybe they'd forgotten something and were trying to fix it. I didn't see anything *happen*."

She hesitated, then added, almost under her breath, "It's not like I saw them poisoning anything."

The words landed hard.

Sarah's pulse spiked. "But you think that's what happened?"

Maya's eyes flicked toward her, then away again. "I don't know what I think. But if I'd spoken up earlier... maybe Roger wouldn't have died."

Sarah didn't answer. The wind filled the silence between them.

Maya pushed her hair back from her face. "I swear, I didn't do anything wrong. But I can't undo any of it, can I?"

She turned to leave.

Sarah watched her walk away, hugging herself against the wind. She didn't notice the figure standing across the promenade, half-concealed behind a rusted blue bin and a row of battered deck chairs. The figure stayed still, watching Maya disappear down the stone steps toward the lower promenade. Then, without a word, they turned and slipped out of sight.

As Sarah sat on the cold metal bench outside the station, her thoughts were a tangled mess of worry and exhaustion. The autumn air was crisp, and she pulled her coat tighter around herself, though it did little to stave off the chill that had settled deep in her bones. She had been waiting for what felt like hours, her heart aching with concern for Charlie. She glanced at the clock on her phone for the hundredth time, wishing that somehow time would move faster, or that she would finally hear some news about her son.

The rumble of a train pulling into the station drew her attention, and she looked up to watch for a young man stepping onto the platform. It took her a moment to recognize Charlie's boyfriend, James as he was bundled up against the autumn cold. What she did recognise was the look of worry etched across his face. As he approached, Sarah stood up, her heart breaking a little more at the sight of him.

"Sarah," James called out as he reached her on the platform, his voice rough with emotion. "I got here as soon as I could. I can't believe I wasn't there for Charlie. I should have been at the competition. I knew I should've cancelled my lectures. But I thought… I thought I could make it up by being there for the second day. And now…"

He broke off, running a hand through his hair, clearly distraught.

Sarah stepped forward, placing a steady hand on his arm. "James, no one could've known this would happen. You had obligations at the university, no one is blaming you. Least of all Charlie."

James shook his head, his jaw tightening. "But I'm blaming me. What if I could've stopped it? What if just being there would've made the difference?"

"You can't think like that," Sarah said gently. "There's no way you could've predicted any of this. The second day never even happened. It's not on you."

He looked at her, searching her face for something, absolution, maybe. "He's just a kid. I was supposed to be there."

Sarah offered a faint, reassuring smile. "You're here now. That's what matters."

They began walking slowly back toward her car, the weight of everything unsaid lingering between them. The wind off the seafront nipped at their faces, sharp and bracing.

As they reached the edge of the car park, something in James seemed to shift. His shoulders straightened, the fretful energy in his eyes narrowing into focus.

"Ok," he said suddenly, voice firmer. "Tell me exactly what happened, who was there when Roger collapsed? What did Charlie say afterward? Were the drinks tested? Is there any chance someone tampered with his equipment before the round started? Did anyone else report anything suspicious?"

Sarah blinked, taken aback by the sudden shift in tempo. "James…"

He pushed on, more to himself than to her. "It doesn't add up. The reaction Roger had, it was immediate. That narrows things down, right? Someone would've had to act quickly. Maybe even brazenly. Were there any gaps in the timeline? Was anyone unaccounted for?"

"James, stop." Sarah held up a hand, and he halted mid-step. "I know how you feel. I do. But I don't have the answers to all the questions you're asking. Not yet."

He stared at her for a moment, breathing hard, as though reeling himself back in. Then he gave a small, rueful laugh. "Sorry. It's the way my brain works, if I can make sense of it, maybe I can fix it. Or at least feel less… helpless."

She softened, placing a hand on his shoulder. "There's nothing wrong with wanting answers. We just need to find them together."

James nodded quickly, his voice quiet but firm. "Absolutely. Anything that will help Charlie."

Chapter 14

Robyn sat across from Sarah at a small table in the back of *Sarah's Secrets,* her eyes bright with determination. She had spent the last few days piecing together fragments of conversations, observations, and gut feelings, and now she was ready to present her latest theory. Beside Sarah, James sat with his arms crossed and a barely touched coffee cooling in front of him. His expression was tight, his gaze fixed on the table as though willing it to reveal something, anything, that could help Charlie.

Sarah leaned back in her chair, a frown creasing her forehead as she listened, her fingers absently twisting the ring on her hand. She looked as if her mind was caught halfway between the conversation at the table and the sterile walls of the police station, where her son was still being held.

James hadn't said much since they sat down, but Sarah could feel the tension radiating from him. He was usually the calm one, the one who could analyse a situation with cold logic, but today that composure felt brittle. Robyn, by contrast, was radiating restless energy, poised to speak, her whole body leaning into the moment like a spring about to snap.

"Sarah, I know this might sound out of left field, but hear me out," Robyn began, her voice low but urgent. "What if the real culprit isn't one of the main competitors or even someone we've been focusing on? What if it's someone we barely noticed, someone who's been lurking in the background, blending in so well that we never thought to suspect them?"

Sarah raised an eyebrow, her scepticism evident. "Who exactly are you talking about, Robyn? We've already looked at everyone who had a clear motive."

"That's just it!" Robyn leaned forward, her voice intensifying. "What if this person had a secret vendetta against Roger, something none of us knew about? I've been thinking more about the milk swap and that strange exchange between Eleanor and the porter. What if they were in on it together?"

Sarah folded her arms, her expression remaining guarded. "And what makes you think this porter had a vendetta against Roger? He's just a porter, Robyn. His job is to carry bags and help out around the hotel."

Robyn bit her lip, trying to organise her thoughts. "I overheard something the other day, something that didn't make sense at the time but now feels like it could be important. I was in the hallway near the staff break room, and I heard the porter talking to someone on the phone. He was saying something like, 'He won't be a problem after this weekend. He'll get what's coming to him.' I didn't think much of it then, but now… it could have been about Roger."

James finally spoke, his voice calm but firm. "Couldn't that have been about anyone? A coworker, a bad tipper... it's a pretty vague threat, Robyn."

Robyn opened her mouth, then closed it, frustrated.

Sarah leaned back in her chair, torn. She wasn't sure if she agreed with either of them. The fog in her brain made it hard to follow the conversation properly, half her thoughts were still trapped back at the station with Charlie.

"But what if it wasn't?" Robyn pressed, her frustration growing. "What if this guy has some personal grudge against Roger that no one knows about? We know Roger made a lot of enemies, and not just among the competitors. What if this porter is one of those enemies, someone who felt wronged by Roger and decided to take matters into his own hands?"

Sarah sighed, rubbing her temples. "Robyn, I get that you're trying to help, but accusing someone based on a hunch and an overheard conversation that could be interpreted in a dozen different ways is risky. What if you're wrong? You could ruin someone's life without any solid proof."

Robyn clenched her fists, her frustration spilling over. "But what if I'm right, Sarah? What if this guy is the real culprit, and we're wasting time chasing other leads while he slips away? You can't just ignore this because it's not a sure thing!"

The tension between them hung heavy in the air, each woman holding her ground. Finally, Robyn took a deep breath, trying to calm herself. "Look, I know it's a stretch, but I can't shake the feeling that there's more to this. If we don't at least look into it, we could miss something important. Let me go back to the hotel, talk to the staff, see what I can find out about this porter. Maybe I'll uncover something that ties it all together."

Sarah shook her head, her voice firm. "Robyn, I appreciate your tenacity, but this is dangerous. We're already in deep with this investigation, and I don't want you getting embroiled in something you might regret. If you push too hard without evidence, you could make things worse."

Robyn stood up, her eyes blazing with determination. "If I don't push, we might never find out the truth, Sarah. I can't just sit around and do nothing. I have to at least try."

Sarah watched her go, worry etched on her face. She understood Robyn's passion, but the stakes were high, and the consequences of making a wrong move could be disastrous. As Robyn left the café, Sarah couldn't shake the uneasy feeling that her friend was about to dive headfirst into something far more dangerous than either of them had anticipated.

As the café door closed behind Robyn, James leaned against the counter, arms folded, staring at the tiled floor.

"I should've been there," he said, barely above a whisper.

Sarah glanced up from wiping the table. "James, we've talked about this. You were studying. No one expected this. No one blames you."

"Yeah, but I do." He exhaled harshly. "If I'd just gone with him that morning, kept him grounded, helped him set up, I could've... I don't know. I should've been by his side. Not stuck in a lecture hall thinking that everything was normal."

Sarah approached him gently. "You love him. That's why this is tearing you apart. But being there physically wouldn't have changed what happened, James. You're here now, and he needs you more than ever."

He nodded, blinking hard. "I just hate not knowing how to help him."

The clock on Sarah's bedside table ticked quietly in the dark, each second marking the slow passage of another sleepless night. She lay on her back, staring up at the ceiling, her mind spinning with the events of the day. The room was still, the only sound the soft rustling of leaves outside her window, but inside her head, a storm raged.

Sarah turned over, pulling the covers tighter around herself, as if the physical comfort could quiet the thoughts that swirled relentlessly in her mind. She couldn't stop replaying the conversation with Robyn, the look of desperation in her niece's eyes, the way her voice had trembled with fear and love for Charlie. Sarah had tried to be strong for her, to be the voice of reason, but now, alone in the dark, the doubts she had pushed down came flooding back.

What if she was wrong? What if by urging caution, she was letting the real culprit slip through their fingers? And worse, what if, in her attempts to protect Charlie, she ended up hurting someone else, someone who was innocent? The thought of accusing the wrong person, of ruining their life based on a hunch or circumstantial evidence, made her stomach twist with anxiety.

Sarah's mind raced back to the past few days, to every decision she had made, every word she had said. She tried to convince herself that she was doing the right thing, that caution was necessary to ensure they didn't make a terrible mistake. But the more she thought about it, the more the weight of responsibility pressed down on her chest, making it hard to breathe.

She turned onto her other side, facing the window, where a sliver of moonlight peeked through the curtains. The pale light seemed almost mocking in its calmness, as if the world outside was oblivious to the turmoil inside her. She wished she could find that same calm, but the fear gnawed at her, relentless and unforgiving.

What if Robyn was right? What if her insistence on being thorough, on not jumping to conclusions, was actually holding them back? Robyn's determination was born out of love and fear for Charlie, but it was also driven by a need to act, to do something. Sarah understood that, even admired it, but she couldn't shake the feeling that it was leading them down a dangerous path.

And then there was the worry about how vehement Robyn had become lately. Sarah knew her niece was fiercely loyal, passionate, and determined to help, but this investigation seemed to have ignited something particularly intense in her. Sarah recognised the frustration behind Robyn's eyes, the subtle tightening of her jaw whenever Sarah gently suggested caution or restraint. It made Sarah uneasy, not because she doubted Robyn's intentions, but because she knew she needed to tread carefully. Robyn's enthusiasm could be a powerful asset, but Sarah worried that a misplaced word or a gentle pushback might crush her niece's spirit or make her feel unappreciated. Finding the right balance, encouraging Robyn's eagerness without letting her feel dismissed, was becoming an increasingly delicate task.

Sarah's heart ached with the weight of it all. She wanted to do right by everyone, by Charlie, by Robyn, by the people they were investigating. But the path ahead was so murky, and every step they took seemed fraught with potential consequences. The fear of making a mistake, of hurting the people she cared about most, loomed over her like a dark cloud, impossible to shake.

She closed her eyes, trying to will herself to sleep, but the worries only grew louder in the silence. She couldn't stop thinking about the lives that hung in the balance, about how one wrong move could have devastating effects. She felt trapped, paralyzed by the weight of her own conscience, and yet she knew that she had to keep moving forward, somehow.

As the night stretched on, Sarah lay awake, wrestling with her fears, her mind churning with the impossible choices that lay ahead. She knew she had to trust herself, trust her instincts, but in the stillness of the night, that trust felt fragile, uncertain. And as much as she tried to reassure herself, the doubts lingered, casting long shadows over her thoughts, making sleep an elusive, distant dream.

Sarah shuffled around the kitchen, her movements slow and tired as she fought through the exhaustion from yet another sleepless night. The dull ache behind her eyes throbbed with every step, and her mind felt clouded, like a thick fog had settled over her thoughts. She cursed herself under her breath, frustrated with the ever-present brain fog that had become her unwelcome companion lately. Whether it was lack of sleep or her hormones wreaking havoc again, she wasn't sure, but she knew something wasn't right.

She sat down at the small kitchen table and stared at the pictures Robyn had taken from Roger's assistant's notes. There was something in them that tugged at her thoughts, something important she wasn't quite grasping. As she thumbed through the images on her phone, her frustration mounted.

"Come on, Sarah, get it together," she muttered to herself, rubbing her temples in a futile attempt to clear her mind. "There's something here. I know it."

Her eyes lazily scanned the notes again, trying to latch onto any clue that might make sense. And then, as she shifted one of the images, her gaze drifted down to the corner of the screen. There, almost unnoticed in Robyn's hurried shots, were pages of Roger's assistant's calendar, accidentally captured when Robyn had been snapping pictures.

At first, Sarah didn't pay much attention to it, it seemed inconsequential, just a jumble of appointments. But then her eyes landed on a familiar name written in bold letters on one of the entries. Coffee shop owner.

Her heart skipped a beat. The word beside it: merger.

"Merger?" Sarah whispered to herself, leaning closer to the screen. "Was Roger doing a deal with another coffee shop owner?"

Her tired brain suddenly began to sharpen, the pieces clicking into place. The coffee shop scene was small and competitive. A merger in their world could easily mean one thing: someone was being pushed out.

"Could Roger have been involved in some kind of business deal?" she wondered aloud. "Was he muscling in on someone else's territory?"

The idea sent a jolt through her, cutting through the haze of exhaustion. If Roger had been negotiating a merger with another coffee shop owner, it could explain so much, the tensions, the resentment. Mergers often meant that one party came out on top while the other lost control of their business. And if Roger had been on the winning side of such a deal, it would have given someone a powerful motive to want him out of the picture.

Her fingers shook slightly as she swiped through more of the photos, looking for more clues. There were other calendar entries, meetings scheduled at odd hours with different names, people Sarah didn't recognize, but that one word, merger, stuck out like a flashing neon sign.

Was Roger trying to force a competitor out of business? Or was someone else trying to stop him from taking over? And if so, had that led to his death?

Sarah's mind raced with possibilities, her exhaustion temporarily forgotten. This could be the missing piece, the thread that tied everything together. She needed to talk to Robyn, to get her thoughts on this, and figure out who this other coffee shop owner was. If Roger had been playing a high-stakes game in the background, someone might have been desperate enough to take him out of it entirely.

She quickly grabbed her phone, her fingers fumbling to text Robyn.

Need to talk ASAP. Think I found something important.

Chapter 15

Inspector Stanley sat across from Charlie once again, his expression calm but focused. The sterile interview room was filled with the quiet hum of tension, and the clock on the wall ticked steadily, marking the passage of time. Charlie sat rigidly in his chair, his hands resting on the table, his face pale but resolute. Stanley had been through this before with him, multiple times, but there was still a lingering sense that something was missing.

"Let's go over this one more time, Charlie," Stanley said, his voice professional but with an edge of persistence. "For the record, you're maintaining that you had no involvement in Roger's death, no reason to harm him, and that everything was just... coincidence?"

Charlie's eyes flashed with frustration, but he forced himself to keep his tone steady. "With all due respect, Inspector, I think you've got the wrong idea. I didn't even *know* Roger, not personally, anyway. This was my first time competing. I'd never even met him before the event."

He leaned forward slightly, trying to hold the Inspector's gaze, his voice gaining strength. "Everything I know about Roger is second hand, things people said about him, stuff I read online. Sure, I'd heard the stories, how he could be harsh, difficult, unfair even, but that's it. I wasn't close to him. I had no relationship with him. Why would I have any reason to want him dead?"

Charlie shook his head, the disbelief evident in his voice. "You're acting like there's some long-standing grudge between us, but there isn't. There *can't* be. He wasn't even judging my round directly. I was just a name on a list to him."

He took a deep breath, willing the tension in his shoulders to ease. "I'm here because I love coffee. That's it. This competition was supposed to be about proving myself, about finally getting a chance to be seen. Killing someone? That's not just out of character, it's insane. You're looking in the wrong direction."

Stanley nodded slightly, taking in Charlie's words, but there was no sign of satisfaction on his face. He was looking for something, anything, that might indicate a crack in Charlie's story.

"You've been consistent," Stanley said at last, tapping his pen thoughtfully against his notepad. "I'll give you that. But consistent doesn't always mean truthful. Sometimes it just means practiced."

Charlie clenched his jaw, clearly fighting the urge to let his temper flare. "I don't know what else to say. I've told you everything I know. I was at my station, prepping for my round. I didn't touch anything that wasn't mine. The milk, the ingredients, none of it. You have to believe me."

Stanley leaned back in his chair, eyes narrowing slightly as he studied Charlie's face. "Then how do you explain the timing?" he asked calmly. "Roger collapsed almost immediately after drinking *your* latte. That's not a coincidence, Charlie. That's cause and effect."

Charlie stared at him, momentarily stunned. "You think I poisoned him?" he said, incredulous. "You really think I'd risk everything, for what? I didn't even *know* the man!"

The inspector didn't flinch. "You didn't have to know him personally. Sometimes motive isn't about hatred, it's about opportunity. Or pressure. Or trying to prove something."

Charlie's hands tightened into fists in his lap. "No. This isn't pressure. This isn't me cracking under competition stress. I was excited, yeah, nervous, maybe, but I didn't do anything wrong."

Stanley regarded him for a beat longer, then added, almost casually, "Interesting, because one of the other competitors mentioned you were acting… odd. That you seemed jumpy. Secretive."

Charlie's head snapped up. "Suspiciously? Is that what they said?" He let out a short, humourless laugh. "Nervous and over-excited, maybe. It was my first big competition, I'd been working toward it for months. Of course I was jumpy. But that's nerves, not murder."

Stanley remained quiet, letting the weight of his words settle.

Charlie leaned forward now, desperation creeping into his voice. "Look, if someone saw something, tell me what it was. Tell me what I'm supposed to have done that was so suspicious. Because I swear to you, I didn't do anything but make a coffee. My coffee. With my own ingredients. That's it."

But even as he said it, a flicker of doubt crept into his mind. Charlie thought back to the competition setup, recalling how rushed everything had been. Hadn't someone been hanging around longer than necessary near the prep area? He shook the thought away, was he imagining things now?

Stanley closed his notebook slowly. "We'll leave it there for now," he said, rising to his feet. "But I suggest you get comfortable, Charlie. Because this investigation? It's far from over."

As the door clicked shut behind Inspector Stanley, Charlie sagged back in the chair, the last of his composure crumbling the moment he was alone.

The silence was deafening. His hands, which had been clenched tightly in his lap, finally unfurled, revealing faint half-moon marks from where his nails had dug into his skin. His pulse still pounded in his ears, matching the rapid beat of his thoughts as they ricocheted around his skull.

Suspicious. Odd. Secretive. That's what they'd said about him? That's what it had come to?

He swallowed hard, trying to remember who had even been around long enough to draw those conclusions. Most of the other competitors had been too focused on their own routines to give him a second glance. He barely knew any of them, just quick introductions, a few polite nods. No real conversations. Certainly nothing deep enough for someone to paint him as some kind of murderer.

How did it come to this?

All he had wanted was a fair shot. A chance to prove that someone like him, new to the scene, unknown, untested, could hold his own in a room full of professionals. He'd poured everything into that moment: every early morning, every failed recipe, every borrowed grinder and late-night clean-up at *Sarah's Secrets*. This was supposed to be the beginning of something, not the end.

Now, here he was. Locked in a room, being told his nerves looked like guilt and that his coffee might've killed a man.

He wiped his face with his hands and let them fall heavily to the table. His knuckles brushed the cool surface, grounding him. The truth was, he was terrified, not of being exposed, but of not being believed.

What if Stanley didn't let this go? What if no one did What if the shadow of Roger's death followed him for the rest of his life?

Charlie let his head drop forward, resting on his folded arms as the adrenaline finally gave way to exhaustion. For a long time, he didn't move, he just breathed. Shaky, uneven breaths that felt like they didn't reach the bottom of his lungs.

But somewhere in the quiet hum of the interview room, something hardened in him. He wasn't going to let this be the end of his story.

They wanted answers? Then he'd find them himself, if he had to. Because the truth was out there, buried in the chaos of competition and gossip and grudges, and someone knew more than they were saying.

And whoever had whispered that he looked suspicious? He hoped they were ready to be looked at too.

Stanley walked down the hall, his mind buzzing with thoughts. Something about Charlie's steadfastness unsettled him, not because it screamed guilt, but because it didn't. He hadn't cracked, hadn't faltered. If he was guilty, he was hiding it well. But if he wasn't… then they were still missing the truth.

As Stanley reached his desk, ready to dive back into the evidence, one of his team members waved him over. "Inspector, you need to see this," the officer said, a note of urgency in his voice.

Stanley raised an eyebrow and walked over to the screen. "What are we looking at?"

The officer leaned forward, clicking through a series of video clips on his monitor. "I've been going through the video footage we managed to gather from the supporters, family members and friends who were filming the competition. Most of it's just what you'd expect, people cheering on their loved ones, but…"

"And?" Stanley pressed, folding his arms.

"And I think I saw something in one of the videos that might be worth looking into." The officer clicked on one particular clip, enlarging it on the screen. "Here, this one. Watch closely."

Stanley leaned in, his eyes scanning the footage. The video was shaky, clearly filmed on a phone, and showed a wide shot of the competition area. People bustled around in the background, competitors at their stations, staff moving between them, and a crowd of onlookers watching the action. It seemed unremarkable at first, but then the officer paused the video, freezing it at a specific moment.

"Right there," the officer said, pointing to the screen. "You see that? In the background?"

Stanley squinted at the image, focusing on the scene behind the competitors. At first, it seemed like just a blur of motion, but as his eyes adjusted, he saw it, a figure moving near the area where the milk bottles had been stored. The person wasn't a competitor. They were wearing staff clothes, but they weren't moving with the usual purpose of the other employees.

"Who is that?" Stanley asked, his tone sharpening.

The officer shook his head. "We're not sure yet, but they were definitely close to where the milk was. And look at this." He played the clip again in slow motion. The figure reached out, subtly adjusting one of the milk bottles before slipping away into the background.

Stanley's eyes narrowed. "That's the porter, isn't it? The one who helped with the competitors' supplies?"

"That's what I thought too," the officer replied. "And it lines up with some of the other statements we've been getting, about that weird exchange between Eleanor and the porter."

Stanley's mind raced as he replayed the scene in his head. It was subtle, easy to miss unless you were looking for it, but it was there, the faintest suggestion that something had been tampered with.

"Good work," Stanley said, his tone serious. "We need to track down that porter and get him in for questioning. And keep looking through the rest of the footage. If this isn't an accident, we're going to find out exactly who's behind it."

The officer nodded, already pulling up more videos as Stanley strode toward the door. The investigation was shifting, and Stanley could feel the weight of it settling in his gut. This was the first real crack in the case, and it might be the one that finally led them to the truth.

As he headed out, the image of the porter's subtle movements lingered in his mind, raising more questions than answers. What had really happened with that milk? And how many more secrets were still hiding in the shadows?

Inspector Stanley sat at his desk, his eyes fixed on the slow, rhythmic tick of the wall clock. It had been forty-eight hours since Charlie Meadows was brought in, and the evidence, or lack of it, was gnawing at him. No matter how many times he combed through the witness statements, rewatched footage, or grilled Charlie from every possible angle, nothing stuck. Nothing concrete. Just assumptions, circumstantial timing, and too many unanswered questions.

He let out a slow breath, rubbing the back of his neck as a ripple of frustration tightened his jaw. He hated letting someone walk away when there were still gaps in the story, but holding Charlie any longer without cause would do more harm than good. And deep down, in that instinctual place where good policing often began, Stanley didn't *feel* like Charlie was the one.

He wasn't proud of the thought, but a part of him was relieved. Relieved he didn't have to keep pushing a young man who, by all accounts, looked more overwhelmed than guilty. But that same relief came laced with urgency. If it wasn't Charlie, then it was someone else, and he needed to find them. Fast. Because the last thing he wanted was to bring Charlie back into that interview room only to realise, too late, that he'd been barking up the wrong tree all along.

With a quiet sigh, he reached for the phone and dialled Sarah's number, already rehearsing the words in his head. After a few rings, Sarah picked up, her voice filled with anticipation. "Inspector Stanley?"

"Sarah, you can come and get him," Stanley said, his tone neutral but carrying a hint of relief. "We're releasing Charlie. We don't have enough to hold him any longer."

There was a pause, and then a burst of excitement from the other end. "Oh my God, thank you! I'll be there right away!"

Stanley hung up, rubbing the back of his neck as he prepared for her arrival. He knew how much this meant to Sarah, but something about the case still nagged at him. He hadn't been able to clear Charlie's name entirely, and there were still far too many questions left unanswered.

A short while later, Sarah burst into the station, her face flushed with a mixture of joy and exhaustion. She rushed over to Charlie, who had just been brought out of the back. Without a second thought, she threw her arms around him, hugging him tightly.

"Oh, Charlie, thank God!" she exclaimed, her voice thick with emotion. Charlie, looking equally relieved, hugged her back.

As they pulled apart, Sarah, caught up in the excitement of the moment, turned to Stanley and impulsively hugged him too. Stanley stiffened for a moment, caught off guard by the unexpected gesture. His arms stayed awkwardly at his sides as Sarah squeezed him, clearly not expecting the hug to go both ways. He gave her a surprised look, and she quickly stepped back, her cheeks flushing with embarrassment.

"Oh! Sorry, Inspector," she said, her voice rushing as she waved her hands in front of her. "Just... thank you so much for letting Charlie go."

Stanley cleared his throat, a small smirk playing at the corner of his mouth as he straightened his jacket. "No problem, Sarah. Just doing my job."

As she and Charlie prepared to leave, Sarah suddenly paused at the door, something flickering in her eyes. She turned back to Stanley, her tone more serious now. "Oh, by the way, before we go... I think you might want to look into Roger's business dealings. There's something there that might have been the reason for his death."

Stanley raised an eyebrow, intrigued. "What do you mean?"

"I can't say for sure yet, but I've seen some things that point to Roger being involved in some sort of deal, a merger with another coffee shop owner. I think he was pushing someone out of their business, and it might have made them desperate enough to take drastic action."

Stanley's curiosity deepened. Roger's death had always felt like more than just a simple accident, but this was the first time someone had pointed toward a potential financial motive. "That's interesting, Sarah. You have anything solid to back that up?"

"Not yet," Sarah admitted, her eyes darting to Charlie, who looked weary but hopeful. "But I think it's worth looking into. There's a name in Roger's assistant's notes that connects to another coffee shop. It could explain why he had so many enemies."

Stanley nodded, his mind already turning over this new lead. "I'll look into it. Thanks for the tip."

With that, she took Charlie's hand, and the two of them headed out of the station. Stanley watched them go, a mixture of relief and curiosity tugging at him.

As he sat back at his desk, Stanley pulled up his notes, ready to dive into Roger's business dealings. The real answers, it seemed, might lie not in the competition itself but in the tangled web of Roger's financial interests.

It was a quiet morning along Castle Road, the charming little street lined with independent shops at the heart of the community, the usual flow of customers weaving leisurely in and out of doorways. Sarah felt a deep sense of relief now that Charlie was safely back at *Sarah's Secrets* with her, but as she stepped outside the shop to retrieve something from her car, her relief faltered. Soft murmurs drifted from nearby, snippets of conversations tinged with suspicion, casting shadows over the peace she had hoped would return.

It was as Sarah turned from her car back toward *Sarah's Secrets* that she noticed the scene unfolding across Castle Road. Outside the Art Gallery, a small cluster of her street neighbours had gathered, their heads bent closely together in what looked unmistakably like a gossiping session. At the centre of the group were Harriet, who owned the gallery, and Greg from the music shop next door. Their voices were hushed, secretive, but their body language spoke volumes.

Sarah slowed her pace, eyes lingering on the group as a ripple of unease coursed through her. She caught Harriet glancing briefly in the direction of *Sarah's Secrets*, her lips pursed in quiet disapproval. Greg nodded in response, folding his arms as if confirming whatever had been said, his expression sombre and serious.

She clearly wasn't meant to overhear, but their judgmental gazes made the intent clear enough. A familiar knot of anxiety formed in Sarah's stomach, tightening with every step closer to her café. Ever since she and Charlie had moved into Castle Road, they'd done everything possible to blend into the close-knit community. But now, with Charlie's troubles becoming public knowledge, it seemed as though all their hard-earned acceptance was slowly unravelling before her eyes.

Harriet's voice dropped even lower, though not low enough to hide her disdain. "I just think we need to be careful about the kind of people we let into this community.

It's one thing to run a nice little café, but it's another when you keep attracting this sort of... trouble."

The words stung. Sarah felt her face grow hot, a mixture of anger and embarrassment bubbling up inside her. But before she could step forward and confront them, another voice broke through the quiet tension of the street.

"I'd be careful about making comments like that if I were you," said Edward Barnes, the owner of the local antiques shop. He stepped forward, his imposing figure casting a long shadow over the pair. His tone was calm but firm, and his gaze fixed on Harriet and Greg with a quiet intensity.

Both Harriet and Greg seemed startled by Edward's sudden appearance, exchanging nervous glances before Greg cleared his throat. "We're just saying, Edward... it's not good for the street. It's not personal."

Edward scoffed, folding his arms across his chest. "Not good for the street? What's not good for this street is people spreading unfounded gossip. Do any of you know what's really going on with Sarah and Charlie? Or are you just jumping to conclusions based on a few police visits?"

Harriet bristled, but there was uncertainty in her eyes. "It's just... twice now, Edward. It's not exactly a good look."

"Twice," Edward repeated, his voice low but commanding. "And what of it? You all were happy enough to take Sarah's business when she first opened up, weren't you? Or was that just for show?"

Greg shifted uncomfortably, clearly caught off guard by Edward's sudden defence. "We're not saying anything about her café, just… you know… it brings a certain kind of attention."

Edward's eyes narrowed. "Attention? Or your own insecurities about change? We've all been through rough patches, people deal with things in their own way. But this street is supposed to be a community. We don't turn our backs on people just because the wind blows a little differently for a while."

Sarah stood frozen in place, watching the scene unfold, her heart pounding in her chest. She'd never expected Edward, of all people, to defend her. In the past, he'd been one of the loudest voices of opposition when she first opened the café. They had only reached an uneasy acceptance of each other after he'd realized she wasn't the problem, his own resistance to change had been. But now, here he was, sticking up for her in front of the others.

Greg opened his mouth to respond, but Edward cut him off with a final, authoritative statement. "Look, if you don't know the whole story, maybe it's best you keep your judgments to yourselves. Unless you'd like someone to start whispering about your businesses the next time things get tough?"

The silence that followed was thick with discomfort. Harriet and Greg exchanged glances, clearly not expecting such a blunt confrontation. Without another word, they nodded awkwardly and retreated into their respective shops, leaving Edward standing there, his arms still folded.

Sarah finally found the strength to approach him. "Edward, I… I didn't expect that. Thank you."

He turned to face her, his expression softening slightly. "Don't thank me, Sarah. You're part of this street, just like the rest of us. People need to remember that."

She nodded, feeling a swell of gratitude she hadn't anticipated. "Still, it means a lot. Especially right now."

Edward shrugged, though there was a glint of understanding in his eyes. "People talk, but it doesn't mean they're right. You've built something good here. Don't let anyone take that away from you."

As Sarah watched him start to walk back towards his antiques shop, the weight of the whispers and judgment felt a little lighter. But the tension in the air remained, she knew that the scrutiny from the community was far from over. The cold shoulders, the suspicious glances, it would all continue, at least for now. But with unlikely allies like Edward stepping in, maybe, just maybe, she and Charlie had a fighting chance to reclaim their place in the street.

Before Edward could get as far as doorway of his shop, the door of the ceramics shop swung open, and Amy popped her head out, her eyes brightening as she spotted them both.

"Sarah!" Amy waved enthusiastically, stepping onto the pavement, her energy almost contagious.

"Hi, Amy," Sarah smiled tiredly, appreciating her friend's ever-cheerful presence. "Sorry, I'm a bit distracted. Everything all right?"

Edward, who had paused at his doorway, turned back to join them, exchanging a quick, conspiratorial glance with Amy before speaking. "Better than all right, actually.

We've just had a very exciting response to our... well, let's just say our 'secret project.' "

Sarah raised an eyebrow, suddenly amused despite herself. "Secret project? I thought that Secrets was my thing."

Amy quickly elbowed Edward gently in the ribs, giving him a playful glare. "Ignore him, Sarah. All in good time."

Sarah gave a weak laugh, shaking her head. "You two are as cryptic as everyone else lately."

Amy chuckled, her eyes darting briefly to Edward with a meaningful look. "Sorry, Sarah, just trust us. It's a good surprise. Promise."

With another quick glance toward Edward, Amy tilted her head subtly, clearly indicating she wanted a word in private. "Edward, can I borrow you quickly? There's something we need to go over..."

"Of course," Edward nodded, giving Sarah a reassuring smile. "Stay strong, Sarah. We're all here for you, whatever happens."

Sarah watched as Amy led Edward eagerly back toward her ceramics shop, their whispered excitement evident. For a moment, curiosity outweighed her worries, leaving her with a welcome, comforting distraction. Whatever her friends were up to, she had a feeling she'd find out soon enough, and maybe, just maybe, it was exactly the kind of surprise she needed.

Chapter 16

Now that Charlie was safely home at *Sarah's Secrets*, Sarah felt even more determined to uncover the truth and ensure justice was served. The weight of suspicion that had fallen on her son had only strengthened her resolve; she knew the real answers lay hidden among the participants of the coffee competition. It was time to push forward and seek the evidence needed to clear Charlie's name once and for all.

With Robyn and Charlie managing the shop, and James keeping a watchful eye on Charlie to make sure he stayed out of trouble, Sarah saw her opportunity to slip away for a bit. She decided her first stop would be Victor Chan's workshop. Victor's name kept coming up in her mind; she needed to understand his perspective on Roger.

Sarah stepped into Victor's workshop, instantly greeted by a rich, aromatic fusion of tea and coffee that filled the air. It was nothing like a typical coffee shop; the space was intimate, almost like stepping back in time into an old apothecary. Shelves lined the walls, stacked high with jars of fragrant teas and exotic coffee blends. The warm wooden tones and soft lighting created a comforting, secretive atmosphere. At the far end, there were only a couple of small tables tucked away in a cosy corner. It couldn't feel less like a chain coffee shop, which made Sarah immediately understand Victor's resistance to Roger's business ideas.

Victor greeted her with a smile, his hands stained slightly from the herbs and coffee beans he worked with daily. "Sarah, welcome. I'm glad you came by. I've been working on a new blend that incorporates traditional Chinese tea elements into the coffee-making process. I thought you might be interested."

Sarah smiled, taking in the unique vibe of the place. "I've heard great things about your techniques, Victor. Mixing tea and coffee seems like a delicate balance. How do you do it?"

Victor motioned for her to follow him behind the counter. "It's all about harmony, like yin and yang. Take the yuenyeung, for example, a blend of brewed coffee and black tea with sugar and milk. It's been a popular drink in Hong Kong for ages. I draw a lot of inspiration from that, as well as other combinations like oolong lattes and jasmine-infused coffee."

As he spoke, Sarah noticed the symbol etched into the glass window and printed on his takeaway cups, a pair of stylised intertwined ducks. "Yuenyeung," she murmured, recognizing the reference to the mandarin ducks that symbolised balance. "It suits your style perfectly."

Victor gave a slight smile, his eyes glinting with pride. "Exactly. It's about creating something unique, something that stands apart from the mass-produced chains.

But that's not easy when you're up against people who… well, don't play fair."

Sarah raised an eyebrow, sensing there was more to his comment. "What do you mean?"

Victor's expression darkened slightly. "The competitions. I've been competing for a couple of years now, and the more I take part, the more I see that the results aren't always about skill or innovation. Sometimes, it feels like the decisions are predetermined, especially when Roger was involved."

Sarah leaned in, intrigued. "You think Roger was influencing the outcomes?"

Victor hesitated for a moment, then motioned for her to follow him into a small back room. There, he opened a neatly organised file cabinet, pulling out a series of folders. Each one contained his entries from past competitions, complete with detailed scores and judges' comments. He spread them out on the table in front of Sarah.

"Look at this," Victor said, pointing to one of the score sheets. "These are my results from competitions where Roger wasn't the judge. Fair scores, consistent feedback, recognition for my innovation. But when Roger was on the panel…" He flipped to another set of entries, showing a marked difference in scores. "It all changed. My scores dropped. Same technique, same blends, but suddenly I wasn't good enough."

Sarah scanned the sheets, her brow furrowing. "That's a pretty big discrepancy."

Victor nodded, his voice growing tight. "It wasn't always like that. I used to get fair marks from Roger, even some praise. But then we had an argument, a disagreement about my business."

Sarah looked up, her curiosity piqued. "Oh? What was the argument about?"

Victor sighed, leaning back in his chair. "He approached me about buying my shop. At first, he framed it as a merger, said he wanted to partner up, that it would be mutually beneficial. But I could see through it. He didn't want a partnership. He wanted to turn this," Victor gestured around the room, "into one of his chain-style coffee shops. Strip it of everything that makes it unique. He didn't understand what I'm doing here."

Sarah glanced around the workshop, taking in the comforting atmosphere, the intimate feel of the place. "This isn't just a coffee shop," she said softly. "It's something special. I can see why you wouldn't want to lose that."

Victor's face softened, appreciating her understanding. "Exactly. Look around, this place is built on tradition and innovation. I mix Chinese tea elements with coffee because it's about blending cultures, not about churning out the same product over and over again. Roger didn't see the value in that. He just saw an opportunity to expand his empire."

Sarah's mind whirled with this new information. "So, after you turned him down, that's when your competition scores started to change?"

Victor nodded. "It felt like retaliation. Roger was influential in the industry, and he didn't take rejection well. I'm not saying he rigged the competitions outright, but let's just say… he had his ways of keeping people like me in check."

The weight of his words hung in the air between them. Sarah could sense the frustration and resentment in Victor's voice. He was passionate about his craft, but Roger's interference had clearly taken a toll on him, both professionally and personally.

"That must've been difficult," Sarah said gently. "It sounds like Roger had a lot of control over the industry."

"He did," Victor replied, bitterness creeping into his tone. "And if you weren't willing to play by his rules, you were sidelined. It wasn't just me, either. He had a reputation for doing this to others, especially anyone who threatened his influence."

Sarah's thoughts raced as she took in Victor's words. Roger's manipulation of the competition, his attempts to buy out Victor's business, these were powerful motives. She could feel the tension in Victor's voice, his desire to protect what he had built, his frustration at being held back. If anyone had a reason to resent Roger, Victor certainly did.

But as she looked around the shop again, Sarah couldn't help but feel that Victor's ambitions went far beyond revenge. He wasn't angry, he was passionate about creating something different, something meaningful. But maybe, just maybe, that passion had pushed him to take matters into his own hands. Sarah felt a surge of anticipation. She was determined to peel back the layers of Victor's complicated relationship with Roger and finally shed some light on the darker corners of the competition.

Leaving Victor's shop, Sarah felt a surge of energy coursing through her. The pieces of the puzzle seemed to be inching closer to some kind of alignment, and she didn't want to lose the momentum. With a deep breath, she decided to see if she could speak to Olivia Green again that same afternoon. The idea of having two productive conversations in one day excited her, but she needed to clear her mind first.

Leaving Victor's workshop with more questions than answers, Sarah felt compelled to speak with Olivia next. As she walked toward the seafront, she replayed their previous conversation in her mind. Olivia had been openly frustrated with Roger's conservative approach, which was sharply contrasted by Victor's deep-rooted passion for tradition. Olivia had seemed eager for innovation, for new and exciting opportunities. But was her ambition strong enough to drive her to take drastic action against Roger? Or perhaps, if Olivia wasn't the one responsible, had she noticed anything suspicious, something or someone who could help Sarah finally unravel the truth?

When Sarah arrived at Olivia's brew house, Olivia greeted her warmly, clearly pleased to see her again. Sarah took a seat, briefly complimenting Olivia on the cozy atmosphere before diving straight into her questions. "Olivia, I've been speaking to some of the other competitors, and there's something I've been wondering. Did you ever notice anything unusual during the competitions, anyone behaving oddly or having arguments with Roger?"

Olivia's smile faltered slightly, her expression thoughtful. "Well, Roger wasn't exactly the easiest person to work with. He rubbed a lot of people the wrong way, me included. But nothing particularly stands out, at least not beyond the usual disagreements. Everyone had their reasons to feel frustrated with him, though. Why do you ask?"

Sarah hesitated briefly, choosing her words carefully. "I'm just trying to piece things together, find out if someone might have had a reason to take drastic action against him."

Olivia raised her eyebrows in surprise, then softened her tone. "Roger could certainly push buttons, but I never imagined anyone would go that far." She paused, her smile returning as she tried to shift the mood.

"By the way," Olivia said, her face lighting up, "I don't know if you're into this kind of thing, but I run a little kombucha masterclass on the weekends. You should come along sometime! It's a fun, hands-on experience. I walk people through the whole brewing process, and we experiment with all sorts of flavours. I think it'd be right up your alley, especially if you're thinking about adding something fresh and trendy to *Sarah's Secrets*!"

Sarah blinked, pulled out of her thoughts by the sudden shift in conversation. It took her a moment to refocus on Olivia's cheerful chatter. She forced a smile, trying to mask her unease. "That sounds... really interesting. I'll definitely bear it in mind."

Olivia beamed, clearly proud of her kombucha-making skills. "Great! Just let me know whenever you want to come by. I think you'd love it. Plus, it's a nice break from coffee every now and then."

Sarah nodded, though her mind was still elsewhere. She could feel herself needing to leave, to process what she had just learned. "Thank you, Olivia. I really appreciate the offer. I'll be in touch, but I should probably get going now."

Olivia didn't seem to notice the slight tension in Sarah's voice. "Of course! Don't be a stranger. It was great to see you again, and good luck with everything at *Sarah's Secrets*."

Sarah smiled politely, making her way to the door, her mind still buzzing with thoughts about Olivia. As she stepped outside and breathed in the salty sea air, she couldn't shake the feeling that something dark had been lurking just beneath the surface of their conversation. And now, as she walked back toward the precinct, Sarah couldn't help but wonder, how far would someone like Olivia go to free herself from the constraints Roger had placed on her?

Inspector Stanley sat across from Helen in a quiet corner of the hotel lobby, the rich scent of coffee mingling with the polished wood and old upholstery. His notebook rested on the table between them, pages filled with quick, slanted handwriting from their last conversation. This time, though, his questions had sharper edges.

"Helen," he began, his voice measured but insistent, "I need you to be straight with me. Earlier, you made it sound like Roger was just difficult to work with, but I've been hearing a different story. Competitors, spectators, even hotel staff have told me that Roger was more than just 'hard to work with.' He was manipulative. He held grudges. And he made sure the people who crossed him paid for it." He tilted his head slightly, watching her. "I need to know, how well did you really know the man you worked for?"

Helen's fingers tightened around her coffee cup, her knuckles whitening for just a moment before she set it down with a sigh. She didn't meet his gaze right away, instead staring out the window as if weighing how much she actually cared about holding onto old loyalties.

"Roger could be a nightmare," she said bluntly. "There. Is that what you want to hear?" She let out a humourless chuckle and leaned back in her chair. "I suppose I got used to it after all these years, covering for him, smoothing things over when he upset the wrong people, defending his decisions even when I didn't agree with them. God, I don't even know why I kept doing it."

Stanley watched her, his pen resting idly on his notepad. Helen exhaled sharply and shook her head.

"I'd made up my mind, you know?" she went on, more to herself than to him. "I was done. This was it, this competition, this weekend. I was tired of making excuses for him, tired of picking up the pieces after he burned yet another bridge."

Stanley's gaze lifted sharply. His stare, cool and assessing, cut through the haze of her frustration.

"Done with him?" he repeated slowly, letting the words settle. His tone was light, but the weight behind it was unmistakable. He didn't blink.

Helen froze, suddenly aware of what she had just said.

She blinked, then let out a breath of dry laughter, shaking her head. "No, Inspector. Don't get excited, I wasn't about to kill him. Couldn't be bothered." She picked up her coffee again, cradling it between both hands. "I just meant that it was time for me and Roger to part ways. He just didn't know it yet."

Stanley held her gaze a beat longer than necessary before jotting something down. Helen arched a brow. "You can write that down all you like, but I had no interest in sending him to an early grave. I was planning on quitting, not committing murder."

For a moment, Stanley seemed to weigh the truth of her words. Then, he gave a slight nod.

"All right," he said, the tension in his voice easing, just a fraction. "Let's talk about what you do know. I've heard Roger had enemies. I imagine after all these years, you'd have a better sense than most of who really had a reason to hate him."

Helen exhaled, shaking her head. "Take your pick." She drummed her fingers against the side of her cup. "Olivia Green. Roger couldn't stand her. He said she had no respect for the craft. Always dismissed her work as gimmicky, but really? I think it got under his skin that she had a following outside of his little circle of 'real' baristas. He liked control, and Olivia was the type who refused to be controlled."

Stanley nodded, making a note. "And Victor Chan?"

Helen's lips pressed into a thin line. "That one was personal. Roger wanted to buy Victor's shop, said he could turn it into something bigger, better. Victor told him to get lost. After that, Roger made sure to downplay Victor's skills at every opportunity. Scores started dipping, invitations started getting lost. It was petty. But that was Roger."

Stanley studied her carefully, taking in the bitterness in her voice, the undercurrent of years of quiet resentment building up, brick by brick.

"You worked for Roger for a long time," he said, his tone almost casual. "You knew how he operated. Do you think it's possible that he was manipulating results? That he was sabotaging people on purpose?"

Helen stared at him for a long moment, something shifting in her expression. Then, she leaned forward slightly, lowering her voice.

"I think Roger did whatever suited Roger," she said flatly. "If he wanted you to win, you won. If he didn't, well, you'd better hope you had some other way of making a name for yourself, because you weren't going to get anywhere with his help."

Stanley nodded, absorbing the words. "One last thing," he said. "Was Roger working on any deals before he died? Anything that might've added more pressure?"

Helen hesitated for only a second before answering. "There was talk of a merger. Something big. He was negotiating with someone, he never told me who. But it mattered to him. More than I realized at the time."

Stanley tapped his pen against his notepad, thoughtful. "And how was he feeling about it?"

Helen let out a tired sigh. "Paranoid," she admitted. "Like someone was going to pull the rug out from under him."

Stanley pushed back his chair and stood. "Thank you, Helen. You've been helpful."

Helen smirked, raising an eyebrow. "See? That wasn't so hard, was it?"

Stanley gave her a small, knowing smile before heading toward the exit. Helen took another sip of her coffee and let herself sink back into her chair, staring at the ceiling.

Roger was gone. And for the first time in years, she didn't have to clean up his mess.

Chapter 17

Inspector Stanley stood in the sitting room of the porter's modest home, his gaze drifting around the space as he took in the immaculate surroundings. Every surface was spotless, the furniture perfectly aligned, and not a single object seemed out of place. Even the small rug in the middle of the room appeared to have been vacuumed in precise, straight lines. It was a level of tidiness that felt almost unnatural.

Stanley considered himself an organised man, bordering, he sometimes acknowledged, on obsessive. There were moments he had to remind himself that his meticulous habits weren't always healthy, that life required flexibility and mess from time to time. Yet, as he studied the unnerving precision of this room, Stanley felt an uneasy ripple. Compared to this, his own particular tendencies seemed casual. Here, control wasn't just a habit, it felt like a compulsion.

Fred Grant, a wiry man with neatly combed hair and a nervous energy, offered Stanley and the constable drinks and after a few minutes of pottering in the kitchen, he returned and placed two cups of tea carefully on coasters in front of them, his movements deliberate and methodical. As

Stanley sat, he watched the porter out of the corner of his eye. The man was fidgeting slightly, his hands twitching as though he wasn't sure what to do with them.

Stanley lifted his cup and took a polite sip, all the while observing the porter's restless behaviour. The man's eyes flickered toward the cups, as if even the slight change in position was unsettling to him. Sensing the tension, Stanley decided to address it head-on.

"You don't need to be worried," Stanley said calmly, placing his cup back exactly where it had been before. "We're just here to ask you a few questions, nothing to be concerned about."

The porter gave a quick, apologetic smile, but his fidgeting didn't stop. "I'm sorry, it's not that, Inspector. It's just... well, I get distracted when things aren't quite like I like them to be. It's something I try to keep under control, but when I'm nervous... it gets more difficult."

Stanley nodded slowly, watching as the porter subtly adjusted the coasters to ensure perfect alignment with the edge of the table. It was clear now: the man definitely had a compulsion for order. His anxiety wasn't about the police visit, it was about the objects around him not being in perfect harmony.

Understanding this, Stanley decided to be careful with his approach. He gently mirrored the porter's movements, making sure his own cup was placed exactly where it had been. This seemed to help calm the man slightly. With the tension slightly eased, Stanley leaned forward.

"I understand, Mr. Grant," Stanley said, his tone even. "But I do need to ask you about something that came up in our investigation. We saw a video from the competition, and in it, you're seen adjusting the milk bottles. Can you explain what made you feel the need to do that?"

Fred's fidgeting stopped as he looked up at Stanley, a flicker of surprise crossing his face. Stanley replayed the scene from the video in his mind: the porter's hands, moving the bottles into alignment, almost obsessively adjusting their placement. He had already begun to suspect that this wasn't about tampering with the contents but rather something else entirely.

The porter hesitated, his hands gripping the edge of his chair. "It's... well, I noticed something off about one of the bottles," he said finally, his voice low. "The lid. It didn't look like the others. It was... different. And I found it distracting."

Stanley raised an eyebrow, intrigued. "Different how?"

Fred blinked, struggling to articulate it. "It wasn't lined up right. The other lids were sealed perfectly, but this one... it looked like it hadn't been closed properly. It was just... wrong. I tried not to notice it, but when I carried the tray from the kitchen to the event, it kept bothering me. So, when I had the chance, I adjusted it. I wasn't trying to tamper with anything, I swear, Inspector. I just couldn't leave it like that."

Stanley exchanged a glance with the constable. His explanation made sense, especially given his compulsive need for order. But the mention of the bottle's lid being "different" caught his attention. Was this just an innocent misalignment that triggered the porter's need for symmetry, or could there be more to it?

"I understand," Stanley said, his voice calm but probing. "But this lid... you're certain it looked off compared to the others?"

Fred nodded emphatically. "Yes. I wouldn't have touched it otherwise."

Stanley leaned back, considering the implications. Fred's compulsive behaviour explained why he had been adjusting the bottles, but if one of the lids truly was different from the others, that could suggest something more. Was this the key to understanding how the milk might have been tampered with? Or was the porter simply imagining it because of his need for order?

"Thank you for explaining, Mr. Grant," Stanley said finally. "It helps us understand the situation better. But I want you to think back carefully. Did you notice anything else unusual about the milk bottles? Anything that seemed out of place?"

The porter shook his head quickly. "No, nothing else. Just that one lid. Everything else seemed normal."

Stanley nodded, standing up to leave. "All right. Thank you for your time. If anything else comes to mind, please don't hesitate to contact us."

Fred stood as well, visibly relieved as Stanley and the constable made their way to the door. As they stepped outside, Stanley couldn't help but feel that they were edging closer to the truth. The porter hadn't tampered with the milk, but his observation about the lid was significant.

As they walked back to the car, the constable turned to Stanley. "Do you think the lid really was tampered with, or was it just his obsession with symmetry?"

Stanley's expression was thoughtful. "Could be either. But if there was something off about that lid, then we need to figure out how and why. It might be the break we've been waiting for."

With that, they drove away, leaving the impeccably tidy house behind, but the unanswered questions about the milk and Roger's death still looming large.

Sarah reached into her bag and pulled out her phone, quickly scrolling through her contacts. After her conversations with Eleanor and Charlie, she knew it was time to reach out to Martin Acton. Could she make it three for three? She hoped Martin would agree to meet with her; he was her best lead now, especially if she wanted to piece together the tangled web around Roger's death.

Her fingers hesitated briefly over Martin's number, her mind flashing back to his tense manner at the latte art contest. But there was no turning back now. Taking a deep breath, she tapped out a quick message:

Hi Martin, it's Sarah from Sarah's Secrets. Do you have some time this afternoon to catch up? I'd love to chat about what happened at the competition. I promise it won't take long, and there'll be brownies in it for you—vegan-friendly, of course!

She held her breath as the message sent, staring at the screen until the reply popped up moments later:

Sure, Sarah. Brownies sound great. I'll stop by around three.

Sarah exhaled with relief, glancing at the clock. She had enough time to bake a fresh batch of her signature vegan keto brownies and set the perfect scene for their conversation. She wanted Martin comfortable and open to sharing whatever information he might have.

Sarah arranged the meeting with Martin Acton in the quieter back section of her coffee shop, *Sarah's Secrets*. She had set the scene with care, choosing a time when the place would be nearly empty, ensuring they wouldn't be disturbed. The low hum of the espresso machine and the occasional clink of cutlery from the front of the shop provided just enough background noise to keep their conversation private. As Martin arrived, she greeted him with a warm smile, leading him to a cosy corner where they could talk.

"Thanks for agreeing to meet with me," Sarah began, sliding a plate of her homemade vegan keto brownies across the table. "I know you've been through a lot lately, but I thought maybe you could help me understand what's really going on with Charlie. He's in a terrible situation, and I'm sure you don't want him to be wrongfully accused."

Martin gave a weary nod, sinking into the chair. "I'll help any way I can, Sarah. I know that I'd only just met him, but I could tell that Charlie's a good guy. It's awful that he's caught up in all of this."

Sarah watched as he picked up one of the brownies, his expression softening slightly as he took a bite. She knew that Martin was vegan, so she'd taken extra care to ensure that these brownies were made with the finest ingredients, free of any animal products. She wanted him to feel comfortable, and maybe the warm, comforting treat would make him more inclined to open up.

As Martin chewed thoughtfully, Sarah gently prompted him. "You mentioned before that you had a strained relationship with Roger. What happened between the two of you?"

Martin sighed, rubbing the back of his neck. "Roger and I... we never really got along. He had this way of pushing people's buttons, you know? Always wanting to be in control, always thinking he knew best. He offered to sponsor me, said it would boost my career, but I didn't want anything to do with him. I didn't trust him, didn't like the way he manipulated people."

He paused, the tension in his jaw visible, then glanced away. "And there's more to it than that," he added quietly. "Something I've never really talked about."

Sarah leaned in slightly, sensing a deeper truth waiting to be uncovered. He picked up the brownie again, but before he could take another bite, he paused. His expression shifted, something between confusion and concern, and then the coughing began. At first, just a throat clear, but it quickly turned into a hacking fit. Sarah's eyes widened as she saw a red rash beginning to creep up his neck.

"Martin, are you all right?" she asked, panic creeping into her voice.

Martin's eyes widened in realisation, his hand going to his throat. "Are you sure these brownies are vegan?" he croaked.

"Yes, absolutely," Sarah replied quickly. "I made them myself. They've got almond flour, coconut oil, cocoa…"

"Oh god, almond…" he gasped, his breath becoming more laboured. "I… I'm allergic."

Sarah's heart lurched. "Oh no. I didn't know! Hold on, I've got something that might help."

She darted to the back room, fingers fumbling as she tore through the first aid kit. Mike had a host of allergies, so she kept antihistamines close at hand. Snatching the packet, she ran back to Martin and handed him the pills and a glass of water.

"Here, take these."

Martin downed them with trembling hands. Slowly, painfully, his breathing began to steady. The red in his face faded bit by bit, and he sagged back in his chair, visibly exhausted.

"I'm so sorry, Martin," Sarah said softly. "I had no idea. I never would've…"

"I know," he managed, voice hoarse. "It's not your fault. I should've said something. I usually check everything, but I guess I let my guard down."

They sat in silence for a moment, the tension ebbing slightly. Sarah looked at him more closely now, her earlier thought returning with more clarity. The resemblance was subtle but there, same sharp features, same intense gaze.

"Martin," she said gently, "did anyone ever tell you that you look a bit like Roger?"

Martin froze, but then, after a beat, he added, "You're not the first person to think it. I used to see it myself… in the mirror, especially when I was angry."

Martin hesitated, then finally said, "There were always whispers growing up. My mum… she never said it outright, but there were hints. She used to work in the same circles as Roger, back when they were both young. And she'd get quiet whenever his name came up."

He gave a dry, humourless laugh. "Once, when I asked her about my dad, she just said, 'Some men don't deserve the title.' I always suspected… but I didn't want to know for sure. I figured if it was true, it would just make everything messier. Especially when Roger came around, acting like he wanted to help me. It felt like… pity. Or guilt. I couldn't take that. So I turned him down."

Sarah's brow furrowed, her heart twisting with the new weight of Martin's confession. "That's a lot to carry."

Martin nodded slowly. "Yeah. I guess that's why I hated him so much. Not just because he was arrogant and controlling, but because part of me was afraid he was trying to make amends without ever admitting what he'd done."

His words hung in the air between them like steam from a forgotten cup of coffee. And as Sarah sat there, still reeling from the near-accident and the deeper revelations it had unearthed, she knew one thing for certain: whatever tied Martin to Roger, it was more than shared blood or bitter resentment. It was part of the story, and the truth, she had to uncover.

Chapter 18

Sarah sat in the corner of *Sarah's Secrets*, the quiet hum of the coffee shop doing nothing to ease the knot of anxiety tightening in her stomach. The note she'd spotted earlier on Helen's scribbled margins, *Check Roger's business storage – inventory list?* buzzed at the back of her mind, a temptation she couldn't quite shake. She stared at the photograph she'd taken on her phone, the words still clear, her fingers itching to delete it and forget she ever saw it.

She knew what she should do. Call Inspector Stanley. Let him take the lead. His face flashed in her mind, serious but kind, professional but understanding. He'd been nothing but respectful throughout this entire ordeal, even when Charlie was his prime suspect. Stanley had followed protocol, yes, but he'd also listened when she spoke, considered her theories without dismissing them outright.

He deserves better than this, she thought, a pang of guilt striking her. *If I go behind his back now...*

But something inside her, a deep-rooted curiosity, or perhaps maternal protectiveness, kept pulling her toward the idea of just going herself. What harm could there be in a quick look? She didn't need to take anything, just confirm what was there. If it led to something important, she'd tell Stanley immediately. It would be as if she'd never been there at all. Just one look.

Before she could second-guess herself, Sarah stood up, grabbed her keys, and headed out the door. She tried to convince herself it was no big deal, just a quick detour, a little more information for the puzzle she was already so deeply invested in. But as she drove toward the storage unit, her hands tightened on the wheel, her conscience gnawing at her.

I shouldn't be doing this, she thought, her pulse quickening as the storage facility loomed ahead. *I should've called Stanley.*

The image of Inspector Stanley's face appeared again in her mind, how he'd look at her if he knew what she was doing now. Disappointment, probably. Maybe even betrayal. After all they'd been through, all the times he'd extended professional courtesies to her, and here she was, deliberately cutting him out of an investigation because...because why? Because she was afraid he might say no? Because she wanted to play detective?

Because it's Charlie, she reminded herself. *I'm doing this for Charlie.*

But even as she thought it, she knew it wasn't a good enough excuse. Stanley was also trying to find the truth. He wanted justice as much as she did.

Still, Sarah pressed on. She found the storage unit easily enough, tucked away in the corner, the dimly lit corridor eerily quiet. But when she reached out for the door, her heart sank at the sight of the combination lock securing it. She stared at it in disbelief, letting out a frustrated sigh under her breath. Of course it was locked. She should have anticipated something like this.

For a moment, Sarah nearly turned around, ready to accept that she'd wasted her time, and that perhaps this was a sign she should have involved Stanley from the start. But then an image flashed vividly through her mind, the photograph she'd taken of Helen's scribbled notes. There had been all kinds of numbers scattered amongst those hurried words. What were the chances one of those scribbles was the combination she needed?

Quickly, Sarah pulled her phone from her pocket, squinting as she flicked through the images Robyn had sent over earlier. She leaned closer, annoyed with her miserable eyesight as the tiny numbers blurred frustratingly. She muttered softly to herself, "Next time you decide to break into someone's storage, Sarah, you might consider bringing your reading glasses."

The word "break" hung in the air. That's what she was doing, wasn't it? Breaking in. Tampering with evidence. Interfering with a police investigation. All things that Stanley would never approve of, and with good reason.

She pinched the screen and zoomed in, peering carefully until one string of numbers finally came into sharp relief. She glanced back up at the lock, her pulse quickening with cautious optimism. Maybe, just maybe, this would be it.

Holding her breath, she carefully twisted the dials, aligning each number as precisely as possible. The lock clicked quietly, releasing. Sarah exhaled slowly, a shaky blend of relief and renewed anxiety washing over her as she pushed the door open.

Inside, the dim, musty space was crammed floor-to-ceiling with files and boxes, a chaotic jumble of Roger's business records. She moved quietly, scanning until her eyes landed on a metal box, partially hidden behind stacks of faded papers and forgotten binders.

Her heart pounded even harder as she picked up the box and unlocked it. Inside, just as Helen's notes had suggested, was the black leather-bound ledger. Sarah hesitated, a pang of guilt making her hand hover over it for a moment longer than she'd anticipated. Just a quick look, she told herself again, even as Stanley's voice echoed in her mind: *"Evidence chain, Sarah. It needs to be collected properly or it becomes inadmissible."*

The ledger was filled with names, dates, payments, Roger's entire financial web, spread out on the pages before her. It was exactly what she had feared: backdoor deals, secret partnerships, and bribes that implicated more than just Roger. Her stomach twisted as she realized the depth of his corruption. She flipped through page after page, each entry confirming that Roger's influence had been rotten from the inside out.

But then, as she prepared to place the ledger back where she'd found it, something caught her eye. A small envelope, poking out from beneath the stack of papers inside the box. Her fingers trembled as she reached for it, curiosity pulling her in despite her better judgment.

She pulled out the envelope and opened it. Inside was a birth certificate, faded but still legible. Her breath caught when she saw the name: Martin Alton.

Sarah's mind raced. Alton? No, it couldn't be a coincidence. This has to be Martin Acton's birth certificate.

She stared at the paper, piecing it all together. If Martin Acton had changed his name from Alton, then he might be connected to Roger by more than just a professional rivalry. Was this the key to everything? Some family secret that had been buried, only to resurface in the most dangerous way possible?

Sarah's hands shook as she stuffed the certificate back into the envelope and returned it to the box. She had seen enough. Too much. This was no longer something she could handle alone. She should've gone to Stanley in the first place. Now, with the ledger and the birth certificate in play, she realized the full weight of the situation.

She locked the box, carefully placed it back where she had found it, and closed the storage unit door behind her, the creaking of the metal sending a shiver down her spine.

Sarah sat in her car, the engine off, her hands resting on the steering wheel as the weight of her actions pressed down on her. The cool evening breeze blew in through the slightly cracked window, but it did nothing to calm the turmoil that churned inside her.

She had just uncovered something huge, Roger's financial ledger, the birth certificate, and with it, a tangled web of lies and deceit that reached far beyond anything she had expected. But now, faced with the reality of what she had done, the ethical implications weighed heavily on her mind.

What if this hurts people? she thought, staring blankly out the windshield. *What if by digging into Roger's past, I'm causing more damage than good?*

But more than that, the knowledge that she had deliberately excluded Inspector Stanley from this discovery gnawed at her. He wasn't just some faceless police officer, he was someone she'd come to respect, someone who had treated her and Charlie with dignity even when the evidence pointed in Charlie's direction. She'd watched him work, seen his commitment to finding the truth, observed how he navigated complex situations with integrity. And what had she done? Cut him out completely because it was easier for her to operate without accountability.

What kind of example am I setting? The thought hit her like a physical blow. All those times she'd lectured Charlie about making good choices, about respecting authority, about doing things the right way, and here she was, breaking into storage units and tampering with potential evidence because she'd convinced herself the ends justified the means.

Her thoughts drifted to the coffee competition contestants, people who had dedicated their lives to their craft. What if the secrets she had uncovered brought down the entire competition? Could she really be the one to expose all of this, knowing it might destroy their reputations, their livelihoods? These weren't just random names in a ledger; they were people she had spoken to, people she had come to understand.

And then there was Charlie. Her son had been through enough, caught in the web of suspicion after Roger's death. Would revealing these secrets make things worse for him? Would it drag him deeper into the chaos, tarnishing his name even more? She had worked so hard to clear his name, to protect him, but now she feared that her actions might end up hurting the very person she was trying to save.

What would Charlie think if he knew I was breaking the law to protect him? she wondered. *Would he be grateful, or would he be ashamed?*

Her heart ached with the weight of it all.

"How did I let it get this far?" she muttered to herself, feeling the sting of guilt in her chest. "Stanley deserved better from me."

Her phone buzzed in the passenger seat, breaking her thoughts. It was Robyn. Sarah picked it up, hesitating for a moment before answering.

"Hey," Robyn's voice was calm, but there was an undertone of concern. "How are you holding up?"

Sarah exhaled deeply. "Not great, Robyn. I'm... I'm starting to wonder if I've made a huge mistake. What if I've gone too far? What if uncovering all of this only ends up hurting everyone, Charlie, the competitors, even the community? And Inspector Stanley..." She paused, the weight of her actions sinking in further. "I shouldn't have excluded him. He's been nothing but fair to us, and I repaid him by going behind his back."

There was a pause on the other end of the line, and then Robyn's voice came through, firm but understanding.

"Sarah, I know you're scared. But I don't think the mistake was looking into this. The mistake was not trusting Stanley enough to include him. This isn't just about Roger's shady deals or a birth certificate. It's about the truth. And sometimes the truth is hard, but that doesn't mean it isn't necessary."

"I just..." Sarah's voice trembled slightly, the weight of her uncertainty pressing down. "What if exposing all of this tears apart the lives of people who don't deserve it? What if this all spirals out of control? And now I've compromised the entire investigation by touching evidence I had no right to touch. Stanley's going to know I went behind his back."

"Listen to me," Robyn said, her voice steady. "You're not the one causing this damage. Roger did that a long time ago with his lies, his manipulation, and his greed. You're just bringing those things to light. And yes, it might be messy, but people need to know the truth. It's the only way we can move forward, Charlie included. As for Stanley..." She paused. "Much as I hate to admit it, maybe it's time for you to come clean. Tell him everything. He might be upset, but I think he'll understand why you did it. He cares about justice, and so do you."

Sarah closed her eyes, letting Robyn's words wash over her. Deep down, she knew her friend was right. This wasn't about her digging where she shouldn't. It was about revealing the truth, no matter how painful or complicated it might be. Roger had built his empire on lies, and those lies were already hurting people. The longer they stayed hidden, the worse the damage could become.

But she also knew she needed to face the consequences of cutting Stanley out. She'd acted as if she couldn't trust him, when all evidence pointed to the contrary. She'd let her fear for Charlie override her better judgment, and in doing so, she might have jeopardized the very case she was trying to build.

"But what about Charlie?" Sarah whispered, her voice barely audible. "What if this blows back on him? I can't bear the thought of making things worse for him."

Robyn's voice softened. "You're doing this *for* Charlie, remember? You've been fighting for his name, for his innocence. This ledger, those secrets, it's the evidence we need. And it's not just about Charlie anymore. It's about our entire community. If we don't bring this to light, then Roger's lies will continue to poison everything and everyone around us."

Sarah let out a shaky breath, feeling the tears prick at her eyes. "I just don't want to be the one who causes everything to fall apart. And I don't want Charlie to see me breaking rules to protect him. What message does that send?"

"It sends the message that you're human," Robyn said gently but firmly. "That you make mistakes like everyone else. That sometimes, when we're scared for the people we love, we don't always make the best choices. Stanley will understand that, and so will Charlie. What matters now is what you do next."

For a long moment, Sarah sat in silence, letting Robyn's words sink in. Slowly, she began to feel the weight on her chest lift, if only slightly. The fear and guilt were still there, but Robyn's support gave her a sense of clarity she hadn't felt in hours.

"Thanks, Robyn," Sarah finally said, her voice steadier now. "I needed to hear that. You're right about Stanley. I need to come clean, tell him everything. He deserves that much from me."

"Any time," Robyn replied. "Now, let's take this to Stanley and let him handle the rest. You've done more than enough. It's time to get Charlie's name cleared once and for all, the right way."

Sarah nodded, even though Robyn couldn't see her. She wiped at her eyes and looked out at the darkening sky. It was time. She wasn't sure what the future held or how the truth would unravel, but she knew she couldn't turn back now. The truth had to come out, no matter the cost. And she would have to face Stanley, admit what she'd done, and accept whatever consequences came with it.

"I'll call Stanley," she said, her voice stronger now. "Let's finish this. Properly this time."

She hung up the call with Robyn and immediately dialled Inspector Stanley's number, her heart racing as the phone rang. When Stanley picked up, his voice was as calm and collected as ever.

"Sarah? Everything all right?"

"No, not really," she said, her voice unsteady. "I... I got a hint, and I went to check something out. Before you say anything, I know I shouldn't have, but there's a hidden financial ledger that Roger kept. It's got everything, his deals, bribes, all of it. And… there's something else. A birth certificate for someone named Martin Alton."

There was a pause on the other end of the line. Sarah could almost hear the gears turning in Stanley's mind.

"Martin Alton?" Stanley repeated. "You think that's Martin Acton?"

"I'm sure of it. I'm at the storage unit now. You need to see this for yourself."

"I'll be right there," Stanley replied, his voice sharp with urgency. "Stay put, Sarah. Don't touch anything else. Text me the exact location."

Sarah hung up, feeling a wave of relief wash over her. She'd made the right decision, finally. But as she sat alone outside the storage unit, the weight of what she had discovered pressed heavily on her shoulders. The minutes ticked by with excruciating slowness, each passing second amplifying her anxiety. She couldn't help but replay the conversation with Stanley in her mind. He hadn't sounded angry, exactly, but there had been a distinct tension in his voice, a professional distance that made her stomach knot with guilt.

In the distance, the flash of lights cut through the gathering dusk. Sarah straightened in her seat, watching an unmarked police car and a forensics van pulled into the storage facility's parking lot. Inspector Stanley emerged from the lead vehicle, his tall figure silhouetted against the headlights. He spoke briefly to the officers accompanying him before striding purposefully toward her car.

Sarah stepped out to meet him, the cool evening air sending a chill through her that had nothing to do with the temperature. Stanley's expression was unreadable as he approached, not the anger she had feared, but something more complex: disappointment tinged with professional focus.

"Sarah," he greeted her with a curt nod. "Where's the unit?"

"Down there," she pointed toward the dimly lit corridor of storage units. "Number 47. I... I should explain…"

Stanley held up a hand, not unkindly but firmly. "Let's secure the scene first. We'll talk after."

The forensics team was already unloading equipment from their van, cameras, evidence bags, gloves, and markers. Two officers began cordoning off the area with police tape, creating a perimeter around the storage unit. The efficiency of their movements, the practiced coordination, made Sarah acutely aware of her amateur intervention. This was how evidence should be handled, methodically, by professionals trained to preserve its integrity.

"I'll need you to walk me through exactly what you did," Stanley said as they made their way toward the unit. "Every detail, Sarah. What you touched, what you moved, what you saw."

His voice carried no accusation, just the steady insistence of someone trying to salvage a compromised situation. Sarah nodded, swallowing hard against the tightness in her throat.

"I used the combination lock, I found it in Helen's notes," she began, watching as Stanley signalled to a forensics officer who immediately photographed the lock. "I opened the metal box in the back corner. That's where I found the ledger and then the birth certificate in an envelope underneath."

Stanley listened intently, his eyes scanning the unit's contents. "And you put everything back exactly where you found it?"

"Yes," Sarah nodded. "As best I could. I was careful."

A flicker of something, perhaps grudging approval at her attempt to minimize contamination, crossed Stanley's face before he turned to the forensics lead.

"Full documentation of everything before it's moved," he instructed. "I want detailed photographs of the layout, then we'll proceed with collection." He turned back to Sarah. "I need you to show the technician exactly what you handled, without touching anything else."

Sarah nodded again, feeling strangely like a child being asked to point out what she'd broken. She stood at the threshold of the unit as the forensics team worked, their camera flashes illuminating the cramped space in bursts of harsh white light. She directed them to the metal box, watching as they meticulously documented its position before carefully opening it.

The black leather ledger looked exactly as she had left it. The technician gently placed it in an evidence bag, sealing it with practiced efficiency. Next came the envelope with the birth certificate, handled with the same careful protocol. Sarah felt a strange sense of relief watching these items being properly processed, as though their official collection somehow absolved her of the impropriety of her discovery.

As the team continued their work, Stanley drew Sarah aside, away from the bustle of activity but still within sight of the unit.

"You understand this complicates things," he said, his voice low and measured. "Chain of custody issues, potential challenges in court."

Sarah's chest tightened. "I know. I'm sorry, Luke. I should have called you first."

Stanley's expression softened slightly at the use of his first name. "Why didn't you?"

It was a simple question, but it cut straight to the heart of her actions. Sarah looked away, gathering her thoughts.

"I was afraid," she admitted finally. "Afraid you'd say no, afraid we'd miss something crucial. And..." she hesitated, "I suppose part of me wanted to be the one to find the evidence that would clear Charlie. As if that would somehow make up for not protecting him better in the first place."

Stanley was quiet for a moment, considering her words. When he spoke again, his voice held a note of understanding beneath the professional exterior.

"I get it, Sarah. I do. But this isn't the way. You could have compromised the entire case, not just against whoever killed Roger, but against everyone implicated in that ledger."

"I know," Sarah whispered, the full weight of her actions sinking in.

"That said," Stanley continued, "you found something significant. If Martin Acton is indeed Martin Alton, and if that ledger contains what you say it does..." He trailed off, his eyes moving to the forensics team carefully packing evidence into sealed containers.

One of the officers approached them, holding up a clear evidence bag containing a small USB drive they'd found tucked into the spine of the ledger. "Sir, you might want to see this."

Stanley nodded, then turned back to Sarah. "I'll need a formal statement from you. Everything you saw, touched, read, in detail. And Sarah?" His expression grew serious again. "No more solo investigations. I mean it. Next time, you call me first. Whatever you find, whatever you suspect, I want to hear it from you directly. Understood?"

There was no anger in his tone, just the firm expectation of a professional who knew all too well how fragile a case could be. Sarah nodded, relief washing through her that he wasn't shutting her out completely.

"Understood. I promise."

As the forensics team finished their collection and began to pack up, Sarah watched the methodical process with newfound appreciation. This was how justice was supposed to work, carefully, meticulously, with attention to every detail and procedure. Her shortcut might have uncovered the truth faster, but Stanley's way would ensure that truth could stand up in court.

The storage unit, now stripped of its secrets, looked oddly bare under the harsh portable lights the team had set up. What had been hidden in shadow was now exposed, documented, and on its way to becoming evidence. Sarah felt a parallel in her own actions, what she had done in secrecy was now in the open, acknowledged and, if not forgiven, at least understood.

Chapter 19

Sarah stood behind the counter at Sarah's Secrets, her hands moving on autopilot as she poured lattes and served pastries to the steady flow of customers. Despite the familiar routine, her mind was elsewhere, weighed down by the investigation she had plunged herself into. The chatter of the coffee shop patrons buzzed around her, but it felt distant, like she was watching everything through a fog. She should've felt connected to the coffee community around her, Southsea had a thriving coffee scene, after all, but instead, she felt isolated.

As she reached for a fresh box of napkins, her gaze landed on her *Sarah's Secrets* notebook, tucked neatly under the counter. She paused, noticing something odd, a faint edge of paper poking from between its pages. Curious, Sarah opened the notebook, and her stomach tightened as she read the words scrawled hastily across the page:

We've seen what you've been doing.

Sarah's pulse quickened. She glanced around sharply, a chill crawling down her spine. Who had left this? When had they managed to slip it into her notebook unnoticed? She forced herself to breathe steadily, closing the notebook quickly and slipping it back beneath the counter, heart hammering.

She was still the newcomer, the outsider. And no matter how much she tried to integrate, the deeper she delved into Roger's death and the murky world of the competition, the more disconnected she felt from the people around her. Even in a room full of familiar faces, she felt the cold sting of loneliness creeping in.

As she handed a cappuccino to a customer, she looked up and, to her surprise, saw Victor Chan standing at the counter.

"Victor," she said, blinking out of her reverie. "I didn't expect to see you here."

Victor offered a hesitant smile, shifting slightly as if he wasn't sure how to start. "Hey, Sarah. I've been thinking a lot since we spoke last. About what you're doing. I feel like... you get it. You understand how deep all of this goes, and I think you're trying to do something about it. Not just for Charlie, but for all of us who were affected by Roger."

Sarah tilted her head, surprised by the vulnerability in his voice. She hadn't expected Victor, who had always seemed so self-contained, to reach out like this. "I'm just trying to find the truth," she said quietly, still caught off guard. "But it's been... complicated."

Victor nodded. "I know. That's why I wanted to talk to you. I feel like you're one of the only people who cares about doing what's right, no matter the cost."

His words weighed heavily on Sarah, but there was something in them that made her stand a little taller. Maybe she was making a difference, even if it didn't always feel like it.

"I've been talking to a few people," Victor continued, glancing around the café as if to make sure no one was listening. "Other competitors who had their own problems with Roger. I think you should meet them. There are things they've been afraid to come forward with... until now."

Sarah raised an eyebrow, intrigued. "You think they'll talk to me?"

Victor's gaze steadied on hers. "They trust me. And I trust you. We've all got stories that might shed more light on what was going on with Roger, things people need to hear. Could you come by my place this evening? I'll introduce you to them."

Sarah hesitated for a moment, feeling the weight of what she was getting into and the memory of the unsettling message fresh in her mind. But then she nodded, determined. "All right. I'll be there."

Later that evening, Sarah, along with Robyn, arrived at Victor's tea and coffee fusion café, a serene space with soft lighting and the rich aromas of oolong and espresso swirling together. Victor greeted them at the door, his usual guardedness giving way to a sense of purpose.

Inside, two men sat at one of the café's low tables, both looking a little anxious but determined. Victor introduced them: Paul, a veteran competitor who had been involved in the coffee scene for years, and Aaron, a younger barista who had competed only a few times but had already crossed paths with Roger's manipulative tactics.

The conversation began cautiously, but soon, as the tension lifted, Paul leaned forward, his voice low but filled with frustration. "Roger tried to bribe me once," he said, his eyes dark with memory. "It was at last year's competition. He approached me late one night, said he needed me to sabotage another competitor's equipment, mess with the settings on their grinder so they'd under-extract their shots."

Sarah exchanged a glance with Robyn, who was listening intently. "Why would he want that?" Sarah asked.

Paul shook his head. "I asked him the same thing. All he said was that this competitor was 'unsavoury competition,' and that they needed to be taken out. He never gave specifics. When I pushed, he got defensive, said I didn't need to know the details. I refused, of course. But after that, things changed. I didn't place as well as I should've. Roger's attitude toward me turned... cold."

Aaron, who had been quietly listening, spoke up next. "Roger never outright asked me to sabotage anyone, but he would constantly undermine my entries. It was subtle at first, but it was clear he had no intention of letting me win. He didn't like that I was pushing new techniques. Said it wasn't the 'right way.' I started to wonder if he was trying to push me out of the scene altogether."

Victor looked at Sarah, his expression grim. "This is what we've been up against for years. Roger manipulated the competition, made deals behind the scenes, controlled the narrative. Anyone who didn't fit into his vision of the coffee world was either forced out or silenced."

Paul exhaled heavily, rubbing a hand over his face. "And it wasn't just competitors. My café, Roast & Hollow, was doing well, until Roger started whispering in the right ears. Suddenly, my suppliers were pulling out, investors backing away. He poisoned everything. And when we shut down... well, that was the end of my career."

Sarah's stomach twisted. "And your business partner?"

Paul nodded slowly. "He took the financial hit harder than I did. He disappeared after we lost everything. I heard he went abroad, but I saw him a few weeks ago. Just in passing. I don't know what he's doing now, but... if he's back, I can't imagine he's forgotten what Roger did to us."

Sarah sat back, absorbing their stories. The image of Roger she had been building was darkening by the minute. He wasn't just a difficult, biased judge, he was actively manipulating the outcomes to suit his own agenda. Her mind flashed to the ledger she had found, filled with the names and numbers of shady financial deals.

Then a thought struck her, ironic, in its own way. "It's funny," Sarah said quietly, almost to herself. "Whoever attacked Roger must've been thinking the same thing as he was. Needing to 'take out the competition.'"

The room fell silent for a moment, the weight of her words settling in.

Victor nodded grimly. "Maybe. But whoever did this... they're not just getting rid of competition. They're after something much bigger."

Sarah looked around at the faces of the men who had been victimised by Roger's manipulation, feeling the burden of the truth growing heavier by the minute.

"Thank you for sharing your stories," she said softly. "I promise, we'll find a way to make this right."

Sarah's discovery at the storage unit had been a significant breakthrough. If the financial ledger revealed what she claimed, bribes, backdoor deals, it could point to motives far beyond a simple coffee competition dispute. And the birth certificate... if Martin Acton was indeed Martin Alton, that family connection could change everything.

Stanley glanced at his watch. The forensics team would be processing the storage unit evidence now. The post-mortem results were due tomorrow morning, and the crime scene analysis should be completed by end of day. He needed those reports to move forward, to understand the physical evidence of how Roger died before he could determine who had the opportunity.

He gathered his notes, organizing them methodically as he prepared to leave the interrogation room. The case was like a well-crafted espresso, complex, layered, and requiring patience to extract the full flavour. But Stanley had never been one to rush an investigation. Time and evidence would eventually reveal the truth, as they always did.

As he stepped out into the corridor, his phone buzzed with a message from the forensic team: "Initial findings from storage unit ready for review."

Stanley nodded to himself. Perhaps the ledger would provide the clarity he needed, a way to cut through the tangle of alibis and point to the one person who had not just the motive, but the means and opportunity to ensure Roger Alton would never judge another coffee competition again.

Three hours later, Inspector Stanley sat at his desk, the glow from his lamp casting long shadows across the clutter of documents that had transformed his usually tidy workspace. The initial findings from the forensics team had been promising enough to warrant an immediate deep dive into Roger's financial records. What had started as a routine examination had quickly evolved into something that made the hair on the back of his neck stand up.

He rubbed his eyes, dry from staring at numbers and entries for hours without a break. The coffee beside him had gone cold, forgotten in the intensity of his focus. The ledger Sarah had discovered was proving to be more valuable than either of them could have anticipated, a meticulous record of not just Roger's business dealings, but what appeared to be a carefully documented history of extortion, bribery, and something else altogether more troubling.

"You were a piece of work, weren't you, Alton?" Stanley muttered to the papers spread before him, as if Roger himself might answer from beyond the grave.

What had initially seemed like mere underhanded deals, kickbacks from suppliers, bribes from competitors seeking favourable judging, had now revealed something far more sinister. Every month, like clockwork, a substantial amount of money was being withdrawn from Roger's account and transferred elsewhere. These weren't business expenses or even the bribes he'd been taking. These were payments going out.

Stanley frowned, tracing the pattern of transactions again with his finger. The rhythm was too consistent, the amounts too uniform. It wasn't tied to any regular business expense or legitimate transaction. The money was leaving Roger's account, but it wasn't going to any company or service he could easily identify. Instead, it looked increasingly like blackmail, Roger was paying someone off. And it had been going on for quite some time.

He leaned forward, cross-referencing Roger's bank statements with the entries in the ledger. There it was: the same transfer, a steady stream of money flowing out. The recipient wasn't a business or a well-known entity, it was a personal account, simply labelled WE.

"Who the hell is WE?" Stanley muttered under his breath.

The payments were too regular, too large, to be a mistake or oversight. Someone had something on Roger, something that made him pay every month to keep it quiet. But without knowing who WE was, the puzzle still had a crucial missing piece.

Stanley grabbed his notepad, quickly jotting down a series of questions. Who was behind this account? Was it tied to Roger's personal life, or was it another competitor in the coffee world with a grudge? Perhaps it was connected to Martin Acton, or rather, Martin Alton, if the birth certificate was legitimate. He needed to dig deeper, but WE was a phantom, a name with no face, no obvious connection to anything else in the records. Whoever they were, they had significant power over Roger.

Just then, the door to Stanley's office creaked open. One of his junior officers stepped inside, holding a folder.

"Sir, we've been tracking the payments Roger made," the officer said, setting the folder down. "They all went to the same account under the name **WE**, but there's no further information on who that is. The account appears to be offshore, deliberately obscured."

Stanley's brow furrowed as he scanned the report. "So, we've got money flowing into an account under a vague pseudonym, carefully hidden from prying eyes. That only makes this more suspicious."

He pushed the file aside, his mind working through the possibilities. The post-mortem would tell them how Roger died, but this financial trail might reveal why. The two were inextricably linked; he was certain of it.

"Do we have any leads on who might be connected to this account?" Stanley asked, looking up at the officer.

"Not yet, sir. But we're digging through Roger's contacts and associates, trying to see if anyone stands out who might be tied to this. And we're looking into the birth certificate angle as well, if Martin Acton is related to Roger, that could explain a lot."

Stanley nodded, knowing it wouldn't be an easy task. This case was becoming more complex with each discovery, and **WE** was at the centre of it all. Whoever they were, they had leverage over Roger, and that leverage could be the key to understanding why someone might have wanted him dead.

"Keep looking," Stanley said firmly. "We need to find out who **WE** is and what they were holding over Roger's head. And get me everything you can on Martin Acton's background, I want to know if there's any official record of a name change."

The officer left the room, and Stanley sat back in his chair, staring at the financial records spread before him. He had a hunch that **WE** was more than just a silent blackmailer, they were a player in whatever game Roger had been involved in. Whether it was tied to the coffee competition or something even more personal, the truth about **WE** was crucial.

The coffee competition's timeline now seemed secondary to this financial puzzle. All those competitors, each with their grievances against Roger, they might have had motives, but did any of them have the kind of leverage that would explain these payments? And if one of them was **WE**, had Roger finally pushed them too far, triggering not just a refusal to pay but a more permanent solution to their conflict?

Inspector Stanley leaned back in his chair, the details of the mysterious **WE** gnawing at him. The offshore account, the regular payments from Roger, it all pointed to something bigger than shady business deals. But no matter how much he turned it over in his mind, he couldn't figure out who or what **WE** was.

His thoughts drifted to Sarah. She had been the one to uncover the tip about Roger's hidden ledger, and it was her tenacity that had brought him closer to this breakthrough. She had a unique perspective, and while she wasn't officially part of the investigation, her involvement had proven invaluable. She might have an idea, something he hadn't considered.

Stanley picked up the phone, his fingers hovering over the dial for a moment. He wasn't in the habit of sharing ongoing investigative details with civilians, but Sarah had more than earned his trust. Besides, she might know something, or at the very least, have a hunch about who **WE** could be.

He dialled her number, waiting as the line rang.

"Hello?" Sarah's voice came through, sounding slightly breathless.

"Sarah, it's Stanley. I've got something I need to share with you. It's about the ledger you brought to my attention."

There was a brief pause on the other end. "Go on," she said, her voice suddenly focused.

Stanley glanced at the papers on his desk, organizing his thoughts. "We've been going through Roger's financials, and we found something interesting. There's a recurring payment, a significant amount of money, going to an account under the name **WE**. It's been happening regularly, and given what we know, it looks a lot like blackmail."

"Blackmail?" Sarah's tone was a mix of surprise and curiosity. "Who is **WE**?"

"That's the problem," Stanley admitted. "We don't know. The account is offshore, and whoever this **WE** is, they've been very careful about staying hidden. I wanted to bring it to your attention because you're the one who tipped me off in the first place. And... well, I figured you might have some thoughts on who or what **WE** could be. You've been in the middle of this investigation, and you've spoken to a lot of people connected to Roger."

There was a long silence on the line as Sarah processed the information.

"**WE**…" Sarah said slowly, as though testing the letters on her tongue. "It could be a person, or it could be a group. Did Roger have any dealings with groups that might've been involved in something shady? Or competitors, maybe, who worked together against him?"

Stanley tapped his pen against his desk, considering her words. "Possibly. But no specific group has come up in the investigation yet. The payments suggest it's something personal, not just business. If it were corporate extortion, I'd expect it to look different."

"I've been thinking," Sarah said, her voice soft but deliberate. "Roger manipulated people, pushed them out of the competition or kept them under his thumb. Maybe **WE** is someone who had a personal grudge against him. Someone he wronged, but who didn't have the power to stop him until they had something on him."

"That's what I'm thinking, too," Stanley replied. "But we need to figure out who had the motive and the leverage. I'm going to keep digging into Roger's contacts, but I wanted to let you know in case something jogs your memory."

Sarah was quiet for a moment, clearly deep in thought. "I'll think about it, Inspector. I've spoken to so many people who were affected by Roger, competitors, business owners. There's got to be a connection somewhere. **WE** could be someone right under our noses."

Stanley nodded, even though she couldn't see him. "Thanks, Sarah. Let me know if anything comes to you. We're closing in on something big, but we need to be careful. Whoever this **WE** is, they had a lot of control over Roger, and that makes them dangerous."

"I will," Sarah promised. "And Inspector… thanks for keeping me in the loop."

"Of course. You've earned it."

Stanley hung up the phone, feeling the familiar weight of uncertainty settle over him. They were getting closer, but **WE** remained a shadowy figure lurking in the background. The next step would be critical, and as much as he trusted his instincts, he knew he'd need every bit of help he could get, including Sarah's sharp intuition.

Whoever **WE** was, they held the key to unlocking the mystery behind Roger's death. And Stanley was determined to find them before they could strike again.

Chapter 20

Sarah ended the call with Inspector Stanley, her mind whirling with the new information about the mysterious **WE** and the regular payments Roger had been making. She slipped her phone into her pocket and continued her walk home from Victor's café, barely registering the familiar streets of Southsea as she passed them.

The conversation with Victor earlier had already left her with plenty to process. His insights into Roger's business practices, the way he'd manipulated competitors and suppliers alike, it had painted an even darker picture of the man than she'd already held. But this revelation about blackmail payments added yet another layer to the puzzle.

"**WE**," she murmured under her breath, testing the initials as her feet carried her automatically toward home. "**WE**... who are you?"

The evening air was cool against her face, but Sarah barely noticed it. Her thoughts kept circling back to all the players in this drama, Martin with his hidden birth name, Olivia and her scrutiny of the milk bottles, Victor's barely concealed resentment, the hotel staff who had witnessed so much. Someone among them knew more than they were letting on. Someone was **WE**.

As she turned the corner onto her street, a sudden realization struck her. They'd been approaching this all wrong. Waiting for Stanley to gather evidence, for the killer to make a mistake, it was too passive. If they truly wanted answers, they needed to force the killer's hand.

By the time Sarah reached the front door of her home, a determined resolve had settled in her chest. She took a deep breath and grabbed her phone, scrolling to Robyn's number and pressing call.

"Hey, Sarah!" Robyn's voice was warm and lively as always, but Sarah could hear the undertone of concern. "What's up?"

"I've been thinking," Sarah began, leaning against the kitchen counter. "It's not just about finding out who killed Roger. We need to expose everything, bring back some integrity to the competitions, to the community."

"What do you mean?" Robyn asked, her voice sharpening with interest.

Sarah paced the kitchen, her free hand gesturing as though Robyn could see her. "Stanley just called me. They've found evidence that Roger was being blackmailed, regular payments to someone or something called **WE**. And with everything else we've discovered, the birth certificate, the rigged competitions, the threats, it's clear that this whole system is rotten to the core."

"So what are you suggesting?" Robyn's tone was cautious but intrigued.

"I know what you mean," Robyn said thoughtfully after Sarah explained further. "But how? It's not like we can go around shouting from the rooftops that we've found shady ledgers and mysterious payments. Whoever's behind this would just go deeper underground."

"I have an idea," Sarah said slowly, the plan beginning to take shape in her mind. "We need to use the killer's awareness of our investigation against them. They're watching us, right? Probably waiting to see what we'll do next."

"Go on…" Robyn's interest was piqued, her voice dropping to a conspiratorial whisper.

"What if we leak some false information? Make it seem like we're about to uncover something huge, something that's going to expose them. If we do it right, they might panic, try to shut us down, or show their hand."

There was a pause, and then Robyn let out a low whistle. "Risky, but it could work. It's like a game of chess, baiting them into making a move."

"Exactly," Sarah agreed, excitement building. "But we'll need help to pull it off. We can't just say we have evidence and hope they take the bait. We need to create a believable scenario, somewhere public. Somewhere they'll feel cornered."

"Somewhere like… a café?" Robyn suggested. "You know, where all the competitors and community members tend to gather. We could stage a conversation, let the news spread organically."

Sarah nodded, a smile tugging at her lips. "That's exactly what I was thinking. And I know just the person to help us, Victor."

"Victor? You think he'll be up for this?"

"I do. He's been hurt by Roger's manipulations just like the others, and he wants to see justice served. If we can get him on board, he can help us get all the competitors together for a 'friendly gathering.' We drop some hints, let them overhear what we want them to hear, and then… we wait."

Robyn laughed softly. "You're a devious one, Sarah. I love it."

Sarah couldn't help but grin. "Thanks. But I want to make sure we do this right. We'll need to loop Charlie in too."

The smile faded as she thought of her son, still shaken from everything that had happened. She knew involving him would be tough, he was vulnerable, still recovering from the accusations and the suspicion that had nearly destroyed him. But he was the key to making the plan work. His presence would make the conversation more believable. If they could draw out the killer, it could finally clear his name.

"I'll talk to him," Sarah said quietly. "He deserves to know what's going on."

"What exactly are you thinking of leaking?" Robyn asked, bringing the conversation back to the practicalities.

Sarah considered this for a moment. "Something specific enough to be believable, but vague enough that we don't tip our hand completely. Maybe… maybe we let slip that Stanley found something in Roger's phone records, calls to a specific number right before he died. A number connected to **WE**."

"And that you've figured out what **WE** stands for?" Robyn suggested, catching on quickly.

"Exactly," Sarah confirmed. "We'll make it sound like we're on the verge of exposing everything, the blackmail, the identity of **WE**, all of it. If the killer thinks we're about to uncover their identity, they'll have to act."

"And Stanley? Are you going to tell him about this?"

Sarah hesitated. "Not yet. I want to run it by Victor first, see if he thinks it could work. Then we'll bring Stanley in. He might not approve of us setting a trap, but if it works..."

"If it works, we'll have caught a killer and exposed the corruption that's been poisoning the coffee community," Robyn finished for her. "I think it's worth the risk."

Sarah let out a breath she hadn't realized she'd been holding. "Thank you. For believing in this. For believing in me."

"Always," Robyn replied warmly. "When do we start?"

Sarah straightened her shoulders, resolve flooding through her. "Tomorrow. I'll call Victor tonight, see if he can get everyone together at his café for a casual post-competition debrief. Something that wouldn't seem suspicious."

"And we'll make sure our conversation about **WE** is just loud enough to be overheard," Robyn added.

"Exactly. Whoever **WE** is, whatever they were holding over Roger, they won't be able to resist reacting when they think we're about to expose them."

As Sarah hung up the phone, a mix of nerves and determination coursed through her. They were taking a risk, no doubt about it. But sitting back and waiting for answers wasn't an option anymore. Not when her son's reputation and the integrity of the entire coffee community hung in the balance.

She glanced out the window at the darkening sky, imagining the web of secrets and lies that surrounded Roger's death. Somewhere in that web was **WE**. Somewhere in that web was the truth.

And Sarah was finally ready to spring her trap.

Later that evening, Sarah sat beside Charlie on the couch, her mug of tea cooling forgotten on the coffee table. She had just finished explaining the plan, watching carefully as her son's expression shifted from confusion to concern to something closer to dread. The silence that followed her words was heavy, punctuated only by the distant ticking of the kitchen clock.

"You want me to sit in a room full of people who probably still think I'm a murderer?" Charlie finally asked, his voice strained. He ran his hands through his hair, a nervous habit he'd had since childhood. "Mum, I still wake up in the middle of the night thinking about the police station. The way they looked at me, like I was..." His voice trailed off.

Sarah's heart constricted. She hadn't been in that room with him, but she'd seen the hollowed-out look in his eyes when he'd finally been released. The experience had left marks that weren't visible but were no less real.

"I know it's asking a lot," she said softly, reaching for his hand. "More than a lot."

Charlie pulled away slightly, standing up to pace the small living room. "You don't, though. You don't know what it was like." His voice wasn't accusatory, just raw with remembered fear. "Sitting there with Stanley firing questions at me, everyone assuming I'd done it. The way they looked at me when I walked out, like I was getting away with something terrible." He stopped, facing her. "What if this goes wrong? What if whoever killed Roger thinks I'm trying to set them up and decides to make sure I take the fall for good this time?"

Sarah saw the tremor in his hands, the tightness in his shoulders, the physical manifestations of his fear. She'd been so caught up in her plan, in the possibility of finally resolving everything, that she hadn't fully considered what she was asking of him.

"You're right," she admitted, meeting his gaze directly. "I don't know exactly what that was like for you. And I should have thought more about what I was asking." She stood up, moving toward him but giving him space. "If you don't want to do this, we won't. We'll find another way."

Charlie's breathing was shallow, his eyes distant as if he was back in that interview room. "I just... I can't go through that again, Mum. Being looked at like I'm guilty, having my every word dissected. Stanley treated me like a criminal, and he was being *nice* compared to some of the others."

"I promise you won't be alone this time," Sarah said, careful not to push. "Robyn and I would be with you every second. Victor too. The whole point is that we'd be controlling the situation, not them."

Charlie sank back onto the couch, shoulders hunched. "And what if it works? What if whoever did this panics and decides to shut us up?" His voice dropped even lower. "What if they come after you because of me?"

Sarah hadn't considered that angle, that Charlie's reluctance might stem from worry for her safety rather than just his own trauma. The realization made her heart swell with both pride and sadness.

"Charlie," she said gently, sitting beside him again. "I understand if you don't want to do this. Really, I do. But I need you to understand something too." She waited until he looked at her. "I'm not going to stop trying to clear your name completely. Whether you're part of this plan or not, I'm going to keep pushing until we find the truth."

Charlie studied her face, a small, rueful smile tugging at his lips. "You never did know when to let things go, did you?"

"Not when it comes to the people I love," she replied simply.

He was quiet for a long moment, his internal struggle visible in the tightness around his eyes. "If, and it's a big if, I do this, you need to promise me something."

"Anything," Sarah said.

"We have a signal. Some word or phrase that means 'this is too much, I need to leave right now.' And when I use it, we go. No questions, no hesitation."

Sarah nodded immediately. "Absolutely. We could use... 'new coffee shipment'? Something that wouldn't sound strange in conversation but that we'd recognize."

Charlie considered this, then nodded slowly. "And you'll talk to Stanley beforehand? Make sure he knows what we're doing so he doesn't think I'm actually confessing to something?"

"I promise. He'll know the plan before we set anything in motion."

Charlie took a deep breath, releasing it slowly. The tension in his shoulders didn't disappear entirely, but it eased somewhat. "Ok" he said finally. "I'll do it. Not because I want to, believe me, I don't, but because I can't keep living under this shadow. I need my life back."

The relief Sarah felt was tempered by the knowledge of what this was costing him. She reached out, and this time Charlie allowed her to take his hand. "Thank you," she said softly. "I know how hard this is. I wouldn't ask if I thought there was another way."

Charlie squeezed her hand, his eyes vulnerable but resolute. "Just... don't leave me alone in there, ok? Not for a second."

"Not for a second," Sarah promised, her voice steady and sure. "We go in together, we face this together, and we leave together. No matter what happens."

He nodded, and in that moment, despite the fear that still lingered in his eyes, Sarah saw a glimpse of the strength that had carried him through everything so far, a quiet resilience that reminded her so much of his father. Whatever came next, they would face it as a family. It was the only way they knew how.

The next afternoon, Victor's café had been transformed into a haven of sorts, a neutral ground where those affected by Roger's death and the subsequent chaos could gather. Victor had pitched it as an informal support group, "a chance to decompress and share our experiences," and the response had been better than Sarah had dared hope.

Nearly everyone had shown up. Olivia sat by the window, absently stirring a cappuccino. Martin occupied a corner table, keeping a polite distance but clearly observant. Maya chatted with a few other competitors near the counter, while several staff members from the Queen's Hotel, including the young waitress Gemma, huddled together, their expressions a mix of curiosity and uncertainty. The atmosphere was subdued but communal, as if everyone recognized they were bound together by the recent events, whether they liked it or not.

Charlie walked through the door with Sarah and Robyn, and the café fell momentarily silent. Sarah felt her son tense beside her, his breathing shallow. She gave his arm a subtle squeeze, reminding him of their promise: together in, together out.

"Charlie," Victor called warmly from behind the counter, breaking the awkward silence. "Glad you could make it. I've been saving that single-origin Ethiopian for you to try, I think you'll appreciate the notes."

The deliberate normality of Victor's greeting seemed to ease some of the tension. Conversations gradually resumed as Victor guided them to a strategically positioned table near the centre of the café, close enough to be overheard by most, but not so conspicuous as to arouse immediate suspicion.

"Everyone's here," Victor murmured as he set down three cups. "I told them we all needed to come together, support each other through the investigation. No one wants to look like they're avoiding the group."

Sarah nodded, her eyes scanning the room. "Perfect. Thank you, Victor."

Charlie sat stiffly in his chair, his fingers wrapped too tightly around his mug. He was trying to appear casual, but Sarah could see the strain in the set of his shoulders, the careful way he avoided direct eye contact with anyone besides their small group.

"You all right?" she whispered, leaning toward him.

"Fine," he replied tightly. "Let's just get this over with."

Robyn slid into her seat, her back to most of the room so she could speak without her expressions being too visible. "Remember, we don't want to be too obvious. Just loud enough to plant the seed."

Sarah took a steadying breath and began their carefully rehearsed conversation, her voice pitched just above her normal speaking tone, not shouting, but clear enough to carry to nearby tables.

"I've been going back and forth about what Stanley told me", she said, stirring her tea. "About those regular payments Roger was making."

Several heads turned subtly in their direction. Olivia's spoon paused mid-stir.

"The ones to that mysterious account?" Robyn asked, matching Sarah's volume. "**WE**, wasn't it?"

Charlie shifted uncomfortably but played his part. "It still doesn't make sense to me. Why would Roger be paying someone off? I thought he was the one with all the power."

"That's what makes it so interesting," Sarah continued, careful not to look around the room too obviously. "Someone had leverage over him. Something he didn't want getting out."

A few feet away, Martin set down his cup with a little too much force, the ceramic clinking sharply against the saucer. His face remained neutral, but Sarah noted how still he had become, like a predator listening for prey.

"And now the police think they've traced the account?" Robyn asked, her incredulity perfectly calibrated. "They actually know who **WE** is?"

Sarah nodded solemnly. "Stanley said they found something in Roger's phone records. Calls to a specific number right before he died, the same number connected to the **WE** account."

The café had grown noticeably quieter, the ambient conversation dropping as more people tuned in to their discussion. Maya had stopped mid-sentence, her attention clearly diverted toward their table. One of the hotel staff, a young man Sarah recognized but couldn't name, was watching them with undisguised interest.

"I just don't know what to do with this information," Sarah said, feigning concern as she looked at Charlie. "If the police really do have evidence linking Roger's payments to someone here in the coffee community... I mean, we have to support the investigation, right?"

Charlie's jaw tightened, but he nodded. "I guess so. I just... I didn't expect it to lead back to someone we know."

Robyn leaned in, her voice carrying just a bit more than necessary. "We're talking serious stakes here. If this gets out, it could destroy someone's career, their whole life. But we can't just sit on it. If Roger was being blackmailed and it's connected to his death..."

She let the implication hang in the air, heavy and provocative.

Victor approached their table again, setting down a plate of biscotti with deliberate casualness. "Whatever you decide, Sarah," he said, his voice clear and steady, "just know you've got support. We can always arrange a more private meeting to discuss sensitive matters, just the people who really need to be involved."

The strategic ambiguity of his offer, who exactly were "the people who really needed to be involved"? was perfect. It created a sense that lines were being drawn, that some people were in the loop while others weren't.

"Thanks, Victor," Sarah said warmly. "I appreciate that. I just... I need to think about the right way to handle this. It's all happening so fast."

As Victor moved away, Sarah watched the ripple effect of their conversation spread through the café. People were exchanging glances, some concerned, others suspicious. A few seemed to be deliberately avoiding eye contact with anyone else. Near the counter, Olivia had pulled out her phone and was texting rapidly, her brow furrowed.

Charlie caught Sarah's eye, a silent question in his gaze: *had it worked?*

Sarah gave him a subtle nod. The trap was set. Now they just needed to wait and see who would take the bait.

She took a sip of her tea, maintaining the appearance of casual conversation while her mind catalogued every reaction in the room. Whoever **WE** was, they had just been put on notice. They would believe that Sarah, Charlie, and Robyn were close to exposing them, that the police were closing in. And cornered people made mistakes.

The carefully orchestrated whispers had been planted. The next move belonged to **WE**.

Chapter 21

Inspector Stanley leaned back in his chair, the post-mortem report spread open in front of him. The sterile scent of paper and ink mingled with the lingering aroma of the strong coffee he had been nursing for the past hour. He ran his eyes over the neatly typed results once more, the pieces finally clicking into place. The evidence they'd been waiting for, the missing link, was right there in black and white.

He stood abruptly, folding the report with precision and slipping it into his coat pocket. This couldn't wait. Within minutes, he was in his car, heading toward *Sarah's Secrets*, his mind racing through the implications of what he'd discovered.

The bell above the café door jingled as Stanley stepped inside. The familiar warmth enveloped him, a stark contrast to the clinical environment he'd just left. Sarah was behind the counter, steaming milk for a customer's latte, but her eyes immediately locked with his across the room. She registered the intensity in his expression and quickly passed the steamer to Robyn.

"Cover for me?" Sarah murmured, already untying her apron.

She met Stanley halfway across the coffee shop, not bothering with pleasantries. "You found something."

It wasn't a question.

Stanley nodded, gesturing toward a secluded corner table. "We need to talk."

As they settled into their seats, Stanley pulled out the report and laid it between them with deliberate care. Sarah leaned forward, her fingers hovering over the pages, almost afraid to touch them.

"The lab results confirmed what we suspected about the milk," Stanley began, his voice low. "It wasn't just regular milk in that bottle, it was almond milk. But that's not all they found."

He tapped a highlighted section of the report. "The bottle contained three distinct sets of fingerprints: Charlie's, which is expected given his proximity during the competition; the porter's, who admitted to rearranging the bottles on the tray; and a third set that was partially smudged."

Sarah's eyes narrowed as she processed this information. The net was drawing tighter. "And the third set? Do we know who…"

"Not yet," Stanley cut in. "They were careful, but not careful enough. Left partial prints that the lab is still trying to enhance." He paused, then delivered the crucial detail. "But there's something else, something that might be the key to everything. The lab found traces of kombucha in the milk residue."

"Kombucha?" Sarah's head snapped up, her eyes widening as the word triggered an immediate cascade of connections in her mind. The investigation's disparate threads suddenly converged with startling clarity. "Olivia," she breathed, the name escaping her lips before she could even process the thought fully.

Stanley's eyebrows rose. "Olivia Green? What about her?"

Sarah's words tumbled out rapidly, her hands gesturing as the pieces fell into place. "When I visited her brew house last week, she couldn't stop talking about her kombucha experiments. It's her new passion project, she has fermentation jars everywhere, special equipment, the works. She was practically evangelical about it." She leaned forward, her voice dropping. "Stanley, she had kombucha all over her workspace. If she handled the milk bottles..."

"The transfer would be inevitable," Stanley finished, his expression darkening. "And Olivia had motive. Roger had blocked her career advancement for years."

"Not just blocked," Sarah added, remembering details from their conversations around the trap they'd set. "Olivia once told me that Roger had effectively blacklisted her from major competitions after she refused to use his preferred suppliers. She was furious about it, said he'd cost her years of her career."

Stanley's jaw tightened. "And if she knew about his nut allergy..."

"She did," Sarah confirmed grimly. "Everyone in the inner circle knew. Roger made a big deal about venues being nut-free whenever he judged."

Stanley sat back, taking a deep breath as the weight of their discovery settled between them. "So we have motive, opportunity, and now physical evidence linking Olivia to the tampered milk."

"It's more than that," Sarah said, her mind racing ahead. "Remember what Martin said about seeing Olivia inspecting one of the milk bottles unusually closely? What if she wasn't checking for tampering, what if she was making sure her tampering hadn't been discovered?"

Stanley nodded slowly. "And the **WE** payments... could Olivia be **WE**? Was she blackmailing Roger all along?"

Sarah frowned, considering this. "It's possible. If she had something on him, something that could damage his reputation irreparably..."

"And when blackmail wasn't enough, she decided on a more permanent solution," Stanley concluded.

He gathered the report, his movements deliberate and precise. "We need to move quickly. If Olivia realizes we're onto her, she might disappear or destroy evidence."

Sarah reached across the table, catching his wrist. "Let me come with you. I've built a rapport with her. She might be more forthcoming if I'm there, less defensive."

Stanley hesitated, weighing the risks. "This isn't a social call, Sarah. If we're right, we're about to confront a murderer."

"I know," Sarah said, her voice steady despite the chill that ran down her spine. "But I also know that people tell me things. And right now, we need Olivia to talk."

After a moment's consideration, Stanley nodded. "All right. But you stay behind me, and if I signal you to leave, you go immediately. No questions."

Sarah agreed, already reaching for her coat. As they headed for the door, she caught Charlie's eye across the café and gave him a subtle nod. The trap they'd set at Victor's had worked, but not in the way they'd expected. Instead of forcing someone's hand, it had bought them time to find the physical evidence they needed.

The pieces were falling into place with terrifying speed. As they stepped outside into the crisp afternoon air, Sarah couldn't shake the feeling that they were rushing headlong toward a confrontation that would change everything. The truth about Roger's death was finally within reach, and it tasted bitter.

Twenty minutes later, Stanley and Sarah stood outside Olivia's brew house, the evening light casting long shadows across the pavement. The shop's warm glow spilled out onto the street, illuminating bottles of various shapes and colours displayed in the window. Through the glass, they could see Olivia moving behind the counter, methodically arranging kombucha bottles and checking labels.

Stanley exhaled slowly, the tension in his shoulders easing slightly for the first time in days. After weeks of dead ends and false leads, they finally had tangible evidence pointing to a specific suspect.

"Ready?" he asked, glancing at Sarah.

She nodded, a cautious optimism settling over her. "Let's end this."

The bell chimed softly as they stepped inside. The shop smelled of fermentation, sweet and tangy with undertones of herbs and tea. Olivia looked up from her work, her expression brightening momentarily at the sight of Sarah, then faltering as she registered Stanley's presence. Her hands stilled on the bottle she'd been labelling.

"Inspector," she greeted, her voice carefully neutral. "Sarah. What brings you both here?"

Stanley stepped forward, his posture straightening with the confidence of a detective who finally had the upper hand. "Miss Green, I'm afraid I have some questions for you regarding Roger Alton's death. We've uncovered evidence that I believe you might be able to explain."

A flash of something, alarm, perhaps, crossed Olivia's face before she smoothed her expression. "Evidence? What kind of evidence?"

Stanley maintained steady eye contact, watching her reactions with practiced precision. "The forensics team found traces of kombucha in the milk that killed Roger Alton."

The words hung in the air between them. Sarah watched as Olivia's face drained of colour, her fingers tightening around the bottle she held until her knuckles turned white.

"Kombucha?" Olivia repeated, her voice higher than normal. "That's... that doesn't make any sense."

"Doesn't it?" Stanley countered, gesturing around the shop. "You work with kombucha daily. Your fingerprints are all over this place. If you handled the milk bottles after working with your ferments..."

"No," Olivia cut in sharply. "No, that's impossible. I didn't touch those bottles. I haven't been anywhere near them!"

Sarah felt a flutter of satisfaction mixed with sadness. Olivia's reaction, the immediate denial, the rising panic, only confirmed their suspicions. She exchanged a glance with Stanley, who gave her an almost imperceptible nod.

"Olivia," Sarah said gently, stepping closer. "We know about your history with Roger. How he blacklisted you, how he blocked your career advancement when you refused to use his suppliers."

"That doesn't mean I killed him!" Olivia exclaimed, setting the bottle down with enough force that the liquid inside sloshed dangerously. "Yes, he was awful to me. Yes, he damaged my career. But I was finally moving on, creating something new with my kombucha line. Why would I risk everything I've built?"

Stanley's voice remained calm but firm. "Perhaps because moving on wasn't enough. Perhaps you wanted justice, or revenge."

Olivia's eyes darted toward the door, a brief calculation that didn't go unnoticed by either Sarah or Stanley. The inspector subtly shifted his weight, positioning himself more firmly between Olivia and the exit.

"We also know that someone was blackmailing Roger," Stanley continued. "Regular payments to an account marked simply as **WE**. Would you happen to know anything about that, Miss Green?"

"This is insane," Olivia whispered, her breathing becoming more rapid. "You think I was blackmailing him too? Based on what, traces of kombucha? Do you have any idea how many people drink kombucha these days?"

"But not many who handle it daily, who had access to the competition area, who had motive," Stanley countered. "Miss Green, I think it would be best if you came down to the station with us. We can discuss this further there."

Sarah could sense the relief emanating from Stanley, the satisfaction of finally having a suspect whose guilt seemed increasingly likely with each defensive response. It was a feeling she shared, though tempered with disappointment. She had liked Olivia, had seen her as another victim of Roger's manipulations. The possibility that she had taken such extreme measures was disturbing.

"Olivia," Sarah said softly, "if there's an explanation, now's the time. Whatever happened with Roger,"

"Nothing happened!" Olivia's voice cracked with desperation. "I didn't kill him! I didn't blackmail him! Yes, I work with kombucha, but that doesn't make me a murderer!"

Her eyes filled with tears, a detail that might have moved Sarah more if not for the overwhelming evidence stacked against her. Stanley seemed similarly unmoved.

"Olivia Green, I'm detaining you for questioning in connection with the murder of Roger Alton," he stated formally. "You're not under arrest at this time, but I must caution you that anything you say may be given in evidence."

As Stanley secured the cuffs around Olivia's wrists, Sarah caught his eye. There was a subtle but unmistakable look of vindication there, the expression of a detective who had finally caught his quarry after weeks of frustration. For Sarah, the feeling was more complicated, relief that Charlie would finally be cleared completely, satisfaction that Roger's killer would face justice, but also sadness that the culprit was someone from their tight-knit coffee community.

Olivia looked over her shoulder at Sarah as Stanley guided her toward the door. "Sarah, please," she pleaded, tears now streaming down her face. "You know me. I wouldn't do this. There has to be another explanation for the kombucha. Please believe me."

The desperation in her voice gave Sarah a moment's pause, but the evidence was too compelling to ignore. Sometimes the most obvious solution was the correct one, no matter how much you wished it wasn't.

"I'm sorry, Olivia," she said quietly as Stanley opened the door. "But the truth needs to come out."

As they stepped outside into the cooling evening air, Sarah felt the weight of the past weeks beginning to lift. While questions still remained, particularly about the mysterious **WE** and whether Olivia had acted alone, it seemed the central mystery was finally reaching its conclusion. Charlie would be exonerated, Roger would have justice, and *Sarah's Secrets* could return to being just a coffee shop rather than the centre of a murder investigation.

The case wasn't fully closed, but for the first time since Roger collapsed on that stage, Sarah allowed herself to believe that it soon would be.

Inspector Stanley leaned forward across the small, starkly lit interrogation room table, his gaze fixed intently on Olivia Green. She was hunched in the metal chair opposite him, her hands clenched tightly in her lap. Her usually sharp eyes were rimmed red, her face flushed from the strain of maintaining her composure. He'd been pushing her hard for the past hour, trying to break through her defiant front, but so far, she hadn't given him what he needed.

"Let's go over it again," Stanley said, his voice low and steely. "You told us that you've been experimenting with kombucha, working on new blends, yes? So tell me, Olivia, what does your process look like? Where do you make it? How do you bottle it? And how is it that traces of it ended up in the very bottle used to kill Roger?"

Olivia shook her head, her hair falling messily around her face. "I...I don't know!" she stammered. "I'm careful, I swear. Everything's sanitised. The kombucha shouldn't have been anywhere near those bottles. I don't know how..."

"Then tell me exactly how you do it," Stanley demanded, leaning in closer. "Step by step. I want every detail."

Olivia stared at him, her eyes wild with a mixture of fear and frustration. She looked down at her trembling hands, then back up at him, as if searching for a way to make him understand. But there was no sympathy in his gaze, no sign that he was going to let up.

"Fine!" she snapped, her voice cracking. "I brew the base tea, ferment it with a SCOBY…"

"Don't use technical jargon with me," Stanley interrupted sharply. "Explain it like I've never heard of kombucha before. I want to know exactly what you do."

Olivia's breath hitched, and she clenched her fists, her nails digging into her palms. "I mix the ingredients in a sterilised jar, cover it, and let it ferment for a few days. Then I strain it, add flavours, and bottle it up in glass bottles. I seal the bottles tightly, just like any other drink. But I don't use milk, almond or otherwise, anywhere near the kombucha. It doesn't make sense!"

Stanley's jaw tightened. He could feel his patience slipping, the urge to just arrest her building like a pressure valve about to burst. But he held back, forcing himself to breathe slowly. He needed more, he needed something concrete.

"And what about the bottles, Olivia?" he pressed. "Where do you get them? Could you have mixed them up with something else?"

"I get them from a supplier downtown," Olivia said, her voice rising in pitch. "They're clean when I get them, and I wash them again before I use them. I don't mix them up. I'm not stupid."

"Clearly, something went wrong," Stanley said icily. "And if you didn't mix them up, how did your kombucha end up in the milk bottle?"

"I *don't know!*" Olivia shouted, her eyes brimming with tears of frustration. She took a shuddering breath, glaring at him through the haze of her anger. "If you're that interested, why don't you come to one of my classes and see for yourself?"

Stanley paused, his eyebrows lifting slightly. "Your classes?" he repeated, his tone making it clear he thought this was just another evasion tactic.

"Yes," Olivia bit out, her voice dripping with sarcasm. "It's a class I run in the evenings, ok? I teach people how to make kombucha, explain the fermentation process, show them how to bottle it properly. If you think I'm some kind of crazed killer, then maybe you should come see how boring and normal it actually is!"

Stanley leaned back in his chair, studying her with thinly veiled scepticism. *Convenient timing for this revelation*, he thought. His years of experience had taught him that suspects often invented details when cornered, throwing out anything that might distract from their guilt. This had all the hallmarks of such a diversion.

"Evening classes," he said flatly. "How long have you been running these supposed classes, Miss Green?"

Olivia huffed, crossing her arms defensively. "Once a week, on Thursdays. It's not a big deal. I only started a few months ago, and it's been slow. Not a lot of people are interested in brewing kombucha in their kitchens, believe it or not."

Stanley made a noncommittal sound, unconvinced but methodically noting the information. Even the most desperate fabrications sometimes contained elements of truth, and he couldn't afford to dismiss anything outright.

"And the people who attend these classes," he continued, his tone making it clear he doubted their existence, "who are they? Do you keep records? Names? Contact information?"

Olivia hesitated, as if sensing his disbelief. "I...uh, sometimes," she admitted. "There are a few that have come by more than once. I don't keep detailed records, but I have a sign-in sheet for liability reasons."

"Can you name any of them?" Stanley pushed. "Anyone who's taken an interest in your process?" His scepticism was evident, but procedure demanded thoroughness.

She shifted uncomfortably in her seat, the anger beginning to drain out of her, replaced by a wary caution. "Why does it matter? It's just a class. People come, they go, and I'm not..."

"Answer the question," Stanley snapped, his voice sharp.

Olivia flinched, then glared at him defiantly. "Fine. One of the competitors, Eleanor, came by once or twice. She said she was curious about what I was doing. I thought she was just trying to pick up some new techniques, but..."

"Eleanor?" Despite his scepticism, Stanley couldn't help but take note. "Eleanor Wren?"

"Yes," Olivia spat. "Eleanor Wren. She came in, took notes, asked me a bunch of questions. I thought it was harmless. She didn't seem that interested, just... nosy."

Stanley's eyes narrowed. He still believed Olivia was their prime suspect, but he'd been a detective long enough to know that dismissing potential leads was how cases went cold. Eleanor Wren had been on their radar before, albeit peripherally. If there was even a chance that Olivia wasn't making this up...

"Did she handle any of the equipment?" he asked, his tone still doubtful but slightly less dismissive. "Any of the bottles?"

Olivia looked marginally relieved at his apparent interest. "I...I don't know. Maybe? She was there during bottling once, I think. I let people help out sometimes, but I didn't think anything of it."

Stanley maintained his sceptical expression, unwilling to let Olivia see that her mention of Eleanor had registered as potentially significant. In his mind, this was most likely a desperate attempt to shift blame, but he couldn't entirely dismiss it without verification.

"I see," he said neutrally, making a show of jotting down notes. "And you can provide proof of these classes? The sign-in sheets you mentioned? Receipts from participants?"

"They're at the shop," Olivia said quickly, hope flickering in her eyes. "In my office. I can show you."

Stanley stood abruptly, his chair scraping against the floor. "Miss Green, you'll remain here while we check the validity of your claims. If these classes turn out to be fictional, it will only make your situation worse."

Olivia's face fell slightly at his continued suspicion. "So... you don't believe me."

"What I believe," Stanley said evenly, "is that the evidence still points strongly to you. But we'll verify every detail, including this story about classes and Eleanor Wren's attendance."

He turned toward the door, his expression stern. "Officer Jenkins will be in shortly to take a formal statement from you. I suggest you use this time to consider whether there's anything else you'd like to tell us, preferably the truth this time."

As he stepped out of the interrogation room, Stanley's mind was working rapidly. He still considered Olivia their most likely suspect, the kombucha evidence was too compelling, her motive too clear. But he couldn't ignore the mention of Eleanor Wren, even if it was just a desperate deflection.

Pulling out his phone, he dialled his junior officer. "Mills, I need you to check something. Go to Olivia Green's brew house. Look for any evidence of kombucha classes, sign-in sheets, receipts, teaching materials. And specifically, see if there's any record of Eleanor Wren attending."

He paused, then added, "And while you're at it, pull everything we have on Eleanor Wren. Her background, her connection to Roger Alton, her whereabouts during the competition. It's probably nothing, but we need to be thorough."

As he ended the call, Stanley felt the familiar weight of an investigation at a crossroads. He was confident they had their killer in Olivia Green, but experience had taught him that assumptions could be dangerous. If there was even a grain of truth to her claim about Eleanor, he needed to know.

The kombucha evidence still pointed squarely at Olivia. But until every lead was exhausted, every stone turned, he couldn't afford to let tunnel vision blind him to other possibilities, no matter how unlikely they seemed.

Chapter 22

It was mid-morning at *Sarah's Secrets*, and for the first time in days, Sarah felt like she could actually breathe. The shop hummed with its regular rhythm, customers coming and going, the espresso machine hissing, Charlie expertly crafting lattes at the far end of the counter. With Olivia in custody, the investigation seemed to be reaching its conclusion. The nightmare was finally ending.

Sarah wiped down the counter, allowing herself a small smile. Perhaps now they could all start to move forward. Charlie was gradually returning to his old self, the shadow of suspicion lifting from his shoulders. Even the coffee community had begun to heal, tentative plans for a new competition already in the works, one without Roger's toxic influence looming over it.

During a quiet moment between the morning rush and the lunch crowd, Sarah leaned against the counter and pulled out her phone. It was time for some digital housekeeping. She began scrolling through her photo gallery, deleting the images she'd collected during her amateur sleuthing, pictures of notes, timelines, and lists she'd compiled.

"No need for these anymore," she murmured to herself, thumb hovering over the delete button on a photo of a list she'd scrawled days ago, possible suspects and their connections to Roger.

The bell above the door chimed softly, and Sarah glanced up automatically. Her casual smile froze slightly when she saw Victor Chan holding the door open for Eleanor Wren. They looked like any other pair of colleagues stopping in for coffee. Sarah hadn't seen either of them since that tense gathering at Victor's café, where they'd set their trap.

"Morning," Victor called across the shop with a friendly wave. "Two of your specials, if you don't mind."

Sarah nodded, tucking her phone away. "Coming right up."

As she began preparing their drinks, she watched them settle at a corner table. They were deep in conversation, their heads bent close together. Something about the way Eleanor's hands moved as she spoke, precise, controlled gestures, reminded Sarah of Roger. The same calculated grace.

While waiting for the espresso to pull, Sarah absently pulled out her phone again, returning to the photo she'd been about to delete. Her eyes drifted over the list of names and initials she'd jotted down when trying to map out all the players in this drama:

VC - Victor Chan - coffee shop owner, pushed out by Roger OG - Olivia Green - competitor, blacklisted MA - Martin Acton (Alton?) - competitor, family connection? WE - ???

Sarah frowned at the last entry. She still didn't know who WE was, the mysterious recipient of Roger's regular payments. Stanley hadn't shared any updates on that front. Probably still investigating, she thought, her eyes drifting back to the other initials.

And then something clicked. Something so obvious she nearly dropped her phone.

VC, OG, MA...

All initials listed first name then surname. Except...

Her eyes darted to Eleanor, calmly stirring her tea at the corner table.

Eleanor Wren.
WREN. ELEANOR.
W.E.

Sarah's heart began to pound as the realization crystallized. It wasn't some mysterious third party or shadowy organization. It was Eleanor Wren, her initials reversed, either by mistake or deliberate obfuscation in Roger's records. Eleanor was WE.

Her hands trembled as she set the phone down, mind racing to connect the dots. Eleanor Wren had been blackmailing Roger. The payments, the control, it had been her all along, working from the shadows while presenting a composed, unremarkable front to the world.

But why? What leverage could she possibly have had over someone as powerful as Roger?

Sarah's gaze drifted back to Eleanor just as the other woman looked up. Their eyes met across the shop, and for a split second, Sarah forgot to breathe. Did her face betray her revelation? Could Eleanor somehow read the realization in her expression?

Eleanor tilted her head slightly, her eyes narrowing almost imperceptibly before her lips curved into a small, polite smile. She raised her cup in Sarah's direction, a simple gesture that suddenly felt loaded with unspoken meaning.

Sarah forced herself to nod back, her mouth dry. She turned away quickly, pretending to adjust the espresso machine as her mind whirled. If Eleanor was WE, then what did that mean for the case? For Olivia?

With shaking fingers, she pulled out her phone again and quickly texted Inspector Stanley:

Need to talk URGENT. Just realized, WE = Eleanor Wren. Her initials backward. It's HER.

She hit send, then glanced back at Eleanor. The woman was still watching her, that same inscrutable smile playing at the corners of her mouth. Did she know? Could she somehow sense that Sarah had figured it out?

Sarah took a steadying breath, trying to maintain her composure. She couldn't let Eleanor suspect anything was wrong. Not until Stanley could act on this information.

She finished making the drinks and carried them over to Victor and Eleanor's table, forcing her hands not to shake.

"Here you are," she said, setting down the cups with practiced ease. "Let me know if you need anything else."

"Thank you, Sarah," Eleanor replied, her voice smooth as silk. "Your café is always so... revelatory. I can see why everyone shares their secrets here."

Sarah's blood ran cold at the deliberate emphasis Eleanor placed on those words. She met Eleanor's gaze and saw it then, a flash of something calculating behind the woman's serene expression. A predator's awareness.

"Enjoy your coffee," Sarah managed, stepping away from the table.

Sarah slipped the phone back into her apron, her heart hammering against her ribs. She returned to the counter, going through the motions of wiping down surfaces and checking inventory, all while keeping Eleanor in her peripheral vision.

The seemingly peaceful morning had transformed into a razor's edge of tension. Olivia Green was in custody, but the real puppet master had been sitting in Sarah's café all along, calmly sipping her tea while Sarah unwittingly served her.

And now Eleanor knew that Sarah knew.

The coffee shop was empty now, chairs neatly tucked against tables and the hiss of the final rinse cycle from the dishwasher providing the only sound. Sarah moved through *Sarah's Secrets* with practiced efficiency, wiping down counters and emptying the last dregs from the coffee urns. The routine was comforting, almost meditative, a stark contrast to the turmoil in her mind.

She glanced at her phone for the tenth time in as many minutes. Still nothing from Inspector Stanley.

"Don't panic," she murmured to herself, methodically arranging clean mugs for tomorrow's opening. "He's probably still processing Olivia. Interviews take time."

But the knot in her stomach tightened. Stanley should have responded by now. Her text had been clear: *WE = Eleanor Wren. Her initials backward. It's HER.*

The moment of realization still felt electric in her memory, that split second when the puzzle pieces had shifted and suddenly revealed the truth. Eleanor Wren had been hiding in plain sight all along, cleverly disguised behind reversed initials in Roger's records.

And now Stanley was interrogating the wrong person while the real culprit walked free.

Sarah checked her watch. 9:15 PM. The streetlights outside cast long, spectral shadows across the empty street. Southsea seemed unnaturally quiet tonight, or perhaps her nerves were simply amplifying the silence.

"He's doing his job," she told herself firmly, flipping the sign on the door from "Open" to "Closed." "He can't just abandon an interview because of a text message, even if it changes everything."

Still, she couldn't shake the unease that prickled along her spine. Eleanor had seen the recognition in her eyes this morning. She had known that Sarah had figured it out. And now, hours later, with darkness settled outside, Sarah felt exposed, as if the café's windows had become too transparent, too revealing.

She reached for the door lock, keys jingling in the silence. The streetlights flickered briefly, casting dancing shadows that made her heart skip. Just the usual power fluctuation, she told herself. Nothing to worry about.

Just as the key slid into the lock, movement reflected in the glass door made her freeze. A figure appeared on the other side, stepping into the spill of light from the café.

Sarah's heart lurched painfully as a face pressed close to the glass.

Eleanor.

The woman stood perfectly still, her expression composed but her eyes burning with something cold and dangerous. She looked immaculate as always, not a hair out of place, her outfit pristine, but there was a tightness around her mouth that sent a chill through Sarah's body.

Eleanor lifted a hand and rapped lightly on the glass, her fingernails clicking like tiny hammers of doom.

"Open the door, Sarah," she said, her voice muffled but perfectly audible through the glass.

Sarah's hand trembled on the lock. "Eleanor, what are you…"

"Open. The. Door." Each word came through with measured precision, soft but edged with steel.

Sarah hesitated, her mind racing. She could retreat to the back office, lock herself in, call Stanley again… but her phone was on the counter, and Eleanor was watching her every move with predatory focus.

Before she could decide, Eleanor's hand moved to the door handle. With a forceful shove, she pushed against it. Sarah realized with horror that in her distraction, she'd turned the key the wrong way, unlocking rather than locking the door. The door swung open, and Sarah stumbled backward as Eleanor stepped inside and closed it firmly behind her.

"Eleanor…" Sarah began, her voice unsteady.

"Don't," Eleanor interrupted sharply. "I saw your face this morning, Sarah. I watched the realization dawn. You know."

Sarah backed away slowly, trying to keep the counter between them. "I don't know what you're talking about."

"Please," Eleanor cut her off, her tone filled with contempt. "Don't insult my intelligence. You figured it out. The payments. WE." She took a deliberate step forward. "You know it's me."

Sarah's back pressed against the espresso machine, the metal warm against her spine. "I…I haven't told anyone," she lied, hoping to buy time.

Eleanor's laugh was brittle, lacking any warmth. "Now that is a lie. You're not the type to keep explosive revelations to yourself, Sarah. Your moral compass wouldn't allow it." Her eyes narrowed. "So who knows? That niece of yours? Charlie?"

Sarah's heart was hammering so violently she was certain Eleanor could hear it. She swallowed hard, steadying herself against the counter.

"Inspector Stanley," she admitted finally. "I told Inspector Stanley."

Eleanor's face hardened, the last vestiges of her pleasant mask falling away. "Of course you did," she said, her voice low and dangerous. "Always doing the right thing, aren't you, Sarah? Well, it won't matter. By the time he realizes his mistake with Olivia, I'll be far from here."

A chill ran down Sarah's spine. "You're leaving?"

"Obviously," Eleanor replied coldly. "But I need to make sure you won't complicate my departure."

She moved suddenly, grabbing a chair from the nearest table and dragging it to the centre of the room. The legs scraped harshly against the floor, the sound jarring in the quiet café.

"Sit," she commanded, gesturing to the chair.

Sarah remained frozen, her eyes darting toward her phone on the counter. Eleanor followed her gaze and smiled thinly, stepping over to snatch the device before Sarah could reach it.

"Looking for this?" she asked, slipping the phone into her pocket. "Sit down, Sarah. Now. Or I promise, this will become much more unpleasant than it needs to be."

With no viable options, Sarah lowered herself into the chair, her eyes never leaving Eleanor's face. She had to keep her talking, had to buy time. Maybe Stanley would realize his mistake. Maybe someone would walk by and see them through the windows.

"I know everything, Eleanor," she said, working to keep her voice steady. "About Roger. I've seen the financial records, the payments. I know you've been blackmailing him."

Eleanor's expression remained unchanged, but something flickered in her eyes, a cold amusement.

"I know why you killed him," Sarah continued, drawing on newfound courage. "He finally stood up to you, didn't he? He was going to stop the payments, maybe even expose you."

Eleanor's lips curled into a mocking smile. "Is that what you think happened? That Roger Alton, that pompous, self-important man, finally found his backbone?"

"Yes," Sarah insisted. "He realized what kind of person you really are."

Eleanor's smile vanished. She leaned closer, her perfectly manicured hands resting on the arms of Sarah's chair, trapping her.

"Roger was a coward," she hissed, her voice vibrating with barely contained fury. "He spent his entire life building this persona of the powerful coffee mogul, but underneath? He was weak. I didn't kill him because he threatened to expose me, Sarah. I killed him because he didn't deserve the power he had. He didn't deserve any of it."

Sarah stared at her, horrified by the cold calculation in Eleanor's eyes. "So you, you killed him because you wanted to take his place?"

"I killed him because he was pathetic," Eleanor whispered, her face inches from Sarah's. "And because I could."

She straightened up, crossing her arms as she regarded Sarah with disdain. "You know what finally broke him? It wasn't the blackmail. It wasn't the threats. It was the truth about Martin."

Sarah's eyes widened involuntarily.

"Oh yes," Eleanor continued, her smile sharp as a blade. "The great Roger Alton, moral arbiter of the coffee world, had an illegitimate son he'd abandoned. I found hospital records, birth certificates, it was all there if you knew where to look. Martin's mother was just another woman Roger used and discarded during one of his 'coffee expeditions.' "

Eleanor's eyes glittered with dark satisfaction. "You should have seen his face when I confronted him with the proof. The mighty Roger Alton, terrified of scandal. Terrified of being exposed as the fraud he was."

Sarah felt a chill ripple through her. "That's why you were blackmailing him."

"That was just the beginning," Eleanor said, voice hardening. "He deserved so much worse than blackmail. Do you know what the 'Wren' in Wren Enterprises used to mean? Legacy. Excellence. We were respected, until Roger destroyed us. He undercut our prices, stole our suppliers, spread rumours about quality issues. My grandfather's business, built over decades, collapsed in months."

Sarah blinked, piecing together this new information. "Roger put your family out of business?"

"He didn't just put us out of business," Eleanor snapped, raw fury breaking through her controlled exterior. "He erased us. Made sure Wren meant nothing in the coffee world. My parents were so ashamed they couldn't even look me in the eye when I said I wanted to resurrect what we'd lost."

Her jaw tightened, and for the first time, Sarah saw the wounded pride beneath the polished facade, years of resentment festering beneath the surface.

"I remembered everything," Eleanor continued, quieter now but no less intense. "Every humiliation. Every betrayal. I used his secrets to control him, to make him suffer. But it wasn't enough, because deep down, he still believed he was superior."

She leaned closer again, her voice dropping to a whisper. "So yes, Sarah. I killed him. I killed him because he destroyed my family without a second thought. Because he abandoned his own son. And because I wasn't going to let him keep winning."

Chapter 23

Robyn sat on the sofa, her foot tapping nervously against the floor. She glanced at her phone for what felt like the hundredth time, willing it to light up with a message from Sarah. She knew her aunt's routine inside and out. Sarah always closed up the shop around this time, always gave Robyn a quick call or text as she was heading out, just to check in and talk about the day. But tonight, the phone remained silent.

Something was wrong. She felt it deep in her gut.

It wasn't like Sarah to skip their usual chat, not after everything that had happened earlier. Don't panic, Robyn told herself, gripping her phone tighter. Sarah's probably just busy. Maybe she had to take a few extra minutes locking up. Maybe she's fine.

But even as she tried to rationalize, her worry only deepened. With every passing minute, the dread gnawed at her. What if Sarah had confronted Eleanor? What if something had happened?

Robyn's heart pounded, indecision tearing at her. She had to do something. But what if she was overreacting? What if Sarah was fine, and she was just being paranoid? She could already imagine the look on Sarah's face if she barged in, all worked up over nothing.

But then she thought of Sarah, alone in the dark coffee shop and her fear solidified into something colder, sharper.

"No," Robyn whispered to herself. "Something's wrong. I know it."

Her fingers hovered over her contacts list, trembling slightly as she scrolled to a name she hadn't called in weeks. Luke Stanley. The last person she'd expected to reach out to. She'd been so angry at him, so frustrated by how he'd treated Charlie, how he'd dismissed their concerns. She had thought she'd never forgive him.

But right now, none of that mattered.

"Swallow your pride," she muttered, pressing the call button before she could talk herself out of it.

The phone rang once, twice, three times. Robyn pressed it tighter to her ear, silently willing him to answer.

Inspector Stanley sat across from Olivia Green in the dimly lit interrogation room, fatigue etching lines in his face. They'd been at this for hours, and though her story about Eleanor Wren attending the kombucha classes seemed far-fetched, he couldn't dismiss it entirely. Not until he'd verified it.

"So you're saying Eleanor specifically asked about the bottling process?" he asked, watching Olivia's face for any sign of deception.

Olivia nodded wearily. "Yes. She seemed particularly interested in how the bottles were sealed. I thought she was just being thorough."

Stanley's jaw tightened as he made another note in his pad. Something about this wasn't adding up, but he couldn't quite put his finger on what.

A vibration from his pocket interrupted his thoughts. He ignored it, probably the forensics team with results he'd already reviewed. He'd check it after finishing with Olivia.

But then it vibrated again. And again.

With a frown, Stanley pulled his phone from his pocket, ready to silence it. The name on the screen made him pause.

Robyn Marsh.

Sarah's niece. The young woman who had glared daggers at him throughout Charlie's questioning, who had made it abundantly clear that she held him personally responsible for her cousin's ordeal. She hadn't spoken a word to him in weeks, and now she was calling.

"Excuse me," he said to Olivia, standing abruptly. "I need to take this."

He stepped out into the corridor, pressing the phone to his ear. "Robyn? What's…"

"Sarah's in trouble," Robyn cut in, her voice tight with urgency. "She's not answering her phone, she's missed our usual check-in, and after what she discovered about Eleanor today…"

"Wait, slow down," Stanley interrupted, his mind racing to catch up. "What did Sarah discover about Eleanor?"

"She didn't tell you?" Robyn's voice rose in alarm. "She sent you a text hours ago!"

Stanley pulled the phone from his ear and quickly checked his messages. There it was, a text from Sarah timestamped several hours earlier, buried under notifications he'd been ignoring during the interrogation:

Need to talk URGENT. Just realized, WE = Eleanor Wren. Her initials backward. It's HER.

His blood ran cold as the pieces suddenly clicked into place.

"When was the last time you heard from her?" he demanded, already striding down the corridor toward the exit.

"This afternoon, right after she figured it out," Robyn replied, her voice shaking slightly. "She said she was texting you immediately. But now she's not answering, and she always checks in after closing the shop."

Stanley cursed under his breath. "I'm heading to the shop now. Stay where you are."

"Like hell I will," Robyn cut in fiercely. "That's my aunt, and I'm already on my way."

Stanley knew better than to argue. "Fine. But when you get there, do not go inside. Wait for me. If Eleanor is there…"

"I know," Robyn said grimly. "Just hurry."

Stanley ended the call and sprinted toward the parking lot, his mind racing. WE wasn't a shadowy organization or a mysterious blackmailer. It was Eleanor Wren, her initials reversed. So simple, yet so easy to miss. And if Sarah had confronted her, or if Eleanor suspected that Sarah knew…

He yanked open his car door, barking orders into his radio as he started the engine. "This is DI Stanley. I need immediate backup at *Sarah's Secrets* coffee shop on Castle Road. Potential hostage situation, suspect Eleanor Wren. Approach without sirens."

As he peeled out of the station parking lot, Stanley's grip tightened on the steering wheel. Sarah had reached out to him when she made her discovery, trusted him with the information, and he'd failed to see it. Now she could be in danger because he'd been focused on the wrong suspect.

"Hold on, Sarah," he muttered, pushing the accelerator harder as he swerved through the evening traffic. "Just hold on."

Stanley drove like a man possessed, his knuckles white on the steering wheel as the streets of Southsea blurred around him. He shouldn't have been surprised to hear from Robyn, but the raw fear in her voice had shaken him to his core. He knew she'd been angry with him, resentful even, after everything that had happened with Charlie. He had tried to do his job, tried to follow the evidence, but in the process, he'd hurt people he genuinely respected. Robyn most of all.

But she'd called him now. And that meant something. It meant she trusted him, at least enough to set aside her anger when it truly mattered. And if Sarah was in danger...

Stanley gritted his teeth, his mind racing through possibilities. Eleanor was desperate, dangerous. If she thought Sarah was going to expose her, she wouldn't hesitate to get rid of her. The fact that she'd already killed once, with such calculated precision, made her infinitely more dangerous. He only hoped he wasn't too late.

He pulled up in front of *Sarah's Secrets* in record time, barely remembering to put the handbrake on before jumping out. The headlights of his car briefly illuminated the shopfront, the sign flipped to "Closed," but the front door slightly ajar. A cold dread settled over Stanley as he approached, his hand instinctively reaching for his radio to call for backup.

"All units, this is DI Stanley. I need immediate assistance at *Sarah's Secrets*, Castle Road. Possible hostage situation."

The radio crackled with confirmation as he cautiously approached the door, every sense heightened. The streetlights cast long shadows across the pavement, and the normally inviting café now seemed ominous, like a trap waiting to be sprung.

"Sarah?" he called softly, easing the door open with his fingertips. The interior was dim, illuminated only by the weak glow of the emergency exit sign. The tables were empty, the chairs neatly arranged. But something felt off, like the air itself was holding its breath.

He stepped inside, footsteps deliberately quiet on the wooden floor. His eyes adjusted to the dimness, scanning every corner, every shadow. And then he saw them.

Sarah stood in the centre of the room, her face pale and strained, her body rigid with tension. Across from her,

Eleanor stood with her back to Stanley, her posture unnaturally still. She was holding something, a knife, he realized with a jolt of horror. A small, sharp blade that glinted ominously in the low light.

"Eleanor," Stanley said quietly, his voice steady despite the hammering of his heart. "Put the knife down."

Eleanor stiffened, her shoulders hunching slightly. Slowly, she turned her head, her eyes narrowing as she saw him. "Inspector Stanley," she murmured, her voice silky and dangerous. "Just in time for the finale."

"It's over," Stanley said firmly, taking a measured step forward. "We know everything. About Roger, about the blackmail, about WE. There's nowhere left to run."

But Eleanor just smiled, a chilling, twisted expression that seemed to transform her elegant features into something almost feral. "You think this is the end?" she whispered. "After everything I've done? After everything I've sacrificed?"

Sarah's eyes met Stanley's across the room, not panicked, but alert, determined. She gave him the slightest nod, a silent acknowledgment of his presence, of her trust.

Stanley held Eleanor's gaze, his expression resolute. "Yes," he said softly. "I do."

The shop fell utterly still, the only sound the distant hum of traffic and the barely perceptible wail of approaching sirens. For a moment that seemed to stretch into eternity, no one moved.

Then, slowly, almost reluctantly, Eleanor's grip on the knife loosened. She glanced back at Sarah, her smile fading into something more complex, bitterness mingled with an almost wistful resignation.

"You should have stayed out of it, Sarah," she murmured. "You shouldn't have started digging. This was never your fight."

Sarah found her voice at last, steady despite everything. "It became my fight when you tried to frame my son."

Eleanor's expression flickered surprise, perhaps even a hint of respect. She looked down at the knife in her hand, then with a sudden motion, let it clatter to the floor.

Stanley moved forward then, stance cautious but determined. "Eleanor Wren, I'm arresting you on suspicion of the murder of Roger Alton, conspiracy to commit blackmail, and attempted assault. You do not have to say anything, but it may harm your defence if you do not mention when questioned something which you later rely on in court. Anything you do say may be given in evidence."

As the words of the caution filled the quiet café, Eleanor's shoulders sagged slightly, not in defeat, but as if a great weight had been set down at last. Her gaze flickered to Stanley, then back to Sarah. And for a moment, just a moment, there was something almost like regret in her eyes.

"Maybe it is over," she murmured. "But remember this, Sarah, sometimes doing the right thing isn't enough to make you a winner."

The distant sirens grew louder, blue lights now visible through the café windows, casting rhythmic flashes of colour across the walls. Backup was arriving, the final act of a drama that had begun with a single cup of tampered milk and spiralled into a web of decades-old vengeance.

Sarah watched as Stanley carefully secured Eleanor's wrists with handcuffs, her mind still reeling from the confrontation. It was over, truly over. Charlie was exonerated, Roger's killer caught, the mystery solved. Yet as Eleanor's words hung in the air between them, Sarah couldn't help but wonder who, if anyone, had truly won in this twisted game.

As Eleanor was led toward the door, her head still held high despite the handcuffs, she paused beside Sarah, leaning close enough to whisper.

"We're more alike than you think, Sarah Meadows. We both protect what's ours, no matter the cost."

Before Sarah could respond, Eleanor was gone, escorted into the waiting police car. Stanley remained behind, his face etched with relief and concern as he turned to Sarah.

"Are you all right?" he asked quietly.

Sarah nodded, the adrenaline beginning to ebb, leaving her suddenly exhausted. "I think so. I just... I need to call Charlie. And Robyn. They'll be worried."

Stanley nodded, understanding in his eyes. "Of course. I'll need a statement, but it can wait until tomorrow."

As he turned to leave, Sarah called after him. "Luke?"

He paused, turning back.

"Thank you," she said simply. "For believing me. For coming when it mattered."

Something shifted in Stanley's expression, a softening, a warmth that hadn't been there before. "Always," he replied.

Sarah sank into a chair, the events of the past week washing over her like a tide. From the moment of Roger's collapse to this final confrontation, nothing had gone as expected. Secrets had been unearthed, lives changed, a killer caught.

Sarah's Secrets had certainly lived up to its name. But as she sat in the quiet aftermath, Sarah knew that some secrets were best brought into the light, no matter who won or lost in the telling.

Robyn's car skidded to a halt outside the coffee shop, her heart hammering against her ribs. The café's windows glowed with blue flashing lights from the police cars parked outside, casting eerie shadows across the familiar shopfront. She flung her door open and sprinted toward the entrance, not even bothering to close it behind her.

Please let her be alive. Please, please...

As she burst through the door, the bell jangling discordantly above her, Robyn froze at the tableau before her. The scene felt surreal, like walking into a photograph: Sarah standing shakily in the middle of the café, pale but upright; Inspector Stanley carefully securing handcuffs around Eleanor Wren's wrists; uniformed officers moving in measured patterns around them, speaking in low, professional tones.

The tide of relief hit Robyn with such force that she nearly staggered. The knot of terror that had been coiled in her stomach since Sarah missed their check-in call dissolved, leaving her light-headed.

"Sarah!" she cried, her voice cracking with emotion.

Sarah turned at the sound of her name, exhaustion etched into every line of her face. When their eyes met, something in Sarah's expression crumbled, the brave front she'd been maintaining giving way to raw vulnerability.

Robyn crossed the distance between them in seconds, wrapping her arms around her aunt and pulling her close. Sarah felt smaller somehow, fragile in a way Robyn had never associated with her strong, resilient aunt. She could feel Sarah trembling against her, fine shivers that ran through her entire body.

"I thought..." Robyn's voice broke, tears welling up unexpectedly. "When you didn't call, and then your text about Eleanor..."

"I'm ok," Sarah whispered, her voice unsteady but determined. "I'm ok now."

Robyn tightened her embrace, as if she could physically shield Sarah from what had just happened. The fear that had driven her across town at breakneck speed was beginning to subside, replaced by a fierce protectiveness.

"Did she hurt you?" Robyn pulled back just enough to search her aunt's face, her hands gently cupping Sarah's shoulders.

Sarah shook her head. "No. She had a knife, but..." Her eyes drifted toward Stanley, who was now speaking quietly to one of his officers as Eleanor was led toward the door. "Inspector Stanley arrived just in time."

Robyn followed her gaze, watching as Eleanor was escorted outside. The woman who had seemed so elegant, so perfectly composed whenever Robyn had seen her in the café, now looked diminished somehow. But there was still a coldness in her eyes that sent a shiver down Robyn's spine, even in defeat, Eleanor Wren radiated danger.

As the officers guided Eleanor out, Inspector Stanley turned back toward them. The harsh overhead lights caught the silver at his temples and the lines of fatigue around his eyes. He looked exhausted, but there was something else in his expression as he looked at Sarah, relief, and perhaps something deeper.

Robyn had spent the last week resenting this man, blaming him for the suspicion that had fallen on Charlie, for the stress that had nearly broken their family. But now, seeing him standing in the aftermath of whatever had happened here, she felt something shift inside her.

He had come when it mattered most. He had believed Sarah when it counted. Their eyes met across the shop, and Robyn felt the last vestiges of her anger begin to dissolve. Without hesitation, she mouthed two simple words: *Thank you.*

Stanley's face softened, the professional mask slipping just enough to reveal genuine emotion. He gave her a small, tired nod of acknowledgment.

Robyn watched his face, suddenly seeing Stanley, *Luke*, in a new light. Not as the stern, suspicious detective who had made Charlie's life hell, but as a man who had admitted his mistake and had risked himself to save her aunt.

"Will you be ok to get home?" he asked, his gaze now including Robyn in his concern.

"I'll drive her," Robyn said, finding her voice at last. "I'll make sure she's safe."

Luke nodded, his eyes lingering on Robyn's for a moment longer than necessary. "Good. I'll check in tomorrow." He hesitated, then added, "Charlie should know that his name is completely cleared now. Eleanor confessed to everything."

The weight of those words settled over them like a blanket. *Charlie was cleared.* The nightmare that had begun with Roger's collapse at the competition was finally, truly over.

As he turned away to rejoin his officers, Robyn slipped her arm around Sarah's waist, supporting her as they moved toward the door. The night air felt cleaner somehow, as if the resolution inside had cleared away more than just the immediate danger.

"Let's get you home," Robyn murmured, guiding Sarah toward her car. "Charlie's waiting. He's been worried sick."

Sarah leaned against her, drawing strength from her niece's support. "I think we all have a lot to talk about," she said, her voice growing steadier with each step away from the café. "But right now, I just want to hug my son and have a very strong cup of coffee."

Robyn laughed softly, the sound releasing some of the tension that had built up inside her. "I think that can be arranged."

As they reached the car, Robyn glanced back at the shop. Through the window, she could see Luke standing in the centre of the coffee shop, his shoulders straighter now as he directed his team. For a moment, their eyes met again across the distance, and Robyn felt an unexpected warmth spread through her chest.

Chapter 24

Robyn perched on a chair near the front window of *Sarah's Secrets*, carefully draping gossamer-thin fake cobwebs across the display. The delicate strands captured the soft afternoon light, creating tiny prisms that danced along the glass. Charlie stood below her, balancing a cardboard box of Halloween decorations against his hip while passing up a collection of small plastic spiders, which Robyn strategically positioned throughout the web.

"Too much?" Robyn asked, glancing over her shoulder at Sarah, who watched from behind the counter with her hands resting on her hips.

Sarah shook her head, amusement dancing in her eyes. "Not at all. Just... maybe don't make them too realistic. I don't want to terrify anyone into spilling their coffee."

Robyn grinned wickedly, dangling one of the larger spiders in front of Charlie's face. "I think we'll be fine. Unless Charlie decides to start hiding these in people's drinks."

Charlie's eyebrows shot up in mock innocence. "Would I ever?" He handed her another small arachnid, his smile widening mischievously. "Though I was considering slipping a few into the cookie jar just to liven things up."

"Charlie!" Sarah groaned, tossing a dish towel at him. "If anyone screams and drops a mug, you're on cleanup duty for a week."

Charlie laughed, catching the towel mid-air and flinging it back to her. "Don't worry, I'll behave. For the most part."

As Sarah watched them, warmth bloomed in her chest. It was remarkable how much lighter everything felt now that the storm had passed. After all they'd endured, the long hours establishing the business, the emotional turmoil of Charlie's wrongful arrest, the fear and uncertainty surrounding Eleanor's actions, seeing them like this again was a balm to her soul. Smiling, joking, working together as though nothing could shake them.

Sarah's mind drifted over the past week, cataloguing the whirlwind of new faces that had entered her life since the competition. The network of coffee enthusiasts she'd connected with, the suppliers who'd reached out after hearing about Sarah's Secrets, even a local reporter who'd asked for an exclusive on their "triumph over adversity" story. Her life had expanded in ways she couldn't have anticipated when she first opened the shop's doors.

"I can't believe how much we've been through already since we opened this place," she said softly, her gaze sweeping around the cozy shop. The flickering lights from the small decorative pumpkins they'd placed on each table cast a warm, inviting glow, and she felt a surge of pride at how far they'd come.

Charlie looked up, his expression turning reflective. "I didn't realize a simple coffee competition could be so dangerous," he admitted, shaking his head.

"Dangerous?" Robyn snorted, stepping down from the chair. "That's the understatement of the century."

Sarah studied Charlie's face carefully. "Does that mean you're put off competing again?" she asked gently.

Charlie hesitated, his gaze thoughtful as he surveyed the café. Then he shook his head, the hint of a smile playing at his lips. "Not completely. But I might... give it a few months before diving back in."

"Perfectly understandable," Sarah agreed. "Take all the time you need."

Charlie nodded, his eyes warm as they met hers. "Anyway, we've got other priorities for now," he said, gesturing around the shop. "Like this place."

The café had transformed over the past weeks, evolving from a simple coffee stop into a space that invited people to linger. The flickering candles on each table, the subtle aroma of cinnamon and nutmeg infusing the air, the soft glow of fairy lights strung along the walls, all of it combined to make the shop feel more like an intimate gathering place than just a café. It was exactly what Sarah had envisioned when she'd proposed extending their hours into the evening, and seeing it come to life filled her with satisfaction.

"We've created something special here," Sarah said quietly, her gaze moving from Charlie to Robyn and back again. "And I think this evening venture will only enhance it."

Charlie nodded, his eyes tracking across the ambient lighting and the comfortable corners they'd designed. "Yeah," he agreed, pride evident in his voice. "It feels like we're developing a whole new dimension to the business. Somewhere people can escape, especially when the weather turns colder."

Robyn stepped closer to Sarah, her smile genuine. "And people already love it," she added, nodding toward the small group of customers lingering at the tables, sipping lattes and chatting softly.

Sarah's heart swelled at their words. They'd all worked so hard to reach this point, and now they were finally seeing the fruits of their labour. But even as she basked in their optimism, a practical thought surfaced.

She reached behind the counter and pulled out a small, neatly folded flyer, handing it to Charlie with a smile.

"What's this?" he asked, unfolding the paper curiously.

Sarah grinned. "It's an advertisement. If we're extending our hours, we're going to need more help around here. You two have been incredible, but with the holiday season approaching, I think it's time we brought in some extra hands."

Robyn raised her eyebrows, peering at the ad over Charlie's shoulder. "We're hiring?"

"That's the plan," Sarah confirmed with a nod. "The evening shifts are going to get busier, and I don't want any of us burning out."

Charlie looked contemplative as he scanned the flyer. "Makes sense," he agreed. "And if we're serious about making this evening concept work, additional staff would definitely help."

"Exactly," Sarah leaned against the counter, crossing her arms. "It'll give us more flexibility, and if we find someone with a passion for coffee, or even just enthusiasm and willingness to learn, we can train them. That way, when the rush hits, we'll have a solid team in place." She paused, a thoughtful expression crossing her face. "Actually, I was thinking about that young waitress from the Queen's Hotel, Gemma. Remember her?"

Charlie tilted his head, recalling. "The one who overhead all that stuff about Roger's judging practices?"

"That's the one," Sarah nodded. "She seemed sharp, observant. The way she handled herself during all that chaos was impressive. I was thinking of seeing if she might be interested in joining us."

"Poaching staff from the competition?" Robyn teased, grinning. "Scandalous."

Sarah laughed softly. "Well, given our apparent knack for finding ourselves in the middle of one drama or another, having someone around who pays attention to details and keeps her cool might not be a bad thing."

Charlie chuckled. "Can't argue with that logic."

Robyn's smile widened, and she exchanged a glance with Charlie. "Looks like we're expanding, huh?"

Sarah nodded, her expression bright with anticipation. "Looks like it. Are you both ok with that?"

"More than ok," Charlie said firmly. "We want this place to succeed as much as you do. And besides," he added with a wry smile, "it'll be nice to have someone else around to help manage the spider collection."

Robyn laughed, nudging him lightly with her elbow. "We'll add that to the job description, 'must not be afraid of Halloween decorations or Charlie's pranks.' "

Sarah chuckled, shaking her head. "I'll start putting the word out tomorrow. Whether it's Gemma or someone else, I'm sure we'll find the right person. This place... it's becoming more than just a coffee shop. It's becoming a community."

Charlie and Robyn shared a warm look before turning back to her, their eyes reflecting shared pride and affection.

Robyn said softly. "And you're at the heart of it."

Sarah blinked rapidly, touched beyond words. She looked at the two of them, her family, her team, her support system, and felt a surge of gratitude so powerful it nearly took her breath away.

"Thank you," she whispered. "For everything."

Charlie shrugged, his smile teasing. "Hey, you're stuck with us now. No backing out."

"Yeah," Robyn added with a mischievous grin. "We're not going anywhere."

Sarah laughed, the sound light and unencumbered. "Good," she said, her voice thick with emotion. "Because I wouldn't have it any other way."

As the afternoon sun slanted lower through the windows, casting long golden fingers across the shop floor,

Sarah felt a sense of contentment settle over her. Despite all the unexpected twists their journey had taken, or perhaps because of them, Sarah's Secrets had found its place in Southsea. And with new faces, new opportunities, and her family beside her, Sarah couldn't wait to see what came next.

The bell above the door jangled merrily as a gust of cold air swept into the coffee shop. Sarah looked up from the espresso machine to see a cluster of familiar faces bursting through the entrance, bringing with them the scent of rain and the sound of laughter. Charlie, who had been methodically wiping down tables, straightened up, surprise melting into pleasure.

"Well, well," Martin announced, shaking raindrops from his jacket like a dog after a swim. "If it isn't Southsea's most controversial coffee artist!"

Behind him, Olivia, Victor, and Maya filed in, their cheeks flushed from the chill outside. The coffee shop suddenly felt warmer, more alive.

"The barista rebels have arrived," Olivia declared, giving Charlie's shoulder a playful nudge as she passed. "We've come to pay our respects after what the Portsmouth Evening News is calling 'Latte-gate.'"

Charlie groaned but couldn't suppress the smile tugging at his lips. "You braved this weather just to take the mickey out of me?"

"We prefer to call it 'solidarity,'" Victor said, unwinding his scarf and dropping into a chair with theatrical exhaustion. He ran a hand through his damp hair. "Also, some of us are suffering serious coffee withdrawal. The stuff at my place tastes like dishwater since I've experienced your brews."

"At least your coffee wasn't judged by someone's corrupt long lost father," Martin added, earning a ripple of laughter.

Sarah emerged from behind the counter, wiping her hands on her apron, warmth spreading through her chest at the sight of Charlie's friends rallying around him. "I'd offer you lot free drinks, but Charlie's been sulking so much I'm worried he's forgotten how to make them."

"Mum," Charlie protested, colour rising to his cheeks.

"What? It's only the truth," she replied, winking at the others.

The conversation flowed easily as they settled in, raindrops racing down the windows while the espresso machine hissed and purred in the background. Inevitably, talk turned to the news that had broken that morning, the regional heat had officially been cancelled pending investigation.

"Can't say I'm shocked," Olivia sighed, cradling her mug between her palms. "The whole competition needs an overhaul after that fiasco."

Martin leaned back in his chair until it balanced precariously on two legs. "Still, we were something special up there. All that talent, and no proper final to show for it."

A contemplative silence fell, broken only by the gentle drumming of rain against glass. Then Maya sat forward suddenly, her eyes bright with inspiration.

"So let's have one."

Charlie blinked. "What, now?"

"Here," Martin said, the front legs of his chair hitting the floor with a thud as understanding dawned on his face. His grin was infectious. "Our own underground championship. No judges, no politics, just us."

"Winner gets eternal glory," Victor proposed.

"And that chocolate hazelnut thing I saw in the display case," Olivia added, pointing toward the pastry counter.

Sarah watched the exchange, arms folded across her chest, enjoying the way life had returned to Charlie's eyes. "Sarah's Secrets could definitely host an unofficial final," she offered. "Though I should warn you, my judging might be even more biased than Roger's."

The group erupted in laughter.

"We'll take our chances with nepotism this time," Victor declared, already rolling up his sleeves.

"All right then," Sarah announced, clapping her hands together once. "Let the completely unauthorized, thoroughly unprofessional, shamelessly biased final commence!"

As the others began playfully jostling for position behind the counter, Charlie arranging milk pitchers and cups with mock solemnity, Sarah noticed Martin hanging back, his gaze fixed on the rain-streaked window. Something in his expression, a quieter, more contemplative look than his usual confidence, caught her attention. She made her way over to him.

"Everything all right?" she asked softly, standing beside him at the window.

He nodded slowly, eyes still on the grey world outside. "Yeah. Just needed a moment."

She waited, the silence between them comfortable, not pressing.

When he spoke again, his voice had lost its performative edge. "It's true, isn't it? Everything about Roger. The nepotism. The timeline." He paused, swallowing visibly. "The affair with my mother."

Sarah felt a pang in her chest. "Oh, Martin…"

"It's ok," he said quickly, finally meeting her eyes. "Strangely, I feel... lighter. I spent so many years trying to measure up to his standards or pretending I didn't care about them. Either way, he was always there, this shadow looming over everything I did."

He exhaled, a slow, deliberate breath. "Now I can finally just make coffee because I love it. Not because I'm proving something, or rebelling against something."

Sarah placed a gentle hand on his arm, feeling the damp wool of his sleeve. "For what it's worth, I think you've already made your own name. Your coffee speaks for itself."

Martin's smile was small but genuine. "Thanks, Sarah." He straightened his shoulders, as if physically shrugging off a weight. "Now, let's see about winning me that chocolate hazelnut thing."

Just as the impromptu contest was taking shape, Charlie arranging judges' scorecards made from napkins, Victor warming up with exaggerated stretching exercises, the bell above the door chimed again. This time, Amy stepped inside, followed closely by Edward, both of them wearing secretive smiles that immediately captured everyone's attention.

"Sorry to interrupt what appears to be a very serious athletic event," Amy called out, raindrops glistening in her curls. "But we've got a little announcement that can't wait."

Edward cleared his throat dramatically and produced an official-looking envelope from inside his jacket. With ceremonial precision, he unfolded a certificate bordered in gold. "Sarah Meadows, proprietor of Sarah's Secrets," he announced, his voice carrying to every corner of the café, "you have been officially selected as Southsea's Best New Business of the Year. Congratulations!"

The café erupted into cheers and applause. Sarah stood motionless, genuine shock rendering her speechless as colour flooded her cheeks.

Amy crossed the room in quick strides and enveloped Sarah in a tight embrace. "We couldn't wait another minute to tell you," she whispered, her voice thick with emotion. When she pulled back, Sarah saw tears of joy shimmering in her friend's eyes. "After everything that's happened over these last few months, you've earned this ten times over."

Edward grinned widely. "The trophy's still being engraved, but the prize money's ready to be transferred to your account."

Sarah pressed her fingertips to her lips, her heart hammering against her ribs. "I...I don't even know what to say. This is incredible."

"Speech!" shouted Martin, and the others took up the call, applauding rhythmically.

Sarah laughed, shaking her head. "No, no speeches," she insisted, waving her hands to quiet them. "I've had quite enough of public speaking lately." She took a steadying breath, emotion making her voice tremble slightly. "But I do know exactly what this money's going toward."

Another cheer rose from the group as Amy squeezed her hand. For the first time since the competition disaster, Sarah saw unguarded happiness in Charlie's expression. Amy bit her lip suddenly, exchanging a guilty glance with Edward. "There's, um, one more thing you should probably know, Sarah." She tucked a strand of hair behind her ear nervously. "Those mysterious notes in your journals? The slightly cryptic ones?"

Sarah's eyebrows rose. "That was you?"

Amy nodded, wincing apologetically. "Me, Edward, and a few of your regular customers. We thought it would be a fun way to build up to the announcement, you know? Little hints that something exciting was coming." She grimaced. "We didn't exactly predict the timing would coincide with... everything else. Talk about unfortunate synchronicity."

Sarah stared at her for a moment before bursting into laughter, real, unburdened laughter that seemed to release weeks of tension. "My God, Amy, you nearly gave me a heart attack! I was convinced someone was threatening me!"

Amy's expression was comically contrite. "Lesson thoroughly learned. No more cryptic notes." She squeezed Sarah's hand. "Next time we'll just say things outright like normal people."

Sarah wiped away a tear of mirth, suddenly aware of the warm circle of people surrounding her, friends, family, and community who had stood by her through all the chaos. As the rain continued to patter against the windows, Sarah's Secrets felt like exactly what she'd always intended it to be: not just a coffee shop, but a haven.

"Right," she said, composing herself with a deep breath and a smile that reached her eyes. "I believe we were in the middle of hosting Southsea's most exclusive underground coffee championship. Shall we continue?"

As the group cheered again and returned to their positions, Sarah caught Charlie's eye across the room. He gave her a small nod, a private acknowledgment between them, they'd weathered the storm, and somehow, against all odds, had found themselves exactly where they needed to be.

Sarah fidgeted with the numbered paddle in her lap, the plastic edge digging into her palm. The community hall smelled of furniture polish and stale coffee, its wooden floors creaking beneath rows of folding chairs. Beside her, Charlie sat with studied casualness, but she noticed how his eyes kept darting to the items displayed at the front.

"Next up," the auctioneer announced, his voice echoing through the sound system, "lot number twenty-three. A La Marzocco espresso machine, commercial grade, barely two years old." A few paddles lifted around the room. Sarah observed with clinical detachment, calculating replacement costs in her head.

The auctioneer nodded, tracking bids with practiced efficiency. "Sold, to number forty-two." He cleared his throat. "And now, our final lot of the day: an industrial coffee roaster."

Sarah's heart stuttered. The roaster stood gleaming under the hall's fluorescent lights, its copper and steel surfaces reflecting possibility. It was beautiful in the way only purposeful things can be solid, reliable, built to create.

Charlie's posture changed instantly. He leaned forward, elbows on knees, his face betraying the excitement he was trying to mask. "That's the exact model we were looking at online," he whispered, a hint of reverence in his voice.

"Starting bid at two thousand pounds," called the auctioneer.

A paddle went up across the room. Then another.

Charlie's hand twitched toward Sarah's arm. "Mum," he murmured, "you don't have to…"

But Sarah had already raised her paddle, her movement decisive. She met the auctioneer's eyes directly.

"Two and a half thousand to the lady in blue," the auctioneer noted.

The bidding quickened. Each time a new offer came, Sarah countered without hesitation. She felt Charlie tense beside her with each increment, but she kept her face neutral, her breathing steady. This wasn't impulse, this was investment.

"Three thousand," called a voice from the back.

Sarah lifted her paddle. "Three and a half."

A moment's pause stretched across the room.

"Three and a half thousand going once... twice..." The gavel struck. "Sold, to number twenty-nine."

Charlie exhaled slowly beside her. Sarah allowed herself a small smile as she signed the paperwork, paid the deposit, and arranged for collection later that afternoon.

In the warehouse behind the hall, Sarah circled the roaster like it was some magnificent creature she'd somehow managed to tame. The afternoon light slanted through dusty windows, catching on the machine's surface. Charlie was already examining the mechanics, his fingers tracing connections and components with the reverence of someone who understood craftsmanship.

"It's in good condition," he said, voice low with appreciation. "Previous owner must have barely used it."

Sarah nodded, running her palm along the cool metal curve. "No history. No baggage." She met his eyes meaningfully. "Just possibilities."

Charlie straightened up, a smile breaking through his careful composure. "Kind of poetic, isn't it? After everything that's happened... something brand new begins."

She felt a tightness in her chest, that particular ache of watching your child heal from wounds you couldn't prevent. "You deserve something good, Charlie. We both do."

He walked around to stand beside her, both of them facing the roaster. "Where are we even going to put this beast? The shop's already packed."

Sarah laughed, the sound bouncing off the warehouse walls. "We'll make it work. Maybe move those shelves by the window..."

"Or sacrifice the reading nook," Charlie suggested, bumping her shoulder lightly with his.

"Absolutely not. That's sacred space." She wrapped an arm around his waist, leaning into him briefly. "We'll figure it out."

They stood there together, contemplating their future in the gleam of copper and steel. Sarah felt something settle inside her, a certainty that had been missing for too long.

What Charlie didn't know, what she hadn't told him yet, was that the roaster was only part of her plan. On her phone, saved in a folder labelled "Next Chapter," was the advertisement that had caught her eye last week: a vintage coffee van painted turquoise and cream, its retro charm impossible to resist.

The roaster was just the beginning. *Sarah's Secrets* was about to hit the road.

She smiled to herself, already picturing Charlie's face when she showed him the photos. After everything they'd been through, this new adventure felt exactly right, a fresh start wrapped in the comfort of what they already knew and loved.

Just coffee. Family. And the open road ahead.

Thank You for Reading

I hope that you enjoyed my second book in the Sarah's Secrets series! It's been a joy for me to get to know the characters better while writing this new story and I'm so grateful to have you as a reader.

If you'd like to show your support, one of the best ways is by leaving a review on Amazon. Reviews, whether short or long, help authors more than you might think. They not only let me know what you liked, but also signal to others that Sarah's Secrets is worth discovering.

I'd truly appreciate any feedback you have, and if you'd like to see more from Sarah, Charlie, Robyn and Sarah's Secrets, your reviews are the best way to let me know!!

Thank you for being part of this adventure – I hope to see you again soon in Mocha Madness!!

Mocha Madness

A Sarah's Secrets Mystery - Book 3

Southsea's favourite coffee shop is brewing up something big.

With the Glorious Festival on the horizon, Sarah Meadows is juggling lattes, logistics and a mobile coffee van named Tallulah – not to mention navigating the ambitions and anxieties of her small but fiercely loyal team.

But when the headline act collapses in front of thousands, what should have been a dream weekend turns into a nightmare. One that no amount of caffeine can fix.

Secrets simmer beneath the surface, on stage, backstage and even within Sarah's own team – as rivalries flare, loyalties are tested, and Sarah finds herself pulled into her most high-profile mystery yet.

Music, mayhem, and murder are on the menu!